INTERVENTION

WILLIAM CAIRD

One Printers Way
Altona, MB R0G 0B0
Canada

www.friesenpress.com

Copyright © 2022 by William Caird
First Edition — 2022

All rights reserved.

No part of this publication may be reproduced in any form, or by any means, electronic or mechanical, including photocopying, recording, or any information browsing, storage, or retrieval system, without permission in writing from FriesenPress.

Vadim Kirpichev, God does not exist (Scientific Proof) 2003.
The reader will recognize some of his work in the captain's argument against the existence of God.

Cover art by author

ISBN
978-1-03-915924-2 (Hardcover)
978-1-03-915923-5 (Paperback)
978-1-03-915925-9 (eBook)

1. FICTION, DYSTOPIAN

Distributed to the trade by The Ingram Book Company

Revelation 3:15-16
Jesus Said: "So then because thou art lukewarm, and neither cold nor hot, I will spue thee out of my mouth. Because thou sayest, I am rich, and increased with goods, and have need of nothing; and knowest not that thou art wretched, and miserable, and poor, and blind, and naked.

Acknowledgements

Many thanks to Lorraine Iversen, my sister Nancy and my daughter-in-law Hailey, for all their help correcting my writing over the years.

Introduction

THIS BOOK WAS A HUGE challenge for me. I had to learn to distance myself from the story, because there were many times during the writing process that I was forced to push the envelope far past my comfort zone for the sake of drama, complexity and sexual tension.

I had to be a little cruder than I was at ease with, to develop the villainous character of Captain Dick and a little too sexually graphic to describe some of his escapades, as well as the tension between the protagonist and Eve Anna.

Chapter One

"EVERYONE MAKES MISTAKES, it's only human."

"Yes, I know, but it was such a stupid mistake."

"That's the thing about mistakes, Eve Anna. Sometimes you can make a colossal mistake and the repercussions are almost nil. The next time you might make a tiny mistake that could cost you your life."

I was handing back the results from the term exam to my grade twelve English class. Class 12A, my favourite of all the groups I teach here at Stephen Hawking High. It is made up of a great bunch of kids. Eve Anna had just expressed her annoyance over missing a perfect mark because of a silly mistake. Eve Anna and I have always had a special rapport. Her beauty and her youthful exuberance are a constant source of fascination for me. I am sure it is no secret to the rest of the class that she is my *teacher's pet*.

"Ninety-nine is an excellent achievement," I tried to reassure her as I held out the corrected copy of her test. "I can tell you studied hard."

"Thanks, Teach." As she reached out for the papers our fingers met. Her touch was very soft and yet electric. She smiled and made my knees go weak. I loved the shape of her lips: the outline of Cupid's bow over the upper lip, the gentle rounded curve of the lower, and the flushed fullness of the pair.

Teach: that is what all my students call me. I accept that title because I believe it is a mark of respect. Having the students appreciate you as a teacher is invaluable, because we have so few disciplinary tools these days. Some of the teachers at the school scream at the children when they are misbehaving. It does not take long for the students to become desensitized to this, and after a couple of days the screaming trickles off their backs like water off a duck. I have tried asking a troublesome teen to leave the classroom; but in many cases that is exactly what they want, and what I consider to be a punishment turns out to be a reward. There is never an easy solution. Most misbehaviour gets its seed from boredom. The only method of counteracting that is to make learning interesting and fun. I think that is one of a teacher's biggest challenges and a hurdle that a lot of my peers are never able to master.

After returning all the exam papers to their respective owners, I stepped to the front of the class and wrote out their reading assignment for the weekend: *Hamlet*, Act five, Scene Two.

"I'm happy with everyone's test results," I announced. "Most of you seemed to have an excellent understanding of the play."

Helena put up her hand.

"Yes, do you have a question about the exam?"

"What was the answer to number twenty-one? We never discussed that in class, did we?" Helena was another student that was always at the top of the class. She was a tall, slim, good-looking blond. Sports was her biggest passion, but she excelled in all the other classes as well. She was probably the most popular teenager in high school, especially with the boys.

"I wondered if anyone would ask me that question." I looked around the room noticing everyone seemed to have the same disillusioned expression on their faces. "Relax, you were only marked on the first twenty questions. I just wanted to see if anyone had an opinion as to what Shakespeare was trying to imply in Act Five, Scene One, when Hamlet asked the sexton: *'How long hast thou been a grave-maker?'* And the sexton replied: *'it was the very same day that young Hamlet was born; he that is mad, and sent to England.'*"

There seemed to be twenty-nine blank faces looking back at me. Then Nicole put up her hand. I was surprised; even though she is a very intelligent girl, she rarely contributes her thoughts to the rest of the class. Nicole is what the other students refer to as Gothic. She only wears the colour black, always seems to be in a dark, pensive mood and rarely smiles. I have heard the kids say, behind her back, that she worships the devil.

"Yes, Nicole, please share your thoughts with us."

"I think that since the sexton started digging graves the very day that Hamlet was born, Shakespeare was insinuating that being born is the first step on our journey towards the grave."

"Very good, Nicole. Of course, Shakespeare was right, but he didn't have to lay it out so bluntly for us. What do you think?"

"Isn't the journey the most important thing here? Not the fact that we are all bound for the grave," Eve Anna said, not sounding completely sure of herself.

"Thank you, Eve Anna." Being a student of philosophy, I was loving where this conversation was headed. "What about in *As You Like It* when Jaques said, *'all the world's a stage, and the men and women merely players'*. He breaks down a human life into seven stages and paints a rather stark and unglamorous picture of our existence: our journey to the grave."

Helena put up her hand, and I nodded for her to respond.

"I'm just a kid. I don't feel that way, but I haven't been crowded into the everyday humdrum of the workplace yet. Some days my biggest worry is whether my skirt matches my blouse."

All the other students laughed. I smiled and motioned for her to continue.

"My mom and dad, that's another story. They seem to be caught in this big rut that they can't seem to get out of. They are so busy trying to make money, they have no time for themselves or their family. I know they feel insignificant and out of control, like rats on one of those little wheels. There are so many people in the world now; one person just seems to get lost in the whole... ."

"You mean they, like most of us sometimes, feel like a tiny cog in the giant social mechanism. Unfortunately, it sounds as if they have been caught in the repressive jaws of a giant consumer trap, set by corporate advertising and dictated by social whim." Since I had written these words in my journal only two days earlier, it was convenient for me to recite them from memory.

"Exactly." Helena seemed glad I expressed what she was trying to say.

"I know what you mean about there being too many people in the world and about us all being crowded together in an almost smothering closeness," I said in an effort to continue the discussion. "I certainly do not have all the answers to this problem. Smarter and more powerful people than I have been grappling with this dilemma since the twentieth century. There are too many people living in poverty, which leads to too much terrorism and crime. I think it is a real shame we all have to go through a metal detector before we can enter the school and have armed guards standing at the door and riding the buses, trains and passenger planes."

Even though it was Friday and this was my last class, I was sorry to hear the bell ring. Before I had a chance to dismiss the class, the principal burst into the room. I was a little taken aback, because he was always courteous enough to knock. He had a strange, anxious expression on his face.

"Sorry to barge in like this. This letter just arrived for you." He held out the letter to me; his hand was shaking violently. "It... it's from NASA."

Suddenly my heart started beating out of control, and a huge lump formed in my throat. Could this be the letter I had been waiting for all this time? I was feeling light headed; so rather than reach out for the letter I had to grab hold of my desk to keep myself steady on my feet. Then I slipped into my desk chair and asked the principal to read the letter for me. He clumsily opened the envelope and unfolded the letter. Still retaining my sense of humour, I decided to dismiss the class.

"You may gather up your things and go home now if you like, class."

"Yeah, right." I heard a voice call out from the back row. "I'm not waiting until Monday to hear the news." Since the entire class was still stuck in their seats, I looked back at the principal to give him the go ahead.

"Dear C. M. Morris: English teacher, Stephen Hawking High School," he began. "Your submission to our Civilian Flight Program Contest has been examined closely, along with almost three-hundred other high school entries. As you know, we are looking for two groups of students: three boys and three girls, along with their chaperones, to fulfill the requirement of our mission. Our NASA staff has selected you and three female students of your choice to take part in an upcoming W.S.S. mission. Congratulations, you and three of your students are going into space."

There was a gigantic roar of approval from the classroom. Everyone was whistling, cheering, jumping up and down, and hugging each other. The principal walked up to me and shook my hand; then he passed me the letter. The students were all huddled around my desk now, excited and anxious to hear what I had to say. I was unable to speak. Going into outer space was something

I had dreamed of since I was a teenager. And which three, of all these wonderful students, would I pick to go with me?

"Well, don't just sit there, say something!" Helena had her arms folded across her delectably full bosom; her eyes were gaping at me, and she sported a facetious grin.

I stood up. My whole body was trembling. It was one of those moments where you are in the spotlight and everyone expects you to have something profound to say, but nothing comes to mind.

"Naturally it's a great honour," I fumbled for the words. "I would also like to say that I would be proud and confident going into space with any student in this room. Unfortunately, I'm only allowed to take three girls with me; so, it is going to be a very difficult decision. I still can't believe this is happening to me. Anyway, have a good weekend, and I'll see you all on Monday."

The principal shook my hand again vigorously, as if he was trying to prime a pump. Then the students each gave me a hug or shook my hand and wished me a good weekend. Eve Anna lingered behind with artful coyness.

"Are you going to take me with you?" she asked; her eyelashes fluttering like a butterfly's wings, displaying a flirtatious impetuousness. The motion drew me into her dreamy hazel eyes,, that sparkled with a mischievous light.

"Actually, I have decided not to take anyone from this class." I had a serious tone in my voice, so at first, she could not tell I was jerking her chain. Her confident smile collapsed into a pitiful frown for the split second she was unsuspecting of my trickery. Then her smile returned, even larger than before.

"You devil," she squealed. "You are going to take me, aren't you?"

"Yes, you know I'm going to take you. How could I leave my favourite student here on earth while I'm out gallivanting around in outer space?"

"Oh, thank you so much!" She sprang forward, wrapped her arms around me, and gave me a big hug. The warmth and youthful firmness of her body against mine was like a penetrating infusion of some indescribable, tender-sweet nuance that was hers and hers alone. I savoured it and sopped it up like a withering plant would take in water. I wanted to hold that sweet nymphet in my arms for a long, long time; but of course, I had to release her at once, for my thoughts were straying far beyond the boundaries of an appropriate teacher-student relationship.

I cleared my throat as I pulled away, pretending to alter my focus to the work on my desk.

"Don't tell a soul until I officially announce the names on Monday," I said, desperately trying to divert my train of thought. Eve Anna, however, was inadvertently making it very difficult for me, because she was twisting her lovely locks of hair around her index finger. She always makes me think impure thoughts when she does that. I could drown in her hair; it is rich and glowing like a dark Irish stout: sparkling and effervescent, with amber highlights.

"Okay, Teach. I'll see you on Monday. Have a good weekend."

Thankfully she was ready to leave. She made a tiny wave, followed by a swirl; then she headed for the door.

"You too, Eve Anna." I was incapable of removing my eyes from the faded seat of her jeans as she walked out of the class room. I was flushed and gently quivering. *Get a grip, you dumbass*, I thought to myself. *She is your student and eight years younger. Have a brain!* But I did not want to have a brain; in spite of my secret oath, I wanted her!

I reminded myself that I needed to stop having these ridiculous thoughts, because I could never act on them; partly because of my pride in my profession and partly because of my strong moral upbringing. I instantly diverted my thoughts to the letter on my desk, which I had not finished reading. NASA had everything worked out beautifully. We would train through the month of July. Then we would have a week's rest before our scheduled lift-off, which was slated for the seventh of August. Our mission onboard the World Space Station would be only one week long. We were to return to Earth on the fourteenth and be de-briefed by the seventeenth. That would allow us ten days to complete our space experiment and make our hypothesis before having to return to the classroom on August 28th. Travel to and from the W.S.S. would be on the new 'Single Stage to Orbit' vehicle. The boys' team was from New York City, and their chaperone was a science teacher named... .

"Adam McGinnis!" I jumped to my feet in total surprise. He was a long-time acquaintance of mine. We grew up together in North Dakota. He and I were very close, right up until the last. It was an ugly scene when we parted. Adam never forgave me for what I did to him. We have not spoken since our last time together. I was apprehensive because I knew it would be awkward working alongside him on our mission.

I gathered up everything I needed for the weekend, left the school and headed for my apartment. I was thinking about Adam and me the whole time. I was confident we could mend our differences.

Chapter Two

AS I SAT IN THE crowded subway car, staring blankly at the armed guard standing across from me, I was trying to imagine Adam and my conversation when we met again after all these years. Over and over, I formulated what I wanted to say in my mind. It was essential that we start again with a clean slate. I had to let him know that it was important that we renew our friendship, but everything else had to remain the same.

As childhood friends we were inseparable. We shot prairie dogs and crows together. We played sports and rode horses together. We were like apple pie and ice cream: we belonged together. When we became teens, Adam changed. He began to look at me in a different light. As much as I loved him, I could never feel for him what he felt for me. I was not attracted to him sexually the way he was to me; in my heart it would be morally wrong. Adam was crushed when I told him the reason we could never be together. There were angry and hurtful words used, such as "freak" and "queer." We never looked each other in the face again.

When we came to my stop, most of the people herded out like cattle; there was the usual pushing and shoving and ill-mannered discourse between the passengers as they stepped off the train. The multitude seemed to look right through me with their hollow eyes, regarding me as nothing more than an obstruction or hindrance in their path. It seemed curious to me that each one of these many bodies, shuffling to the surface, was a unique individual with separate thoughts and feelings; each with their own hopes, dreams, and fears. Most of them would have their own families that they cherished and loved—bringing meaning to their lives. Maybe some of them were happy, but most lived in quiet desperation: being discontent with their overcomplicated urban lives, that were burdened with a constant irritability which grated on them like rats chewing at their soul.

I was glad to get above ground in spite of the fact that it was terribly cold outside. The wind tore at my jacket and stung my face as I walked towards my apartment. I wished I had worn more clothes. I always cursed the children at my school for walking around half frozen, because they are too fashion conscious to cover up with something warm. I am a perpetual nag on the subject. "When I grew up back in North Dakota it was fashionable to be warm," I always say. I never let on that today's North Dakota teens are probably also dressing in a way that I would consider unsuitable.

The guard to my apartment building was standing outside having a smoke when I arrived. We had idle chitchat over the fact that it was finally Friday while he opened the door for me.

"How were all the little brats today?" he asked with a friendly smile, leading me into the back room where I had to check my handgun. I unlocked the tiny storage locker and pulled my .45 out of my backpack. I popped the magazine then pulled back the slide to be certain it would be put away unloaded.

"The brats?... driving me one step closer to early retirement," I joked as he passed his metal detector next to my body and searched through my back pack.

"You're good to go," he said, escorting me to the elevator. "Have a nice evening."

"You too." I turned my back to him and entered the elevator. I thought about what a shame it was, that we had to take all these precautions to protect ourselves these days.

Dude, my cat, casually looked up from his comfortable spot on the back of the couch when I entered my dark apartment.

"Don't bother to get up on my account," I said to him for my own amusement. He stretched and yawned, then went back to sleep. "I'm glad to see you too." I could not help but chuckle to myself as I turned on some more lights to keep the place from seeming lonely. Then I headed for the liquor cabinet. I mixed myself a nice whiskey sour and relaxed on the couch beside the cat.

"What should I make for supper, Dude? What about microwave hotdogs and orange death?" I was referring to the macaroni and cheese that comes in the box.

My cell phone rang. It was lying right beside me.

"Hello."

"Rock, it's Adam. How ya doin'?"

"I'm fine thanks. Where are you calling from?" My heart increased its tempo dramatically.

"I'm in town and I was wondering if I could take you out for dinner?"

"That would be great. I was just wondering what I was going to make for myself. Do you know where I live?"

"Yes, your mother gave me your address. I can be there in about forty-five minutes. Is that okay?"

"That would be fine." This was all so unexpected I could hardly contain myself.

"It's great to hear your voice again, Rock. I can't wait to see you. It has been far too long."

"This is a wonderful surprise. See you." I hung up and hurried to the bathroom. I had just enough time to catch a shower. I had to be in and out, dry my hair, change clothes, and be down stairs before he arrived.

As I stood naked, drying my hair in front of the mirror, I took time out from my thoughts of Adam to admire my well-structured body. It was a ritual of mine. With my blond hair fluttering in the hot breeze, my eyes were pleased with the tightness of my abs. My arms, which I was holding above my head, were a bit too delicate for my liking, but still had respectable contours. I tried to work out whenever I could. I ran my free hand down my left side, following the becoming lines of my trim body. I turned and checked out my ass over my shoulder. It was my best feature. Man, I have a damn fine behind. Adam could not help but be impressed with the way I have kept myself in shape. My shortness was my only true fault, other than maybe my vanity. I just like to be the best I can be, and I always try and encourage that quality in my students.

I dressed in black pants and wore a blue shirt and tie to bring out the aqua in my eyes. I wore my holster under my jacket so that I could carry my gun. I did not like to be without it at night. I went down stairs, collected my side arm, and waited for Adam. I was becoming very nervous in expectation of his arrival.

He stepped through the door. I could feel every excited beat of my heart. He looked a little more mature than the last time I saw him, otherwise he was exactly the same: tall and solidly well-built; the features of a hard-working farm boy that was fed plenty of beef and potatoes with homemade whole wheat bread and fresh cow's milk. Dark hair and green eyes complimented his down-home handsome face and big country boy smile.

"Rock, I can't tell you how good it is to see you." Adam always called me by my nickname; he gave it to me years ago.

I could tell he wanted to give me a manly hug, but I put out my right hand and he received it warmly.

"It's great to see you too. What brings you to Boston?"

"I came to get scrod." He laughed. "No, seriously, I came to help you celebrate. Congratulations by the way."

"Congratulations to you as well." I gave him a friendly slap on the back. "I guess we can celebrate together."

"That's the whole idea." He put his hand on my shoulder and motioned towards the exit.

"Wait a minute. I just found out maybe three hours ago. How did you get here so fast?"

"Promise not to tell?"

"Of course. You know me, always a model of discretion." I smiled and winked.

"I have a friend at NASA. He phoned and spilled the beans a week ago."

We stepped through the door and I pointed down the street.

"This way. I know you like sea food. There's a wonderful restaurant down the street that still accepts cash and serves the freshest fish in town."

"I've been resisting getting a microchip implant as well, but there are getting to be fewer and fewer business that will accept any other form of payment these days; before long, being without a personal identity chip will mean total detachment from modern society." Adam shook his head in disgust as he spoke.

The governments of the world were not forcing the sheeple to participate in the identity chip program, but it was being strongly promoted as an essential convenience. In reality, it was a convenient tool for them to track your every purchase and your every movement. Unfortunately, it was becoming impossible to get by without one.

"Remember in the bible, they warned us that the 'Mark of the Beast' was coming. I never expected it would be in my lifetime." As I said this, I was thinking about how the Bible also said that if you took the mark and engaged in the system you would be rejected from Heaven.

"Are you packing?" he asked, diverting our thoughts away from a depressing subject matter.

"Yes, I am. Why?"

"It's just that I feel a lot safer knowing you have your piece. Do you still carry that old .45 Colt Government model? The one your grandfather gave you."

"I'd never part with it."

"I'm surprised you haven't traded up to one of those new caseless composites. You know, the ones with the electronic ignition. They only weigh a fraction of that old cannon."

"It's partly the expense and partly the sentiment involved. Sure, it's heavy, but there is something about the feel of steel and wood that makes me feel more confident."

"Don't get me wrong. You're one of the best shots I know. I've seen what you can do with that thing. Two thugs with those fancy modern guns wouldn't stand a chance against The *Rock*."

"I love it when you lay it on thick like that." We both laughed. Adam knew he could gain some points by complimenting me on my marksmanship.

We caught up on all the news in each other's lives while we walked down the street. Adam was assistant principal at his school in New York. He was enjoying his life as a science teacher. He said he was dating lots, but has never been in a steady relationship. Apparently, he roomed with another guy to save on rent, because the rent on apartments in New York is brutal. I told him about my school and my cat and how I was still sworn to celibacy. I was shocked at how dull my life sounded when I reduced it to cold, hard facts.

The restaurant was not fancy, but we did not come for the ambience. The waiter seated us at an intimate table for two next to the kitchen. I ordered a Pilsner Urquel and Adam asked for a Stella Artois. When our drinks arrived, I raised my glass and made a toast.

"Here's to long-lost drinking buddies." I looked at Adam and suddenly became sentimental against my will. As hard as I tried, I could not stop tears from moistening my eyes. Seeing this, Adam was also overcome by his emotions, and he too became a little teary eyed.

"Let's not ever become distant again, Rock," he said, raising his glass with one hand and wiping a tear from his eye with the other. "I've missed you more than you can ever know."

"You're right. Old friends like us should be able to work out our differences." I touched his glass with mine; then there was silence for a moment. I was thankful the waitress came to take our order. Adam ordered the scrod and I asked for the shrimp.

"I suppose you have selected the three boys for the trip. Especially since you knew that we were going a week before I did." I had to throw in that little dig.

"Yes, I have actually. They are three very intelligent and capable young men. I'm sure they'll be a little too metropolitan for your liking, but they'll be perfect for this mission."

"You mean they're sissies?"

"You always had a way of cutting through all the crap, didn't you, Rock. I wouldn't want to take them on a camping trip in the Rocky Mountains, but for something scientific and technical like this, they'll be perfect."

"Don't misunderstand me. I'm not judging. I'm just trying to get a mental picture, that's all."

"What about the girls? Have you made up your mind?"

"I think so; three very intelligent, yet characteristically diverse individuals."

"Sounds intriguing. I can hardly wait to meet them."

His attention was instantly diverted to the waitress. Our food had arrived. She put down our meals and asked if there was anything else we wanted; then she walked away carrying the tray above her head. I could not help but stare at her curvaceous body as she made her way to the kitchen.

"Our waitress has a bodacious little ass, don't you think?" I was trying to make guy talk with Adam, but he had something, or someone, else on his mind. He barely took his eyes off me through the whole meal. Just before the dessert came, he gushed.

"Rock, you look incredible. You still have that magic about you." He reached out and tried to take my hand. "You know I still love you madly, don't you?"

I pulled my hand back in self-defence.

"I suspected as much," I said rather callously. "I was hoping the subject wouldn't come up, especially since you already know my dirty little secret."

"I'm sorry. Truly I am. I thought I was over you, but just one look at you and... bam! You damn near set me on my ass." He bowed his head in pain.

"Adam, you are the sweetest, most kind, and most giving person I have ever had the pleasure of knowing. You are the best friend I've ever had and I love you more than I could love any man; but unfortunately, I could never give you what you want and need. I can never have sex with you. It's the whole gender dysfunction thing I'm uncomfortable with. In my heart I feel it is immoral."

"Rock, come on, how could two people who love each other as much as we do be immoral in the eyes of God? You are the most moral individual I've ever known. From where I'm sitting, it looks like a match made in heaven."

"Think of how it looks to me. From where I'm sitting, one of us is the wrong sex. I can't tell you how I have yearned for a loving relationship that didn't make me feel ashamed. Love and sex just aren't in the cards for me, Adam."

"Just because you haven't been dealt a strong hand doesn't mean you have to fold."

"It's unfair of you to say that. You know I have always tried to do the absolute best I can with the cards God dealt me. I don't feel as if I have been stuck with a losing hand; it's just not well suited to the game of intimacy. A poor hand in poker may turn out to be a winner in a game of wild card rummy."

"Lord knows you've always been a bit of a wild card, Rock. But that's always been part of your charm. Now let's cut through all the metaphoric crap; the bottom line is I love you and I want to be with you forever."

"Adam, this whole conversation is scaring the hell out of me!" I raised my voice and tried to sound firm. "Please tell me I'm not going to lose you over this issue again, because I feel the same way today as I did ten years ago."

"Don't worry, I'm not going to run away mad this time. I think I knew what your answer was going to be, but I just had to try. Can you forgive me?"

"Come on, let's forget about dessert. I'm taking you home with me. We'll have a nightcap and then we can go to bed. Just not in the same room."

"That's sweet of you, Rock. I'd like that." Adam raised his hand to catch the waitress's attention. "Check please," he announced.

"I'd like to pay for my own meal," I said with a self-reliant tone, while counting out the required amount of bills from my wallet.

"If you insist." Adam knew enough not to contest issues of money with me. "Your share comes to one hundred and ninety-two credits."

"A credit sure doesn't go very far nowadays."

"Yes, especially on a teacher's salary."

I was trying to get by on a lousy three hundred and fifty thousand a year since the global economic reset. Now my generation was paying the price for a profoundly corrupt and willfully ignorant episode in world history, where past generations used the fiat money system to steal wealth and resources from the future, so that they could live beyond their means during their lifetimes. They accomplished this, not though personal labour or production, but by printing up money out of thin air and accumulating debt at every level of society until the debt became so immense that it imploded on itself, creating extreme hardship and loss of life throughout the world.

I made the concession of taking Adam's hand as we left the restaurant. He looked down at me with a very contented expression and smiled. We must have appeared vulnerable walking down the street hand in hand, because a tough looking character jumped out of an alley and accosted us. Before I knew it, I was grabbed from behind by his partner, and a knife was thrust in my face.

"Give me your money or I will cut your friend's throat," they demanded of Adam.

For some reason I did not feel panic at all; rather, a sense of calm determination flowed through my entire body. My mind shifted from light heartedness to fierce resolve. I winked at Adam—who had a look of pure terror in his eyes—and slipped my hand under my coat. I drew my .45 from its warm home and clicked off the safety. Then I worked it slowly around behind me without the robbers being aware of what I was doing.

"I think you had better put that knife down, if you know what's good for you!" Adam stated boldly.

"Oh, yea, whatchya gonna do about it, fuck-face."

"I have a gun pointed right at your nuts, asshole!" I tried to sound forceful. As soon as he stepped back to look down, I spun around and stuck the muzzle in his face. Both men dropped what they were carrying and fled. For some strange reason I started to laugh. My heart was pounding wildly and my hands were shaking; but somehow, I saw the whole thing as being funny.

"Rock, what's got into you?" Adam sounded confused and amazed. "We could have been killed."

"I think it must be an adrenaline release or something." I was still chuckling as I picked the knives off the pavement and handed them to Adam. Then I knelt down again to check out a small cooler one of them had dropped. "Did you see the look on that ass-hole's face when I stuck my gun up his nose?"

"You're one tough hombre, Rock." Adam was finally able to relax and smile. He looked at the knives and laughed.

"I may be small, but I'm mighty," I joked, as I opened the lid of the cooler. It contained an ice pack, three scalpels, two loaded syringes, and some freezer bags; a curious collection of objects that held a clue to the thugs' intentions.

"Who was it that said, 'God created men, but it was Samuel Colt who made them equal'?"

"I'm not sure, probably John Wayne or somebody like him." I closed the cooler's lid slowly, and then looked up at Adam.

"These things must have set those poor bastards back eight or nine hundred apiece." Adam was looking at the knives in his hand. "I don't think we'll have any more trouble with them tonight."

"Why, because they lost their blades?"

"No, I'm sure they had to go straight home to change their shorts."

We both laughed hysterically. I put my gun away. Then we resumed our walk back to my apartment. Adam put his arm around me. I allowed it, because I sensed it was a show of friendship and pride more than anything else.

We tossed the cooler and the knives into the first dumpster we came across.

"What has the world come to, Adam? A person can't even walk down the streets without fearing for your life anymore." The stark reality of the hold-up was just starting to sink in, and I felt a cold wave of terror sweep through my entire body. What if the robber had grabbed my arm and wrestled my gun away? Adam and I could have been shot to death with my own firearm. I shook my head; I could not believe I handled the whole thing so calmly.

"With all the terrorism and hate in the world today, I think there's only one solution: it's time for another flood."

"You mean the forty-day and forty-night, Old Testament type of flood?"

"Exactly."

"It may have to come to that," I said, opening the door to my building. I gave my gun a thankful last glance as I put it away in its locker for the night. We went upstairs, and I gave Adam the tour of my apartment. He let on he was impressed with my decorating skills. I made us each a hot toddy, and then we sat on the couch.

"So, this is the Dude," he said, patting my cat on the head.

"He's a good, hard cat," I explained. Then Adam gave me an inquisitive glance, as I expected he would. "Good for nothing and hard on the grub."

We both had a good laugh at the Dude's expense. He was just a barnyard cat that I had brought from home, but he had adapted to city life quite nicely.

"You know, you could sleep in my bed tonight as long as you promise to stay on your own half." I was feeling guilty about making him sleep on my old couch.

"Thanks, but the sofa will be fine. I'd never be able to get to sleep lying so close to you like that. I would just lie there having indecent thoughts, sporting a bone so hard a dog couldn't chew it."

We both laughed again with gusto. It was great that we were feeling at ease with each other in spite of our past history.

"We are going to be all right now, aren't we, Adam?"

"Yes, Rock, I think everything is going to be right with us."

Since there was an awkward silence for a few moments, I asked Adam if he would like to watch the news. He thought that was a great idea.

"Computer." I spoke in a loud enough voice so that it could hear me from the other side of the room.

"Yes, how may I help you?" the computer addressed me.

"Television, local news for Boston."

My large-screen, Integrated Computer Terminal switched on. The rectangular format was split into thirds, displaying three separate newscasts from which I had to choose.

"Channel twelve, please."

There had been a terrorist attack on London, England today. A large bomb was set off during a soccer match killing three-thousand and injuring many more. World authorities were still searching for five missing nuclear war heads that were lost from the inventories of the former Soviet Union. There was a riot in New Orleans as the poor and homeless protested for free access to food, shelter, and medical attention. There had been six homicides in Boston within the last twenty-four hours. Two of the bodies were found with all their vital organs removed. They had been murdered so that their organs could be harvested and then sold on the black market. Apparently, a heart would sell for half a million credits.

"You realize, Rock, that could have been us," Adam admitted. "I didn't want to say anything before, but the stuff in the cooler was kind of a giveaway. The hoodlums had exactly that in mind when they attacked us."

"I kind of suspected as much," I confessed. It was not the first time I had seen incidents of that nature on the news. Actually, it was quite common. But hearing the news anchor give graphic descriptions of similar cases in the same city, on the same night, that ended in death and mutilation, was extremely disturbing. "It's terrible that we can put a price on a human life like that."

"It makes me sick to my stomach to think that we came that close to being eviscerated on the street like a worthless animal. How could anyone do such a thing?"

"There are so many people crowded into the cities these days, I guess they figure one less is no big deal."

"But how do they dehumanize it?"

"Don't ask me to explain the criminal mind. All I know is five-hundred thousand sounds pretty attractive."

"Money really is the root of all evil, isn't it?"

"Don't get me started." I could have gone on all night itemizing the evil and harm mankind has done in the pursuit of the almighty dollar.

"Let's watch something else, shall we? The news is too depressing."

"How about some music?"

"I'd like that."

"Computer... search your music files for Holst, Gustav... The Planets. The Montreal symphony Orchestra... Nineteen, eighty-seven recording with Charles Dutoit conductor. Track seven please... Neptune." I called out my selection. "This is my favourite recording of this piece. Thank goodness it was recorded digitally. It sounds as good today, forty-five years later, as it sounded back then. I love to play this right before bedtime because it relaxes me."

We sat listening quietly for a few moments, enjoying the mystical quality of the music.

"You know what I think about sometimes?" Adam broke the silence.

"I'll play your silly game. What do you think?" I was trying to be a smart aleck.

"It has been over a century since we have had a true musical genius like Mozart, Beethoven, or Tchaikovsky."

"You're right." I thought about the provocative nature of his words, adding my own observation: "And what about architecture. Just think of the amazing structures that were erected centuries ago, like The Taj Mahal, The Parthenon, Notre-Dame and Gaudy's cathedral; they were masterpieces of design. Today our buildings are technological marvels, but they only have one thing going for them: they are just big."

"Look at painting and sculpture. When was the last time we had a Michelangelo, a Monet, or a Van Gogh? There again, not in the last century. I think that says a thing or two about modern humanity."

"Maybe it says something about us?" I am not sure where that came from, but I was shocked by my own words.

"Us as teachers? That's rather profound, Rock. There's much fodder for thought in those words."

And chew on that fodder we did. For over a minute we were pensive. It was a little disturbing for both of us, to say the least. Adam was the first to speak.

"I like this music. It's sort of buoyant and atmospheric, like you are floating in a tall ship on a dead calm sea."

"When I listen to this piece, I think about being lost in space, cut off from all humanity, slowly drifting through the cosmos for eternity."

"That's not really a picture I want to have in my mind under the present circumstances."

"Oops." I did not make the connection until Adam pointed it out to me. "On second thought, I like your analogy better."

We decided it was time for bed. I got Adam settled on the couch; then we said goodnight. When I was almost to my room, Adam reminded me that he loved me. I did not feel awkward telling him I loved him as well. After lying in bed, wide awake for over an hour, a thought occurred to me that I had to share with Adam. I slipped quietly to his side and whispered.

"Adam, are you still awake?"

"Well, yeah." He made it sound like a given. "What's on your mind?"

"I've made a decision about us that I just had to share."

Adam sat bolt upright as if he had been zapped by a mild electric shock.

"What kind of decision?" He seemed to be expecting more than I was prepared to offer.

"I'm not quite sure how to say this, but anyway, here goes. Sometime in the future, when we are past middle age and sexual relations doesn't seem so important to you anymore, if you still haven't found someone, I'll be more than happy to be your companion for the rest of our lives. We could grow old together."

"That's wonderful, Rock." He threw his arms around me and gave me a big hug, then let me go as soon as he sensed I was uncomfortable in his embrace. It was easy to see he was happy with my proposal.

"Remember, no matter what, I'm not giving up my oath of celibacy. It's the only way that I keep my sanity. And I want you to actively pursue a more appropriate mate than myself until you feel you have reached that stage in your life. Only you will know in your heart when that time comes."

"It sounds like a very fair and wonderful arrangement."

"Promise me you'll make a determined effort to find someone else first."

"I promise."

He did not sound very convincing, but I did not persist. We said our goodnights again, and I think we both slept soundly after that; we had a lot more peace of mind about our future and about our friendship.

Chapter Three

A TEN-YEAR-OLD MERCEDES PULLED INTO the parking lot of the Mother Teresa Humanitarian Hospital in Mombasa, Kenya. The car was driven instinctively, through the pouring rain, to a parking spot labelled: "Reserved for Dr. Albert Maxwell". The physician turned off the engine and sat thinking for several minutes before he opened the door. He was worried about a patient in his care. A portly man of medium height wearing a finely tailored suit that was slightly tattered and had seen better days, exited the vehicle. He had salt and pepper greying hair and a moustache. Perched half way down his prominent nose was a pair of wire frame spectacles that gave him an air of undisputable intelligence. The pensive expression on his lightly stubbled face was evidence of his concern. As soon as he wiggled into his trench coat and opened his umbrella, a bolt of lightning struck a nearby tree, creating a cannon shot of thunder that almost brought him to his knees. The flash must have disturbed the heavens, because heavier drops of rain raced to the ground, causing earth and sky to collide in a tumult of dancing water and gushing mud.

Distracted by his thoughts and the rain, the doctor did not see an oncoming car as he stepped out onto the street adjacent to the hospital. The sizzling of skidding tires on wet pavement instantly caught his attention. He lept back awkwardly to escape being struck by the swerving car, but was smacked by the rear panel and thrown off his feet.

The native African man behind the wheel, jammed the car into park and ran to the Doctor's assistance.

"Dr. Maxwell," he shouted. Panic dominated his features. "Are you injured?"

The doctor raised his hand for assistance, looking up at two white eyes and a dark face that blended into the early morning shadows. "No, I'm fine. Just shook up a little, that's all."

"I'm so very sorry, Doctor. You stepped out right in front of me; I didn't have time to react." The man helped the doctor to his feet.

"Yes, it's all my fault. I had a lot on my mind and I wasn't paying close enough attention; just a stupid little mistake."

"You should be more careful, Dr. Maxwell. Next time a little mistake might kill you." The dark man flashed a row of pearl white teeth and made one of his eyes disappear in a wink as he wrapped his arm around the Doctor's waist and helped him across the street.

"I'll be fine from here, thank you. Sorry for the inconvenience." Dr. Maxwell knew the man was one of his many patients, but he was still in shock and could not remember his name.

"God was with you today, good doctor. Farewell and be careful." He was forced to turn and walk away because his car was holding up traffic.

The doctor hung up his sopping trench coat upon entry to his office. He then started trimming his beard with his laser-razor, while he called the head nurse on the intercom.

Intervention

"Nurse Hogen, how is our patient from the Highlands Territory doing?"

"Oh... hello, Dr. Maxwell. Not very well I'm afraid. You had better come down here right away and have a look at him."

"Have you ever seen anything like this before, Nurse?" Dr. Maxwell said, a few minutes later, after seeing his highlands patient.

"No, I worked in a city hospital before I came here. We do not see many diseases of that nature there." She remained silent for a moment. "How about Miss Arubu? She worked here for forty years before she retired."

"Do you think she's well enough to come in and confirm my diagnosis?" Miss Arubu was currently a patient of Dr. Maxwell's. She was having heart trouble and was very weak as a result. "I could go and pick her up in my car, if she is able."

"I'll call her at once."

The doctor got up from his desk and headed for the nurses' station.

"Marjorie is having one of her better days and seems to be in a good mood." Mrs. Hogen greeted Dr. Maxwell with the news as he entered her office. She was still beaming after her phone conversation. Miss Arubu had a way of lifting everybody's spirits. She was greatly missed at the hospital, especially by Dr. Maxwell. They were both very much alike: being two of the most giving, unselfish individuals you would find anywhere. Each of them had devoted their lives to ease the suffering of underprivileged people.

When the doctor arrived back with Miss Arubu, he used the sheltered emergency entrance to help her into the hospital. Miss Arubu was a native African, aged 64 years. She was a large woman, both tall and wide across the middle, giving the impression she was an individual that commanded respect. Her round, cheerful face, however, told another story. She seemed to be in perpetual good spirits with her brilliantly white teeth always displayed in a contented smile, which forced dimples to form in her full cheeks. Her features were care-worn, but her eyes were dark and persistently warm, bright and jolly. She was always a pleasure to work with, never bossy or condescending.

The doctor found disposable body suits for Miss Arubu and himself. They also covered their faces with surgical masks and a visor.

"Are you sure about this, Marjorie? This is a dreadful and, I suspect, highly infectious disease. No one would think less of you if you chose not to go in there."

"I chose to help the sick for over forty years. Why should I stop now? Besides, I'm going to die anyway if they do not find a new heart for me soon." She stretched a pair of surgical gloves over her hands as she spoke.

"You're an angel to be sure. I'm convinced there will be a new heart for you in short order."

"It's sweet of you to say that, Albert. But you know as well as I do, I don't stand a chance in hell of ever getting to the top of the waiting list before my time is up."

Dr. Maxwell just shrugged; he was well aware of just how long the heart waiting lists were.

"By the way, how is your research going? Things were looking very promising before I had to leave." Miss Arubu and the doctor had been working on an anti-rejection drug made from an indigenous plant found in the forests of Kenya. Her grandfather was a native Medicine Man who had shown her many amazing herbal remedies before he died. One in particular showed promise in the field of organ transplantation; more specifically, inter-species transplants or xenotransplantation.

"Remember the pig's heart we put in Elvis the chimpanzee? His new heart is still functioning perfectly."

"Dr. Maxwell! That was six months ago."

"Yes, I know. Isn't it wonderful?"
"Albert, you'll go down in history."
"I couldn't have done it without you."

He placed his hand on her back, and led her into the room. The patient was tossing and turning in his bed and moaning in agony. There was blood on his pillow, that he had obviously coughed up during the night. The doctor pointed out the open lesions covering the unfortunate individual's body and took his temperature, which was extremely high.

Miss Arubu lifted the black man's eyelids, uncovering two infernal red spheres inhabiting sockets once occupied by cool-white human eyes. Then she felt the patient's testes and the glands under the neck to check for swelling. She was holding up one of his hands, looking down rubbing his palms, when he sat up suddenly and coughed convulsively in her direction. She jumped back as fast as she could, but had almost certainly been in his line of fire. She thought she felt a tiny speck of moisture hit her in the corner of the eye, but disregarded that notion because she was outfitted with a visor.

Dr. Maxwell raced to Miss Arubu's side.

"My God, Marjorie. He coughed all over you?"

"Dr. Maxwell, lock the door to this room, and go have a shower with disinfectant soap at once! Then call the Global Institution for Infectious Diseases." Miss Arubu and the doctor hurried to the showers.

•———•

After his shower, Dr. Maxwell met Miss Arubu at the cafeteria.

"Well, what do you think about my patient? Is it Ebola?"

"There has never been a recorded case of Ebola in this part of Africa."

"What the hell could it be then?" Dr. Maxwell was alarmed by the change in Marjorie's expression. He had never seen her look so grim.

"Something worse, something more insidious. Maybe the deadliest form of hemorrhagic fever that mankind has ever experienced. Did you send a sample of his blood away to be analyzed?"

"Yes, of course. I flew one out to Cape Town yesterday, but I don't understand... ."

"The patient will be dead by the time you get the results."

"You're scaring me, Marjorie. What is it?

"Years ago, when I was just starting out as a nurse, I witnessed a similar case that came out of a small village in the highlands territory. The doctor at the time was Francis Licks." Marjorie stopped and covered her face to hide her tears. She felt embarrassed to have the doctor see her this way.

"It's okay, Marjorie. I understand."

"No, you don't!" It was uncharacteristic of her to snap at him. "No one could."

"It's important that I know what happened."

"Maybe we did the wrong thing. I don't know. We didn't have much time; we had to act fast. Dr. Licks and I did what we thought was right under the extreme conditions."

Miss Arubu was becoming hysterical. Dr. Maxwell grabbed her by the shoulders and gave her a gentle shake.

"Marjorie, for God's sake pull yourself together. Calm down, your heart can't take this."

Miss Arubu wiped the tears from her eyes, took a deep breath and then continued.

"We traveled around to all the smaller villages back in those days, administering care out of the back of a Land Cruiser truck. We treated minor infections, mended broken bones; you know, simple country doctoring, nothing fancy. We weren't prepared or equipped to deal with what happened. The man staggered into the village, so close to death it was a miracle he had gotten that far. He had those same ghostly red eyes and bleeding sores all over his body. Inky-black feces was splattered all over his behind, and bloody vomit was all down his front. He gasped and gurgled inside as he struggled to breathe, so that he could choke out his last words. 'They're all dead,' he kept saying. I can still hear his pitiful plea. 'They're all dead. They're all dead.'" Miss Arubu repeated painfully.

Dr. Maxwell squeezed her hand, beseeching her to continue.

"We probably should have taken tissue samples to have analyzed and performed an autopsy, but it just didn't seem worth the gamble. The doctor and I took one look at each other and knew at once what had to be done; we didn't have to say a word. Dr. Licks went straight to the Land Cruiser and grabbed a gas can off the back. We burned him, Dr. Maxwell. The villagers were so petrified at the sight of him, they hauled wood all afternoon to fuel the fire. There was nothing left but ashes when we were done.

"As soon as Dr. Licks started the fire, he turned to me and asked me to strip. I was a bashful young girl at the time, but I was so terrified I undressed in front of the whole village without even giving it a second thought. The doctor and I threw our clothes in the fire; then we rubbed each other down with disinfectant.

"The next day Dr. Licks recruited a handful of men from the village to go with him to the home of the dead man. All I know is, they burned the whole village. Dr. Licks would never speak of the incident after he came back. We stayed at the village until we were sure the disease had been contained; then we went home. The incident was never filed or recorded in any way. Dr. Licks was just starting to practice medicine. He was young and inexperienced the same as me; he didn't need to be grilled by the medical community over the incident."

"Why do you suppose we have never seen another case of that nature until now?"

"I think the virus is a freak of nature; something that normally does not belong in the grand scheme of things."

"Please explain."

"It's my theory that the virus is some sort of genetic hybrid, haphazardly derived from human contact with another animal. The two parent viruses are relatively benign as they are, but when you put them together, they become a killer. As you know, this sort of thing only happens on a very limited scale. The chances of it happening in nature are astronomical; that's why we usually only see this sort of thing once in a lifetime."

"Or in your case, twice."

"Aren't I the lucky one?" Miss Arubu sat staring off into space for a moment. "I talked to a lot of the tribal elders after that, asking them if they had witnessed anything similar to what I had seen. My grandfather was the only one that would talk about it with me. Sometime in his youth, he and his father went to visit a neighbouring tribe. When they got there, everyone was dead from symptoms the same as our patient and the man I watched die in the village. They knew enough not to get too close; they waited until the wind was blowing towards the river, then they left the entire village in ashes."

"If the virus is such an effective killer, why do you suppose it has never spread any further than a single village?"

"In some ways this particular virus is its own worst enemy. It kills so fast and so efficiently it runs out of hosts in short order. But I think we've been lucky in the past, because it emerged in a secluded, lowly populated area. If it had somehow gotten out into the mainstream population, the results could have been devastating."

"My god! What have I got on my hands here, Marjorie?"

"The wrath of God Himself." Marjorie looked into the doctor's eyes with a penetrating stare, emphasizing her seriousness. "You must take every precaution at your disposal."

"Is there anything I can do for the patient?"

"I guess all you can do is prescribe the new antiviral drugs and hope for the best."

"What would your grandfather administer in a case like this?"

"One ounce of straight Canadian whiskey, three times a day."

They both felt relieved to laugh.

Chapter Four

I WENT TO SCHOOL ON Monday the same as usual, but I knew the events of the day would be far from normal. The students of grade 12A filed into class one by one and each glanced at me inquisitively as they passed my desk. Each one was curious, wanting to know my decision. Because of my mischievous nature, I had decided to prolong the announcement as long as possible. When everyone had been accounted for, I got up from my desk and started my lesson for the day.

"At the start of Act five, scene two, Hamlet and Horatio are in a hall in the castle. Hamlet is telling Horatio of the king's plot to have him killed upon his arrival to England. Please open your books to that page. On lines eight to eleven, Hamlet said, *'Our indiscretion sometimes serves us well when our deep plots do pall; and that should teach us that there's a divinity that shapes our ends, rough-hew them how we will'*."

I looked up from my copy of the play to see that none of the class had their books open like I had asked; they were all just sitting there looking dumbfounded. I decided to keep teaching until someone said something. "By this he meant: that no matter how badly flawed our hard thought-out plans are, sometimes God, or fate, has to step in and correct matters."

Finally, it was too much for Helena to bear.

"Come on, Teach. How can you expect us to concentrate on Shakespeare when you know we have something else on our mind?"

"I suppose you want to know my decision concerning the NASA trip?"

A unanimous, "Well, yeah," arouse from the class.

"First, I would like to say that this was a very difficult decision, because any one of you would be suitable for the mission. And of course, NASA excluded half of you from my selection by asking for three girls. Sorry guys." There was a muted rumble of discontentment from the boys. "I'm going to need the full cooperation of all the young men and women in this class that I'm unable to select. The four of us that are going on the mission will need your full moral and objective support." I put down my copy of Hamlet. "Anyway, I've held you in suspense long enough. I have already talked to your parents this morning, while you were on your way to school, so it's a done deal. Eve Anna, Helena, and Nicole are the lucky ones going into space. Congratulations, girls."

There was a variety of screams, cheers, whistles, boos, and cat calls that erupted from the class. Helena burst into tears of joy, Nicole just sat there with a stunned look of unexpected jubilation and Eve Anna tried, unconvincingly, to act surprised. Everyone was out of their desks and crowding around the three future astronauts. That is when I realized I should have waited until noon to make the announcement.

"Well, I guess we might as well kiss our regular classes good-bye for today," I declared.

There was another cheer.

"Sit down please, everyone. Sit down and I'll tell you what I have planned for our space project." There was a slow procession back to their seats. The truth was, I could not think of a decent project when it was time to send the application to NASA. In desperation, I came up with the idea of studying the effects of space travel on memory retention. I thought it was absurd at the time, but obviously someone at NASA liked the idea. I was not going to tell the students this, of course.

"The project I have chosen is going to require quite a bit of work on your part, girls. I want to do several tests of memory retention here on earth under normal conditions. We will also do an equal number of similar tests in outer space. When we get back to earth, we'll compare your scores and make a hypothesis. In other words, does the effect of space travel have any effect on the part of the brain that controls our memory?"

"What kinds of things are we going to be required to memorize?" Nicole asked.

"Just about everything you can think of, Nicole. All the teachers in the school are helping me out with this. They are each contributing four similar projects; two of these you will do on earth and the other two companion projects will be done on board the new World Space Station. With each project you will have fifteen minutes to study the information provided; then you will be asked to exchange the information sheets for a questionnaire on the subject and you will have an equal amount of time to fill that out. There will be a total of one hundred test procedures for each individual. On the space station I plan on doing five hours testing every day for five days. In order to keep the experiment consistent, we'll have to do the same thing here on Earth. Instead of having the usual one week break at Easter, Eve Anna, Helena, Nicole and I will be working on our project in the classroom." There was a cheer of approval from the rest of the class. "Do any of our three future astronauts have a problem with that?"

"I'm not looking forward to the work, but I think the whole concept is exciting. Not only do we get to go into space, but we get to take part in a real scientific experiment." Helena was overflowing with enthusiasm.

"Nicole?"

"It all sounds fine to me."

"Eve Anna?"

"Bring it on." She was always game to try anything.

"That pretty much settles it then. It's outer space, or bust." In an instant I wished that I had used a better choice of words.

Chapter Five

THERE WERE MANY THINGS GOING through my mind as I motored towards NASA headquarters in my chauffeur driven government car. The on-board computer was dishing out digitally composed, synthesized music—which I hated—and it was a constant distraction to my thoughts. I was assured that the Commander of Flight Operations would be there to greet me on my arrival. It was a great honour to be given a personal tour of the facility by such a high-ranking individual. I thought about the girls and what a big responsibility it was for me to be looking out for them on this mission. I thought about Adam and how difficult it was going to be working right alongside him in the close quarters of the space station. And of course, I thought about the danger involved. It was no secret that the new SSTO vehicle was a big embarrassment to NASA. They had spent trillions getting it off the ground, only to find that it was very difficult to fly. There were several near disasters. They had hoped that the giant onboard computers would be capable of controlling the inferior aerodynamics of the SSTO; but, no matter what they tried, the thing had all the grace of a turkey in the air. From what I have read, there are only five individuals that are capable of piloting the craft.

After clearing several security checkpoints, we were at the commander's office building. The driver asked me to wait in the car while he notified his superior. Within five minutes I was shaking hands with a very agreeable gentleman that looked to be in his fifties. We exchanged introductions and the usual pleasantries; then the commander led me to a small, three-wheeled vehicle that we were going to ride on our tour. It was just a modified, battery powered golf cart, but it served our needs perfectly. He showed me the living quarters where the girls and I would be staying during our training and the many different buildings that housed the training devices and simulators. Our next stop was the Single Stage to Orbit vehicle.

It was housed in an immense hanger on the edge of the base. Two armed guards stood at the small entrance door, but made no effort to challenge our entry when they saw my companion. The SSTO vehicle was much larger than I could have imagined. If I had thought about how much fuel it had to carry to get itself into outer space, I would have been better prepared to witness its immensity for the first time. It looked like a giant bullet that had been squashed flat in a vice; and just like its predecessor, the space shuttle, it was covered with heat resistant ceramic tiles. There were several technicians working on the enormous engines, which were the most important contributing factor in the vehicle's special ability to achieve orbit without the luxury of an extra stage or external fuel tanks. There was a tall, heavy-set man in a military uniform standing and overseeing the activity.

"We're in luck," the commander pointed to the large man standing behind the engines, "that's your pilot, Captain Dick." We pulled up beside him and got out of the car, so that I could get acquainted.

"This is Captain Richard Dick. He will be your pilot on this mission."

The big man in the air force uniform turned around slowly and indifferently to take stock of us. He motioned a salute to the commander as a chore of necessity; then looked down at me with annoyance. His appearance was very peculiar and menacing. His mere presence could cause content babies to cry and well-mannered dogs to bite.

He had a receding chin and his forehead sloped back at a sharp angle, causing his already prominent nose to stick out like a snout. I was met with a grunt of disapproval and a bucktoothed sneer. When the commander made the introductions, I put out my hand as a required courtesy. He ignored my gesture of good will, turning his head to look at some imaginary distraction inside the rocket engines, thus revealing a pronounced angular profile that made an inner voice inside me scream, *"rat!"*

"Pleased to meet you," I choked out against all reason.

He was forced to turn and look at me again. His venomous eyes, that were jaundiced and looked like two piss holes in the snow, glared out from under a single dark and gnarly eyebrow that spanned the entire width of his flabby head.

"Weasel! Weasel!" the little voice ranted uncontrollably.

"So, you think you want to take a bunch of snot-nosed brats into space, do you?" he squeaked.

"That seems to be the general idea, according to NASA," I blurted out in self-defence.

"You realize, the whole fucking trip is just a publicity stunt to get more money out of the government, don't you?" His shrill voice grated on me like fingernails down a chalkboard.

"I suspected as much," I said, taking half a step back to distance myself from his foul breath.

"Don't worry, Shorty. I'll get your prissy, high-classed little brats to the station and back safely," he chattered, pointing at me and waving his finger to emphasize his statement. "I'm the best fucking SSTO pilot NASA has got, and don't you forget it."

Shorty! That weasel just called me, Shorty. I could not believe my ears. The nerve of that bastard. I was flabbergasted. I know I am only five-foot f--- all, but that does not give anybody the right to call me Shorty. I wanted to punch him right in his oversized gut, but I reminded myself that my life was going to be in this man's hands and maybe it would be a bad idea to get him more annoyed than he was already. I decided to try and appeal to him politely.

"I would appreciate it if you would call me by my surname, thank you." I was thinking it only proper that he adhere to military protocol.

"I'll think about it, Shorty." He tilted his head back and peered down his beak at me with a condescending expression. Then he turned his back to us and left.

"Well," said the Commander of Flight Operations, "you've met our infamous Captain Dick."

"What an asshole!" I could not hold back my true feelings.

"Many people would agree with you; but the fact of the matter is, he's been with the SSTO program since its inception and knows the vehicle inside out and backwards. He was correct when he said he is the best SSTO pilot at NASA. As a matter of fact, he's leaps ahead of anyone else we have. You couldn't be in better hands."

"I'll have to take your word for it, but it's not going to be easy working with him."

"Richard has a lot of faults, I'll agree. If it weren't for his superior piloting skills, he would have been kicked out of the military years ago. He has an ego twice his own mass, is a notorious womanizer, male chauvinist, and a borderline psychopath; but the problem is, unfortunately the SSTO is a very difficult vehicle to fly. Because there are going to be civilian children and their escorts on board, I'm committed to safety above all else. I hope you can understand where I'm coming from?"

"Yes, I guess I'll just have to make the best of a bad situation."

"One of the main reasons we brought you down here today was to inform you of the risks involved and introduce you to your pilot. If you're uncomfortable with any part of the mission, please do not hesitate to withdraw yourself and your girls from the competition."

"I'm sure that won't be necessary." It was selfish of me to go along with things so unquestionably. My personal desire to get into outer space was clouding my judgment. In my heart I sensed it was a mistake to take six innocent adolescents on such a dangerous and controversial excursion; but I wanted it so badly for all of us, I thought the risk and unpleasantness of the pilot would be an acceptable difficulty.

"Very well then, let's proceed to the cafeteria. We can have a bite to eat and discuss the mission further."

At the cafeteria we talked about the risks involved with the mission: the lift-off, the time aboard the World Space Station, and the landing. I was reminded that the SSTO was basically just a big bomb. The harsh reality being, there was enough liquid hydrogen and oxygen on board at lift-off to level an average size town if it exploded. The commander also talked about our legal rights and the one hundred-million-dollar insurance policy on each of the passengers.

"I hope I'm not scaring you with all this technical nonsense." The commander sounded apologetic. "I just want you to know all the risks, that's all. The odds of anything bad happening are astronomical."

"That's very reassuring, thank you." I knew there was a strong element of risk when I filled out the application for the competition. Life is full of risks. Nothing ventured, nothing gained.

"I'm going to send some permission slips and some release forms home with you. Please see that everyone going on the mission has her parents fill them out. Each individual would be wise to have her own lawyer look at them before she signs." The commander rose from his seat and offered his hand. After we said our good-byes, he left me in the capable hands of the driver who was going to return me to the airport.

I was sick to my stomach on the trip home. The excitement I was feeling on the trip down was replaced with anxiety. It seemed as if I did not get one encouraging thing out of my tour of NASA. The pilot was a dud. The mission was meaningless. The rocket was controversial. Every element of the trip seemed distressing. I tried to remind myself of why I wanted to go in the first place. It was the chance of a lifetime, for me and for the girls. I had to look past all the negative issues and focus on the positive. Any risk was outweighed by the potential gain. It would be very educational and character building for the students. By the time I got home I was feeling silly for being so pessimistic about everything. The trip was going to be a life-altering experience.

Chapter Six

DR. MAXWELL WAS SITTING AT the window of a commercial jet, peering out over the plains of Africa on his way to Cape Town. There was a medical journal in his hands, because he was trying to reacquaint himself with heart transplant procedures. He had performed several in the past, but had not done any extensive surgery – other than his experimentation with animals—since he had moved to the small hospital to help the underprivileged. At his request, Miss Arubu had already been flown to South Africa after her massive heart attack. Since there were no hearts available in the donor pipeline, the doctor had opted to try for a xenotransplantation. It was a highly irregular procedure, banned in most countries. Dr. Maxwell was willing to try this radical approach for several reasons. First and foremost, he was very fond of the patient and felt that the medical system owed Miss Arubu a debt of gratitude for all her years of devoted service. He and Marjorie had agreed that she was the perfect candidate to try out their new anti-rejection drug. She had nothing to lose because her myocardial infarction had left extensive damage to her heart and she would die if left untreated. She had worked side by side with the doctor for fifteen years doing research on the drug; not only was she very familiar with its capabilities, she had a stake in its development.

A heart harvested from a cloned "knock-out" pig raised in a special disease-free environment was being flown in from a facility in Europe. Transgenic Technologies Inc. had used their patented gene-targeting procedure in the nuclear transfer (cloning) process to "knock out" the alpha 1, 3 galactosyl transferase genes, which are responsible for making an enzyme that adds sugar to the surface of pig cells. This is instantly recognised by the human immune system as being foreign, triggering an immune system response, leading to hyper-acute rejection. Dr. Maxwell had taken great care to take every precaution. A prominent heart surgeon and former colleague, Dr. Joe Thornton, was already scheduled to perform the operation with his assistance. Dr. Maxwell had about six months' worth of anti-rejection drug in his possession and was capable of producing enough to keep her alive indefinitely. All the technical issues had been taken care of, only the moral implications remained unresolved. Was this an act of disrespect towards the Creator?

•———•

Because Miss Arubu was asleep when the doctor arrived, he checked all the heart monitors and sat down beside the bed to study her file. This was her third major heart attack. She would have to have her operation at once, perhaps as soon as the pig heart arrived. He had already talked to Dr. Thornton and everything was set to go; nothing to do but wait and worry. While he studied Marjorie's chart, she awoke and spoke to him through the many tubes and respirator.

"How is your patient from the highlands Doctor?"

The doctor stood up at once. He was surprised to hear her voice and answered hesitantly, putting her hand in his before he made a sound.

"Unfortunately, our patient died, Marjorie."

"Were you able to keep the infection contained?"

"Yes, as you know, Doctor Tucker from the Global Institution for Infectious Diseases was there the very next day. They have been at the hospital and at the native's village for several weeks now and we've been given the green light as far as having it contained."

"Thank God for that."

"Aren't you a little concerned for your own health?"

"I've had better days, that's for sure; but I'm in good hands and I have complete faith in our new drug. I have already prayed to God for his help during the operation. It's all up to Him now."

Tears started to swell in the doctor's eyes with her words and he felt obliged to leave before things became too emotional for him. It was important for him to separate himself from the patient in that regard.

"I have to go now, to prepare for the operation. You will be getting prepped soon. You know I'll do the best I can."

"I know this is a real long shot, Albert. If things go wrong, don't hold it against yourself. Promise me that."

"I promise. Good-night, nurse." With these words he turned, stepped through the door and headed for pre-op.

The operation lasted 4 hours and was a complete success. The heart started perfectly and was beating strongly with good rhythm. There were no signs of rejection thanks to Dr. Maxwell and Miss Arubus' new miracle drug. Dr. Thornton and Dr. Maxwell were elated. Their faces were already plastered on every newspaper and television news program on the planet. It was another heart transplant first for South Africa. "Pig's heart beats in human body," the stories claimed. "Turning point for mankind," some boasted. "Surgeons defy God," others warned. No matter what the headline, they were famous. People from all over the globe were phoning wanting them to do interviews. It was a media circus.

When Miss Arubu woke, she called for Dr. Maxwell.

"How do you feel?" the doctor asked.

"Happy to be alive, thank you. The nurses tell me we're famous."

"The only complication as a result of the surgery, I'm happy to say."

"Things are going well then?"

"It's early to tell, but so far, beyond all expectations."

"Do you think I'll finally be able to see my sister in the United States after all these years?"

"All the major American television networks have been phoning constantly, begging you to fly to New York for an interview. I think you could name any price and they would pay. You could easily raise sufficient funds to see your sister in Texas."

"That would be a dream come true; but like you say, it's too early to tell. Lots of things could go wrong in the next few days or weeks."

"Rest now, Marjorie. Save your strength for recovery and don't worry about a thing. I have every confidence things will go well for you and your new heart."

Chapter Seven

THE GIRLS FOUND IT IMPOSSIBLE to contain their enthusiasm after we arrived at the Boston airport. That is when the reality of the trip had finally sunk in. Our medical exam and pre-flight training would start the very next day. Adam and his three boys were taking a separate flight from New York. They would meet us at the NASA dormitory adjacent to the training center. I was happy to hear that we would each have our own room; because as far as I was concerned, sharing a barrack-style accommodation with the girls was out of the question. I am sure bunking in the same room as the girls would have been fine, but why risk the sexual awkwardness if it could be avoided; besides, this would hopefully alleviate any chance of personal temptation.

Since graduation had concluded in the past week, it seemed strange to be going on an outing with three of my students. I should have been headed off on a fishing trip to northern Michigan, instead of taking a field trip to NASA. I was going to have to sacrifice my entire summer holiday and right about now I was having second thoughts. My complete carry-on baggage consisted of work projects for the girls to do in space and at the training centre while we were there. The three girls were sitting in the seats right in front of me and seemed to be getting along better than I expected. Since they never really hung out together at school, I was not sure how they would get along during the trip. If all the laughing and giggling was any indication, it could turn out to be an incident-free excursion. As a matter of fact, they seemed to be having so much fun I could not help but feel a little jealous. It did not seem fair that I was going to have to play the part of the responsible adult and go over their work sheets, while they goofed around and had fun.

As soon as we arrived at NASA, the dorm supervisor informed us that Adam and the boys were already there. I found out which room he was in and then we all went to introduce ourselves. When I knocked on the door, I was startled by the uneasiness that quickly overtook me. There was something about our relationship that still made me uncomfortable. Adam opened the door and emerged as a tower of formidable strength and self-assurance.

"Mr. McGinnis..." I was going to continue by pretending not to know Adam and introduce myself, but he blew my cover almost before I got started.

"Rock!" He grabbed my outstretched hand and pulled me in for a big hug, almost smothering me against his well-developed biceps. "How ya doin'? It's great to see you again."

When I turned around to introduce Adam to the girls their chins were almost resting on their chests. It must have been quite a shock for them to see their teacher engaged in a big manly bear hug with a stranger. Adam called on his boys and we proceeded to get acquainted. Blaine was a tall, skinny, brown haired, baby-faced kid with glasses, who may as well have had *Computer Nerd* stamped on his forehead. He was your classic 98-pound weakling, but it was evident right from the start, that he was very friendly and had a great since of humour.

Frankie was a tall, good looking, Afro-American; but his body type was the exact opposite of Blaine's. He was extremely well built. It was clear he worked out on a regular basis. He was smartly dressed and paid close attention to his appearance. There was an air of complete self-assurance, almost cockiness, about him and you could tell right away that he was one of those people who was his own biggest fan.

Randy was an average boy. He was medium height, medium build and not bad looking. He had dulled blond hair, along with greenish-brown eyes. He was dressed in an old t-shirt and tattered blue jeans. Randy was the shy, quiet type who was obviously uncomfortable around girls. He stood quietly on the periphery of the social circle that the boys and girls had created and awkwardly tried to fit in. I was surprised to see Nicole single him out later and try to make conversation.

Adam and I made the usual small talk while the students became acquainted. He mentioned that this was the boys' first trip outside New York City. I was astounded. I could not imagine what it would be like to grow up without ever knowing what life was like beyond the concrete jungle. How tragic it seemed. They had been insulated from the real world their entire lives. What an unnatural life man has chosen for himself, I thought; and how far removed from our savage, but free, beginnings we have evolved. We have sacrificed so many freedoms in exchange for so few comforts; the masses, so broadly distant from what is real and what is true. How disconnected we have become from God's good earth that brings us sustenance each day and how misplaced our priorities that we put fashion, entertainment and social status ahead of religion, freedom and our union with Mother Earth.

After everyone got acquainted, the girls and I went to our rooms to unpack. The rooms were simple but comfortable. I was relieved to be able to stretch out and relax my aching back. I was lying face down on the bed when I heard a knock at the door.

"Who is it?" I asked without budging.

"It's Eve Anna. May I come in?"

"Come on in, Eve Anna," I said almost begrudgingly. I did not want to be disturbed and I did not want to be alone with her. "Maybe it would be a good idea if you left the door open," I added, as she walked through the door.

"Hey, Teach."

"Unpacked already?"

"Yeah, sure; that didn't take long. The other girls are taking a nap, but I got bored and decided to come and talk."

"A nap, that sounds divine." Hint. Hint.

"What are you doing?"

"Just trying to rest my weary back. The trip was rather tiring." I did not lift my head that I had buried in my pillow, because I did not want to be distracted by her pretty face.

"I could give you one of my famous back rubs."

"That's fine I..." I tried to decline the offer, but she started before I had a chance to finish. After two, maybe three seconds of her gentle fingers nimbly roaming over the contours of my back, I did not want her to stop. No one had ever touched me so tenderly before.

"You have a talent for this sort of thing," I said, surprised that the tension that was pent up inside me could be so easily wiped away by the stroke of her hand.

"Yes, I know," she admitted without humility, as her hands artfully remoulded the muscles on my neck. "So, what's the deal with you and Mr. McGinnis?"

"We lived a mile and a half from each other and played together as kids."

"Just friends then?"

"What else did you have in mind?"

"Oh, nothing. Just curious." The sincerity of her voice hinted she had innocently dispelled all other possibilities.

Eve Anna had me almost to a state of blissful unconsciousness, when I was startled back to reality by the sensual motion of her hands kneading my buttocks. Such intimacy was totally unfamiliar to me. I had no idea that the simple touch of another human being could be so stimulating. I loved how the simple dexterity of her finger tips sent shock waves of pleasure throughout my body. This was precisely the psychologically complex emotional situation I had vowed to avoid. I had to stop it at once, but I had to do it tactfully, without hurting her feelings.

"I don't have any tension down there."

"Yes, but doesn't it feel good?"

"Maybe a little too good, if you get my drift?"

She stopped and then shifted herself to be sitting upright, just inches away from me, at the head of the bed.

"What did you think of the boys from New York?" I asked.

"They were all right, I guess; maybe a little too immature."

"They're seventeen-year-old boys."

"All Blaine could talk about was his precious, virtual-reality games that he plays on his integrated computer terminal. That sort of thing gets lame real fast. The kid is living in a Spec-view fantasy world."

"I've seen those on TV, they look extraordinary." I was ashamed to tell Eve Anna that I had upgraded from a personal computer to an ICT only a few weeks before. It was a long overdue change, because most of the world had joined the giant computer mainframe link over five years ago. Now instead of being restricted to a small computer processor at home, I can rent time with the largest processor bank in the world, having ready access to every book ever written and every piece of music ever recorded. I also like the new system because it has eliminated computer terrorism, pornography, rebel media, web hacking, virus planting and most other Web related crimes. This was only possible because the system is capable of policing itself. The great disadvantage being the total lack of privacy and loss of freedom of speech associated with a centralized computer, owned by a global entity that has never been revealed to the billions of users. Big Brother was always watching and only telling us what it wanted us to hear!

"You have never had a set of Spec-views on?" Eve Anna sounded surprised that I was living in the dark ages.

"Not yet."

"Well, they're really no different looking than a pair of sunglasses with a tiny little receiver on them, but the picture resolution of those little, lens-thick screens is fantastic. It's just like being somewhere else. When you tilt or turn your head, the view changes accordingly. I can see why some people can get carried away with the concept. The applications for something like that are almost limitless."

"I'm thinking of getting a set for taking virtual tours of places around the world. You can explore every major building, museum or coliseum ever built. I've even heard that you can take a virtual tour of the Titanic. That would be amazing."

"I took a tour of the World Space Station just last week. It was exciting to see the structure where we'll be spending time in outer space."

"That would be something."

"Frankie is a little too full of himself for my liking. What do you think?" At first, I thought Eve Anna's thoughts were going off on a tangent, but then I realized she was returning to my original question.

"And Randy?"

"Not sure. The jury is still out on him."

"Are you attracted to any of them?" I am not sure why that popped out of my mouth.

"No... ugh. What's the matter, are you afraid I'll sneak into one of their rooms or something?" Eve Anna's friendly tone was exchanged for sarcasm.

"Sorry, I was just curious. I was asking as a friend, not as your teacher." Eve Anna was sliding off of the bed as I spoke.

"I should go now."

"You aren't going away angry, are you?" I removed my face from its impression in my pillow to see if I could discern what she was feeling. She appeared to be unaffected.

"No, it's time I left you alone, that's all."

"Thanks for the back rub." I thought it best to dismiss the other subject.

"Anytime, see ya," she said, as she closed the door behind her.

I lay back down on the bed and made another bid for a nap. The image of Eve Anna, just before she left my room, was fuse welded to the back of my retinas, causing her subtle feminine curves to linger on my mind until I drifted off to sleep.

•———•

In the morning we were scheduled to have physical checkups. The boys went first, then the girls. As the students came out of the doctor's office, they were escorted away to be checked out on the giant salad spinner or some other type of fancy test equipment. Adam was called up ahead of me. Captain Dick was leaving the doctor's office as Adam was entering.

"Say, Adam." I overheard Captain Dick speak in an uncharacteristically jovial tone. "When the doctor is checking out your prostate gland, make sure he has only one hand on your shoulders instead of two." He laughed like a sick hyena at his own joke and then proceeded down the hallway.

INTERVENTION

"That's good advice, Captain." Adam forced out a smile and then made a funny face as he put his hand over his butt in a motion of self-preservation. "Thanks."

Adam and I met later at the simulator for the control centre of the World Space Station. Taking a regular shift at the controls would be part of our duties as adults onboard the WSS. Our duties at the control centre seemed intimidating at first, but I was soon able to grasp everything that was needed of me. The task was relatively simple: monitor radio transmissions from NASA, watch the display board for any mechanical malfunctions and pay special attention to the sensors searching for pieces of debris that might be on a collision course with the station. If I was aware of any abnormality, I was to take evasive action immediately.

After two hours of instruction, Adam and I were left on our own to play with the simulator. In the middle of one of these tests, Adam asked a provocative question.

"Have you ever wondered what it would be like to make love in a weightless environment?"

"I try not to think about sex in any environment."

"The whole idea fascinates me to no end. Just think of it, Rock. You wouldn't have to use your arms and legs to support your weight, so you would both have complete freedom to touch and intermingle during the act."

"Wouldn't you need to get some purchase somewhere?"

"Purchase on each other."

"You've thought this through, haven't you?"

"It's been a fantasy of mine for years now. Long before I ever imagined I would get into space."

"And who was your partner during these fantasies?"

"If I told you, it might spoil the magic."

"I hate to burst your bubble, but you are aware that the WSS spins on its axis to simulate its own gravity."

"Yes, but there's one room at the center of the hub that is completely free of gravity; and rumour has it, the crewmembers leave that room vacant for just such a contingency."

"Adam, Adam, Adam... you poor sex deprived maniac, you."

"Not sex deprived," he added with a huge smirk on his face. "Just Rock deprived."

"Yeah, well, you're just going to have to get your rocks off somewhere else." I honestly did not want to say that, but I just could not resist the play on words.

The focus of our conversation turned to the more practical day to day functions on board the station and that is where we dwelt for the rest of the day. The days and weeks that followed went by faster that I had hoped, for the summer was almost gone and I did not have any free time to do any of the summer activities that I love. All my time was spent with the girls going over the work sheets for our space experiment and repeating the many simulations pertaining to the space station.

Chapter Eight

THINGS WENT WELL FOR Miss Arubu. Her recovery was nothing short of a miracle. She was on her feet within a week and her heart biopsy showed no signs of rejection. Ten days after the operation she was feeling stronger than she had felt in three years. She was in excellent spirits and kept busy by answering the many cards and letters she had received from friends and well-wishers. She had spoken to the American television networks and had made an agreement with NBC for a substantial amount of money. Miss Arubu had decided to keep just enough to take the trip to see her sister in Houston and keep a little for her retirement; the rest would be her gift to the hospital in Mombasa.

Dr. Maxwell had already received a 20 million dollar advance from Transgenic Technologies and an undisclosed pharmaceutical company, in order for him to continue his research under licence to them. Dr. Maxwell graciously included Miss Arubu in the contract as equal partners. If their anti-rejection drug could be mass produced and passed all the necessary drug trials, the contract would be worth billions. Neither of them would have to worry about money ever again.

Nurse Hogen—who happened to be due for a holiday anyway—had agreed to accompany Miss Arubu on her trip to America. She was more than qualified to give her the medical aid she would require in the first few months of her recovery. Mrs. Hogen's biggest assignment would be to monitor the transplanted heart, to ensure there were no signs of rejection and to administer medication. She would also be in charge of watching Marjorie's diet, which would have to be low in sodium and fat. Since Mrs. Hogen was also a good friend of Marjorie's, she was sure to be invaluable in assisting in her day-to-day needs.

Just three weeks after the operation, Miss Arubu was scheduled to leave for America. Dr. Maxwell went to the airport to see her and Mrs. Hogen off. He and Dr. Thornton gave her a thorough examination the previous day and they were both pleased to give her the confirmation she needed. At the airport, Dr. Maxwell went through a last-minute medical checklist for the ladies to follow.

"And don't try and lift anything more than five kilograms." The doctor made one last addition to his list as he gave Marjorie a goodbye embrace.

"Don't worry a bit," Mrs. Hogen replied, as she hugged the Doctor a fond farewell. "I'll take good care of her."

As the doctor and Mrs. Hogen were in each other's arms, Marjorie started to cough. It was a very mild cough that only lasted a few seconds, but Dr. Maxwell picked up on it right away.

"How long have you had that cough, Marjorie?" Dr. Maxwell rubbed his chin, which both ladies recognised instantly as a sign he was concerned.

"It's just a silly cold bug, that's all. I woke up with the sniffles and an irritation in my chest this morning. I'm sure it's nothing to worry about."

"If it gets any worse, you get her straight to a hospital in the States as soon as possible." The Doctor gave Mrs. Hogen a stern look as he spoke.

"I'll be fine. You're worrying like an old woman."

"We can't be too careful." The Doctor did not need to remind them that her immune system was partly suppressed by the drugs she was taking.

"Goodbye, Albert." Marjorie smiled back with a reassuring grin as she turned and walked towards airport security.

It was shortly after the ladies had checked through security and were comfortably settled in the seats adjacent to their loading gate, that the lady in the chair across from Miss Arubu recognised her. The stranger introduced herself, shook Miss Arubu's hand and expressed what a pleasure it was to meet such an important pioneer in the medical field. This small gesture of esteem started a chain reaction of interest from many other passengers that were seated nearby, waiting to board planes headed for various destinations around the globe. Probably 25 people shook Miss Arubu's hand or kissed her cheek to congratulate her on her achievement. This notoriety continued on the airplane to Amsterdam. Once they were in the air, many of the over three-hundred passengers on the plane had to stop by her seat to say hello, wish her well, or just take a look to see what all the fuss was about. Just like the passengers in the Cape Town airport, these people were bound for all parts of the world. This celebrity-like status continued all the way to New York. Many people at the Amsterdam airport went out of their way to make contact with her as well as did the people on the flight across the Atlantic. The whole experience was so taxing, Miss Arubu was glad she was going to have a couple of day's rest in a New York hotel before she had to do her interview.

•———•

Dr. Maxwell and many of the staff at the Mombasa hospital took time out from their busy schedule to watch Miss Arubu's television interview. Miss Arubu did herself and everybody at the hospital proud. She handled the situation with poise and dignity.

"Do you see yourself as being a hero?" The host asked at one point in the interview.

"A hero would have acknowledged that her time was up and accepted death gracefully. I had nothing to lose and everything to gain from the operation."

"Don't you think putting the heart of a pig into a human being was a breach of medical ethics?"

"Is it ethical to let hundreds of people die every day when we have the technology to help them live, but are too afraid or too righteous to put it to use?" The audience applauded with approval at her response; she had won them over with her bright smile and infectiously warm nature.

"Then let me put the question to you another way. Do you think putting the heart of a pig into a human being is a sin against God?"

"Perhaps it is; but how is it more contrary to the word of the Bible than a lot of the other atrocities man has done in the past, solely in the name of progress and in commerce? When do we reach the point where we say, this is the boundary of science and medicine that we must never cross?"

The host appeared to be intimidated by Miss Arubu's answers to his philosophical questions and diverted his line of questioning to the simple facts pertaining to the surgical procedure and the origin of the miracle drug that facilitated the operation. He asked what she was going to do with all her money and was noticeably astounded when she said she was giving it all to charity. When they had run out of time, he wished her all the luck in the world and hoped that she would be able to keep her good health.

INTERVENTION

Everyone at the hospital stood up and clapped at the end of the interview. They all remarked that she was looking good and seemed to be her old self again. No one except the Doctor had noticed that she was coughing intermittently throughout the interview.

•———•

Two days after Miss Arubu arrived at Houston, Dr. Maxwell received a call from Nurse Hogen. There was no hello or how are you; she just got alarmingly straight to the point.

"Dr. Maxwell, there's something terribly wrong with Marjorie! Her cough is worse; she is finding it hard to breath and she has broken out in a horrible rash. I wanted to talk to you before I sent her to the hospital." There was a short pause on the phone as Dr. Maxwell digested the information and composed himself.

"Does she have blood shot eyes?" The magnitude of his concern was evident in his speech.

"Yes, beet red."

"Do you remember the patient from the Highlands Territory?"

"Yes, of course. But how on earth could it be that? His disease had a very short incubation period. Marjorie was exposed to him almost two months ago."

"I can't explain it, but I know we need to take every precaution. Where are you now?"

"We are at Marjorie's sister's house in Houston."

"Don't let anyone leave the house. Do not take her to a hospital. Call Dr. Tucker from the Global Institution for Infectious Diseases at once. His number should be in with all the other contact numbers I sent along with Marjorie. They have their own small, twin-engine jet and are ready to go at a moment's notice."

"What do I do in the mean time?"

"Give her a massive dose of *Virobloc;* two thousand milligrams. Make sure she has enough to drink, keep her warm and comfortable..." There was a noticeable pause before the doctor finished his prescription. "And pray, Nurse Hogen; pray to God that this is not what I think it is."

"Thank you, Doctor." It was obvious that Nurse Hogen was in tears.

"Tell Dr. Tucker to call as soon as he knows anything." Dr. Maxwell hung up the phone. He was too upset to remember the usual courtesy of saying goodbye.

The next day Dr. Maxwell received the call that he was dreading from Dr. Tucker.

"Albert, I'm afraid I have terrible news."

"Miss Arubu has the same disease that killed the man from the highlands?" Dr. Maxwell said, with a heavy heart.

"Worse than that. Are you sitting down?"

"Worse, how could it be worse?" Dr. Maxwell fell backwards into his chair in dreaded anticipation.

"I'm afraid we have a mutation, parented by the same deadly virus that killed your patient. Nurse Hogen tells me that Miss Arubu had some contact with the patient?"

"Yes, that's true. I had her in to help with my diagnosis. Her name was on the list of people that were potentially exposed. One of your staff checked her out."

"Didn't you take that into consideration before you performed the Xenotransplantation?"

"It never crossed my mind."

"Well, that one little mistake could have devastating repercussions."

"But Transgenic Technologies assured me that the heart was disease free." Dr. Maxwell understood what Dr. Tucker was implying.

"Think about what you just said, Albert. Are you that big of a fool? No matter how sterile an environment the pigs were raised in, what are the odds of not one single virus sneaking past their defences? It goes against all reason. Besides, as you probably know, every species carries its own dormant viruses within its DNA. In this case we are looking at porcine endogenous retroviruses or PERVs."

"So, you think one of these pig viruses mutated with the haemorrhagic fever virus."

"Yes, but here's the kicker. Not only has the disease acquired a longer, more efficient incubation period, it now has stealth capability."

"Stealth?"

"It's a cytopathic virus that lacks the antigens required for protective anti-viral cellular immunity; in other words, a virus that can fly under the radar of the body's immune system."

"My God, Darcy, is that as bad as it sounds?"

"I would classify it as devastatingly catastrophic. I'm afraid you have inadvertently engineered the most perfect killing organism the world has ever seen; billions could die." Dr. Tucker stood silently for half a minute waiting for Dr. Maxwell to reply. "Albert."

"I'm still here, Dr. Tucker. It's all too much for me to absorb. How do you react when someone tells you that you will be responsible for the deaths of billions of human beings? Are you sure you're not over reacting?"

"I hope I'm wrong, but I'm quite sure we have a pandemic on our hands, the likes of which mankind has never seen. I cannot over estimate its severity. Miss Arubu was in contact with hundreds of individuals on her trip from Africa to the USA. Most of these people were enroute to destinations spanning the entire globe. It's the worst-case scenario, Albert."

"What course of action do we have?"

"All I can do is try and contain the outbreak one person at a time; but like I said, it might already be too late. It could be worldwide as we speak."

"How horrible; how very, very horrible. What have I done, Darcy?"

"Goodbye, Dr. Maxwell. I will keep you posted." Dr. Tucker did not have the time or the desire to console his colleague. He had work to do. "Keep in mind you are a potential carrier yourself."

Dr. Maxwell said a few words into the receiver, but soon realized that Dr. Tucker had hung up. He covered his face with his hands and slumped into his chair. Naturally, he was devastated. After several minutes had passed, Dr. Maxwell got up from his desk and opened the glass cover to his firearm collection. He took down an old .455 Webley, which dated back to the Boer war. He then proceeded to fill it with cartridges and placed the muzzle against his temple. Suddenly, he became aware that he was taking the coward's way out.

"I don't deserve to die this way," he said out loud to himself, standing in front of a mirror with the gun pointed at his head. He realized that he must spend his dying days looking after the sick that were soon to be pouring into the hospital. "At least I can do that much," he voiced quietly.

He was painfully aware of his responsibility. He unloaded the handgun and put it back into the showcase. He then walked, almost without purpose, towards the exit of his office; and had no recognition of heaving a dry hacking cough as he stepped into the hallway.

Chapter Nine

I WAS LASHED DOWN FIRMLY into my seat inside the cockpit of the SSTO vehicle, the *Herald of Democracy*. Checked and rechecked, poked and prodded, then left to my own devices in the belly of the beast. A fiery dragon filled to the brim with twinned components ideally suited to combustion; an unprecedented explosive release of force and fire were just a spark and a few seconds away from ignition. The serpent was aimed towards the heavens and the inhospitable realm of space. The dragon's lair was little more than an unlimited expanse of hostile nothingness, but it beckoned me to follow blindly.

I was numb with fear and helplessly trapped by the countdown being sounded off in the background. There was an explosive, crackling roar as the beast trembled and then leapt into the sky. Its fiery breath released clouds of licking flames that swirled all around us. I feared that there were too many flames. Bright orange billows of unfathomably hot gasses enveloped us for what seemed like an eternity. Was this the end? Were we all to be baked alive by this inferno? I closed my eyes, clenched my teeth and braced myself for the worst, but the end did not come.

We were still rocketing skyward, trailing our fiery dragon's tail behind us. I then became aware of the powerful force pushing me down into my seat. My cheeks felt like lead weights being drawn away from my face and my arms were pulled to my sides. Through the thunder of the engines, I could make out our pilot taking telemetry and throttle position orders from Mission Control. It was comforting to hear the words, "systems nominal" come over the intercom. At "T" plus 9 minutes we were beginning our manoeuvres, which would place us in orbit around Earth. Within 45 minutes we were three-quarters of the way around the world and firing the Orbit Manoeuvring Systems engines for the second time, to push us into an even higher and more stable orbit. The payload bay doors were opened to expose the radiator surfaces that were on the insides of the panels. Without these heat exchangers there would be a rapid buildup of heat inside the ship.

"Attention, Crew. This is your captain speaking. Welcome to outer space."

There was a big cheer from all the neophytes on board, myself included.

"All systems are optimal and we are *go* for docking with the WSS. We should be meeting up with the station in twenty minutes."

Because Randy, Helena and I were stuck in the lower level of the cockpit, our view from the windows was restricted. All we could do was patiently wait until we docked with the space station. It was not that difficult because we knew we would be rewarded later. The crew on the lower deck were closest to the escape hatch and were always the first ones to exit the ship. After we docked with the WSS, Captain Dick addressed me from above.

"Astronaut Morris, could you open the equalization valve? Remember to stand back from the vent because you could get a blast of air."

I unfastened my seat harness and proceeded to the front of the vehicle. I popped the valve and there was a small rush of air into the cockpit as the air pressure between the space station and the SSTO equalized.

"You may now open the docking doors."

I rotated the mechanism and released the door. A distinguished looking grey-haired man was waiting there for me, with his hand extended.

"Welcome to the World Space Station," he said graciously. "You're Morris, aren't you? I'm Cauldwell," he added as he shook my hand.

"Pleased to meet you, Cauldwell. It's great to be here."

"Grab your personal things and come on board. Don't worry about the supplies. My crew will make the transfer before we leave."

I got my bag out of the storage cabinet and crawled through the narrow tunnel to get to the main part of the space station. It was still weightless on board the space station, because the rotation that created the artificial gravity had to be shut down for docking. Cauldwell escorted us to one of the observation posts as soon as we had all exited the SSTO vehicle. Captain Dick stayed behind to supervise the unloading operation. The rest of us were able to glide effortlessly down one of the long tubes that connected the central hub to the main part of the station, which was normally subject to a small gravity pull.

There was a large window at the observation post, and the earth that we left behind glowed brightly below us, like a gem mounted in the heavens. This was what I had come to see. This was why I strapped my ass to a rocket and submitted to being blasted into space. It was worth all the risks, just to see my home from this perspective. It was a sight that was both philosophically and spiritually moving and it touched me to the core. It was vast and yet so finite, beautiful and yet so perishable. God gave us a paradise unparalleled in the universe; but unfortunately, its future was left in our unworthy hands.

"Come on, Teach. Give the rest of us a chance."

They were right, I was hogging the window. Cauldwell was waiting for me when I pushed myself away from the porthole.

"I have logged over two-hundred days up here during the five missions I've spent on the station. I never get tired of looking at the view."

"I know I'm going to spend a lot of time poised at that window."

"Would you like to come along while I fire the thrusters to get the station spinning again?"

"That sounds great." I felt honoured that Cauldwell had taken a shine to me and I followed compliantly. He was a seasoned astronaut that I could learn a lot from. It was a rush to glide effortlessly down the corridors on our way to the control room. I was sorry that we were going to activate the gravity system, because weightlessness was way too much fun. I reminded myself that I could always go to the centre of the hub if I wanted to play in a gravity free environment. Astronaut Cauldwell stopped at the carbon dioxide scrubbers first, to show me how to service the unit. It was one of the most important pieces of equipment on board. Next, we stopped to check out the water purification system. Every drop of water we used, or waste that we excreted, was processed and the water reclaimed. When we finally arrived at the control room, Cauldwell explained that we had to wait until we heard from Captain Dick before we proceeded to artificial gravity.

"It's common practice to stow all of the supplies in the absence of gravity," Cauldwell explained.

"That's good thinking."

"What did you think of the trip up?"

"Amazing, absolutely amazing." I did not let on that I thought we were all going to burn up on the launch pad. "It's quite an achievement when you think about it. In a little over a century, we have gone from our first powered flight in Kitty Hawk, North Carolina to a single stage flight into outer space. To be a part of all that is a great honour."

"It's definitely a lot to take in, the first time out."

"My heart is still racing from the excitement."

"Well, it's a real treat having you all here, Morris. We regulars sometimes take the whole program for granted, so it's always nice to receive a fresh dose of enthusiasm from the civilian crews when they arrive."

"It's a shame you have to go back to earth so soon. I'm sure you would have gotten a blast out of all those energetic teens we brought along."

"There's no doubt in my mind."

"Cauldwell, it's Captain Dick here. The *Herald of Democracy* has been shut down and all our cargo has been transferred to the WSS. You can commence gravity whenever you are ready."

"Roger that, go for gravity." Cauldwell floated out of his chair and motioned me to come in closer. "You may as well do this, Morris."

Since I had done it on the simulator many times, I did not let the real thing intimidate me. The first thing was to hit the gravity initialization alarm. It was important to warn everyone, because there would be a slight jolt when the rockets fired. I sounded the alarm three times as prescribed in the manual, then I typed in a coded command for the computer and the thrusters fired. Within two minutes we had forty-five percent gravity, which was the normal amount generated on board the station.

"That was a good job, Morris. But I have to get to the point and tell you why I really asked you down here."

I diverted my attention to Cauldwell immediately. He had an inexplicable expression that alluded to something mysterious. I had only been aboard the WSS for a few minutes and already I was involved in a clandestine conference with the commander of the previous mission. This was definitely not in my flight plan. My heart was pounding with anticipation.

"What's on your mind?"

"I need to warn you about your Captain Dick. The man is dangerous."

"I've had a bad feeling about Dick, right from the first time I laid eyes on him."

"As soon as I saw those pretty young girls you brought on the mission, I knew I had to say something. Watch your back at all times and never leave your girls alone with him. The man is a psychopath and the worst kind of pervert. I have worked with Richard for twenty some years now and I wouldn't trust him any further than I could throw him."

"I can't believe NASA would turn a blind eye to his shenanigans."

"He's one hell of a pilot, but I just thought you should know the whole story. I was pretty sure no one at NASA would have the guts to tell you the truth."

"God bless you for caring."

"At least you'll have a short stay on board; you've got that going for you. Captain Dick will be so busy readying the SSTO for its return to earth, he won't have the time or the energy to get himself into trouble."

"I hope you're right."

"I can carry on here. Why don't you go get hooked up with your students. They probably think you've abandoned them."

I shook Cauldwell's hand for the second time and then left the room.

"Can things get any more complicated?" I thought to myself, as I moon walked slowly back to where I left the girls. Cauldwell's message did not change things all that much. He just confirmed what I had already suspected—the captain was a sleaze-ball.

It was amusing to bound down the hallway at less than half normal gravity, but I sensed one should be careful not to get going too fast in case you stumbled. The results would almost assuredly be unpleasant. Just like me, the kids were trying to perfect their spacewalk. They had already traveled the entire circumference of the station and were closing in on me fast. If I did not pick up the pace, they were going to lap me.

"Hey, Teach. Wait up." Eve Anna called out.

I stopped when I realized I was not involved in a race.

"Isn't this a blast?" Helena was bursting with jubilation. "This is the greatest experience of my life. Thank you for picking me for the mission."

"We've only just begun, right Mr. McGinnis?"

Adam was bringing up the rear and was standing behind all the students with a healthy grin on his face. Because he knew we did not have anything scheduled for today, he was happy to just go with the flow.

"Right you are, Rock. What say we get unpacked, then we can all spend some time in the zero-gravity room."

There was a cheer of approval from everyone present, then we rushed off to our quarters to stow away our gear. Everyone on board had their own personal locker, but the sleepers were meant to be shared. We would sleep and work in shifts. That way we would always have someone in control of the station. The beds were long cylindrical cocoons that closed up to be light tight and sound proof; allowing for a good sleep, whatever the external conditions. The conditions inside were constantly monitored by the computer and could be adjusted to suit the individual's needs. We all had to spend a night in a similar cocoon back on earth, to ensure none of us would become claustrophobic and jeopardize the mission.

After we finished the chore of unpacking, we inspected the washroom facilities. Adam and I did not have to stress the importance of water conservation, because the people at NASA had gone over that many times. Being satisfied with our living area, we headed off to the low gravity room. The enclosure was appropriately padded, allowing for the kind of horse play that six teenagers and a couple teachers, with too much energy, might encounter. We bounced around in that room for an hour and a half. It was more fun that any ride at an amusement park and it was a great ice-breaker for the students. That short time in the hub did more to promote peer bonding than the several weeks together at NASA.

It was soon time for our shift in the control room. Adam and I had to do the rock- paper-scissors thing to see who would go first, because we did not have a coin to flip. Since I lost, it was the perfect introduction for Adam to embarrass me. He told the story of the time he took five dollars off me by using the "heads I win, tails you lose," coin flipping routine, when we were young.

"That was not my proudest moment to be sure. Go ahead and laugh at that poor naive and trusting young kid from North Dakota. At least I was not callous and manipulating like some people." I looked straight into Adam's eyes as I spoke. The students were enjoying Adam's and my camaraderie, but it was time to get to work.

I got the girls started on their assignments right away. There was no sense postponing the workload, because they had a full itinerary. Adam took his boys to the space laboratory and they proceeded to set up their science project before they went to bed. Cauldwell and his crew were already on board their own SSTO vehicle, the *John Glenn*, awaiting their return to earth. Because of the staff exchange, they would use the sleeping facilities on the ship to get their eight hours rest before re-entry. I spent my first shift on the bridge going through a check sequence with a fellow named Marty from mission control. It was interesting work and Marty and I got along fine. After about four hours of doing their assignments on the bridge, the girls decided to go to the galley and take their break. Shortly after that, I had the uneasy feeling that someone was watching me. I turned around just in time to see Captain Dick slink away into the dark hallway. Thoughts of that creep, secretly perusing me from a distance, made my flesh crawl. I called Marty back and got permission to leave my post for a few minutes. The girls were fine when I got there and had not seen or heard anyone for hours. I asked them to microwave me a meal and a cup of coffee and bring them to me as soon as they were ready. I was even more nervous about leaving the girls by themselves now.

When my time on the bridge was almost finished, I received a call from Cauldwell stating they were ready to depart. He requested that I terminate the artificial gravity, so that they could slip their moorings and proceed to re-entry. After they broke away from the station and I had the gravity back to normal, Adam and the boys arrived for their turn on the bridge. I did not linger to chat, because I wanted to get to the window in order to watch the *John Glenn* pull away from the station.

It was exciting to see the SSTO manoeuvre itself away from the WSS on its return trip to earth, but in its wake, there remained much insecurity. I was marooned on a man-made island in space; the only other inhabitants were Captain Dick, Adam and six teenagers. The rest of the flight crew had gone back with Cauldwell and his team. They were to return with the next group of space station inhabitants in seven days and then assist Captain Dick in our return flight to earth. I stood at the window until the *John Glenn* disappeared over the horizon. North America was directly below us. Most of it was in a dark shadow, untouched by the sun. The entire continent was lit up with a busy network of city lights: the luminous display of mankind's existence.

"What a terrible waste of energy," I thought, as I turned and headed back to the bridge. Thousands of tons of carbon were being dumped into the atmosphere every year, contributing to the greenhouse effect, just to illuminate the billions of street lights around the world. Man was a chronic, unrelenting consumer who placed a heavy burden on his environment.

"Well, that's that," I announced as I stepped onto the bridge to greet my team. "We're on our own."

"Don't worry, Teach. They'll be back for us," Helena reassured me.

"Are you girls ready for bed?" I asked.

"About four hours ago." Eva Anna sounded very tired as she spoke. "After all this excitement, I'm just totally zonked."

We relocated to the sleep capsule area. I helped all three of the girls get settled in their cocoons; then I crawled into mine. I was afraid to close myself in, because I would be detached from the outside for eight hours. What if our shady Captain Dick decided to try something with one of the girls while I was asleep? I would be completely unaware of their dilemma. I exited the cocoon and went back to the bridge to ask Adam to check on us from time to time. He said he would. I slept soundly after that.

When we awoke, Captain Dick was already manning his post on the bridge. It was his turn to work a shift in the control room. I sent the girls on ahead to one of the work rooms while I stopped to chat with the captain. I felt it was my duty to try and build a more friendly rapport with the man.

"How's everything going?" I asked, as I entered the control room.

"I could do this shit in my sleep."

I was not really concerned with his abilities during slumber; therefore, I tried again. "Do you have the *Herald of Democracy* ready for re-entry?"

"Everything is on schedule. You aren't doubting my capabilities are you, Morris?"

"Not at all. I have every confidence in your abilities." I did not expect him to get so defensive. I felt I had to defuse the situation with flattery.

"I'm going to need your help tomorrow." The captain was not courteous enough to ask, he just stated the fact bluntly.

"That shouldn't be a problem."

"I want to do an EVA, so that I can check on the exterior of the SSTO. I need you to help me on with my equipment and monitor my activities while I'm outside the station."

"You don't expect any trouble, do you?" I knew that an Extra-Vehicular Activity was not a routine excursion for simple SSTO missions to and from the station.

"No, I just want to take every precaution because of the present conditions." I must have had a bewildered expression on my face, because he continued by clarifying what he just said. "Even though I'm against the hair-brained idea of sending civilians into space, NASA has a lot riding on this mission; and by God, I intend to get you home without incident."

"That's good to know."

"I'll call you tomorrow, when I'm ready for you." Then he turned his back to me and said, "See ya, Shorty."

"Yeah, sure. We'll see you tomorrow." I left the bridge in a state of confusion, amazed that I had just been blown off so coldly.

Chapter Ten

WE ROSE ABOUT FORTY-FIVE MINUTES before shift change the following morning, leaving us just enough time to get cleaned up and have breakfast. The girls and I arrived at the bridge with about two minutes to spare.

"Good morning, Captain." I greeted him cordially, only to be countered with an abrupt reply.

"You and you, stay here,' he said, pointing to Helena and Nicole. "All you have to do is watch the control panel. If any red lights come on, one of you call NASA and the other can come running to get one of us at the *Herald of Democracy*. Any questions?"

Helena and Nichole shook their heads in unison. Obviously, they were to take over the captain's shift while he did the EVA.

"Fine. Morris, you and the gal can come with me." Eve Anna and I followed without argument.

When we crawled inside the SSTO there were two space suits and two jet packs, called Manned Manoeuvring Units, set out and ready to go.

"If anything goes wrong out there, Morris, you'll have to come and get me."

"You realize I only had about a fifteen-minute introduction with one of these."

"That's your problem."

"I see." I'm sure antagonizing me was just Captain Dick's idea of fun, because he was confident in his equipment.

We helped him on with his suit and helmet and then mounted the MMU on his shoulders. I opened the rear airlock doors and helped him inside. The captain equalized the airlock and exited the vehicle. Eve Anna and I followed his progress with the aid of several television cameras that were attached to the station. He checked out the entire surface of the SSTO inside and out. After about thirty minutes of inspection, the Commander radioed that he found a loose hold-down inside the cargo area.

"You guys can relax for a few minutes while I work this back into place."

Eve Anna and I were standing face to face inside the narrow corridor. It was awkward standing so close to each other with nothing to occupy our hands or our eyes. In an instant Eve Anna's face transformed. She suddenly appeared vacant and mystifying, as if I had caught her day dreaming in class. She looked straight into my eyes inquisitively; then she did the strangest thing. Before I realized what was happening, she leaned forward and pressed her lips to mine. Not just a casual glad to have you as a friend kind of kiss either; it was a passionate, lock down the hatches and let's go under for a minute kind of kiss. I was submerged by her powerful sensuality; submarined by her forwardness and her femininity.

When she released me, I surfaced far too slowly; weighted down by the ballast of my heavy emotions. The delayed opening of my eyes betrayed me. She was grinning like a mink in the chicken coop when I was finally able to focus. I was flabbergasted, but primarily I was embarrassed.

"What brought that on?" I choked out, my fingers unconsciously caressing her precious moisture still lingering on my lips. I savoured her essence; it had a distinct sweetness and boldness of character that was reminiscent of tasting honey made from wild bees for the first time.

"Did you enjoy that?" She was devilish the way she asked so nonchalantly and the way she smiled.

What a ridiculous question! Of course, I enjoyed her kissing me; I could not deny the fact. I was fully aware that my overwhelmed expression had given me away.

"Yes. I enjoyed that very much. You're quite the kisser. But I don't understand…?

"I was just testing."

"Testing for what?"

"I was trying to find out if you were festive."

"Festive! I certainly am not. What in the name of God gave you the idea I was festive?"

"I'm not sure. There's something different about you. I can't put a finger on it. I'm sorry."

"You should be sorry. Just between you and me, same-sex relationships give me the willies. The whole idea is detestable. The concept flies in the face of God and His ideals for Christian family values."

"I'm almost sorry to hear that," she returned, distracted.

"What do you mean by that?"

"Oh, nothing really. You just don't seem so mysterious anymore, that's all."

"Mysterious! Honestly, Eve Anna, your imagination astonishes me. What if someone had caught us while you were *testing* me? I could lose my job over something so out of line as kissing one of my students. Let's get back to work."

Eve Anna turned sheepishly to face the monitor. The captain was on his way back to the air lock. I was glad to have something to divert the focus of our attention. Our space walker knocked at the air-lock door. There was a small gush of air as I opened the hatch. The captain pointed to his helmet as soon as he got inside. Eve Anna took off his headgear while I removed his MMU.

"Everything looks good," the captain said with a satisfied smile. It was the first time I had seen him with any expression other than a sneer.

"That's wonderful. Will there be anything else?" I asked, anxious to get out of that cramped space and back to our other duties. Mostly, I wanted to remove myself from the scene of the crime.

"No, that will be all. If you take the rest of this shift on the bridge, I'll trade for yours. I have taken up a bunch of your time and I know you have a project to finish."

"Thanks. That will be fine." I could not help but wonder if Captain Dick had a different agenda. It was not like him to be generous in any way. But, to give him credit, he was a loyal NASA employee, devoted to the success of the mission.

Eve Anna and I left Captain Dick and headed back to the bridge. It was an uncomfortable situation, working with Eve Anna for the rest of the day. Occasionally, when no one was looking, Eve Anna would look at me suggestively and quickly pucker her lips. This playful teasing and taunting lasted the rest of the day and I am sure that I blushed with embarrassment every time our eyes met. What frustrated me the most about the whole affair, is that I am pretty sure Eve Anna was still uncertain about my sexual orientation.

At the end of the day, as I lay awake in my sleep cocoon, I played the kissing incident over and over in my mind. It was my first kiss; at least my first kiss where emotions came into play. I never intended for my life to get this complicated. I had tried to avoid this moment since puberty. I enjoyed the kiss; I loved the kiss, but that was not the problem. There was much more being exchanged than the tender-sweet pressure of our lips and a little moisture. I felt something intense. Since I had never been in a relationship before, I was confused. Was I receiving emotion from her, or was I feeling something unfamiliar stirring inside me? Maybe it was a fair exchange. I could not be sure.

•———•

The next day Eve Anna acted as if nothing had happened. We fell, comfortably I might add, back into our routine of doing our worksheets and minding the control room. In our spare time the girls and I sat by the big window and gazed down at the giant blue marble that was our home. We also spent a lot of time in the zero-gravity room. Later in the day, Adam introduced me to HAM radio. It was customary for the station inhabitants to kill time by talking to people back on the planet. You could talk to radio operators from all over the world. Adam and I talked to people in England, Australia, Canada and Hawaii. It was fun to hear how these people lived and get their impression of what was happening on earth. I seemed to hit it off with a middle-aged man that lived in Canada's far north, near Uranium City, in the province of Saskatchewan. He was a retired teacher named Fred, who wanted to get away from it all. Fred lived by himself, in a cabin on the shore of one of northern Saskatchewan's many lakes. He spent most of his time fishing and painting landscapes, that he sold to supplement his income. I was a little jealous of his lifestyle.

Chapter Eleven

THE FIFTH DAY STARTED OUT the same as any other aboard the World Space Station. I woke the girls and we had breakfast. I had hot oatmeal cereal cooked in the microwave. It turned out more natural that some of the pre-packaged meals. Some of the girls liked the canned fruit with some yogurt.

I had set the alarm a half hour early this morning, so that we could spend some time in the gym. There was a well-equipped exercise room on the station and we were determined not to let ourselves get out of shape during our short time on board. We each had a good workout and were in need of a shower at the end. I called the shower stall first, because it was important for me to get to the shift change, in the control room, on time.

My first activity was to call NASA and go through the daily check list with Marty. We were about twenty minutes into our checklist when the Commander of Flight Operations interrupted our work.

"Commander Gilmore, to what do I owe this pleasure."

"I have news concerning your mission."

"What kind of news?"

"Your return to earth has been delayed indefinitely."

"But the girls and I have classes on the twenty-eighth."

"I'm sorry for the inconvenience. We feel it's in your best interest to stay at the station for a few more days. At least until the situation back here has stabilized."

"What kind of situation?"

"I probably shouldn't worry you until we get all the facts. I would appreciate it if you would tell Captain Dick that his orders have been changed and I would like to talk to him at his earliest convenience."

"Is it the weather?"

"No, the forecast is fine."

"Captain Dick has gone over the *Herald of Democracy* with a fine-toothed comb. He assured me yesterday that everything was in order and set for our return as scheduled."

"The problem exists here on earth. Could you please call on Captain Dick for me?"

"I'm not going anywhere until you tell me exactly what this is all about." I was very unhappy that NASA had put me in this position. The airwaves were silent for a moment and then Commander Gilmore continued.

"I just got off the phone with the President. Have you ever heard of the Global Institute for Infectious Diseases?"

"Yes, I have." Now that I knew we were being delayed by direct order from the President of the United States, I no longer wished to be defiant.

"The Institute has asked the President to declare a state of emergency. Apparently, there has been some sort of outbreak. Six people are dead already."

"I'll talk to the captain immediately. Thanks for your honesty." I had heard enough at this point. Of course, I did not mind extending our mission under the circumstances. The girls would be better off right where they were. I headed for the SSTO as soon as Marty gave me the go-ahead. I hollered into the entrance because I knew that Captain Dick would be sleeping when I got there. Because there was no answer, I crawled inside. I found him still fast asleep in his bunk; he was less than hospitable when I shook him.

"What the fuck do you want?"

"We have a problem."

"Can't it wait?"

"Gilmore wants to talk to you."

"Gilmore!" The man was out of his bunk as if it had suddenly become electrified. "He never calls."

"The mission has been extended because of some type of epidemic happening on earth."

"Wake McGinnis and the rest of the crew. They need to be informed as well."

"We'll meet you on the bridge in ten minutes."

When we were all assembled, the call was made to mission control. Gilmore explained the crisis as best he could. The problem was a killer virus that had mutated from organisms that do not normally coexist, but were thrown together when someone in South Africa tried to transplant the heart of a pig into a human being. There was potential for a global pandemic, because the carrier had been in contact with hundreds of people that traveled to points all over the world.

"So, you want us to stay up here and wait until the disease has run its course?"

"That's correct, Captain Dick. You should have enough water and supplies for a six-month period. We will be sending an unmanned SSTO vehicle with another shipment of supplies as soon as we have a better understanding of your future needs."

"What if some of these viruses hitchhike along with the shipment?" I was sure that they had allowed for just such a contingency, but I had to be positive.

"Don't worry, Morris. We have placed fumigating canisters inside the ship that will be discharged enroute to the space station and everything should be virus free long before you need to get on board."

"Couldn't someone create a vaccine that would allow us to come down early?" Helena asked.

"Apparently, this virus is kind of special. It's like nothing anyone has ever seen before. They tell me a vaccine might take years to produce. Any more concerns."

I am sure there were many, but we were all too shocked by the news to reply.

"I'll call you every day to keep you up to date," Gilmore added.

"Thanks, Commander. Over and out." Dick ended the conversation.

There was an extended period of silence as everyone in the room digested the news. It was a definite blow for the girls to learn they were stranded for what would probably be months. All our lives would have to be put on hold for a while. Now Cauldwell's warning took on a whole new perspective. We were going to be trapped in the station, with that maniac, far longer that Cauldwell or I could have ever imagined.

"I miss my mother," Helena stated an obvious concern for most of the teens on board. It would be extremely hard for them to be separated from their families for such a long time. Already missing my cat, I could only imagine how the students must have felt. Before I knew it, there were three young girls crying on my shoulders. Consoling distraught females was not one of my strong points, but I did the best I could. Our, not so esteemed, captain stomped out of the control room in disgust and headed back to his bunk. He did not seem to be impressed with the girls' unprofessional display of emotions. Everyone calmed down eventually and we were able to discuss the situation logically.

INTERVENTION

"We just have to make the most of a bad situation. I'm sure we'll be able to talk to our families periodically and we'll be kept up to date on their wellbeing." I waited to see if Adam had anything to add and then I continued. "This doesn't have to affect your plans of attending university this fall. I'm confident arrangements can be made so that you may take all your classes online. Most universities provide that kind of service for first year students. Adam and I would be happy to assist you in getting signed up and help with your studies. Since there will be very few distractions, it's likely you will complete your work in half the time. From what I've seen so far, it seems like we all get along; it's very important that we keep it that way. Is there anything you'd like to add to that Adam?"

"Let's all accept this as a challenge. There will certainly be many more hurdles to jump before we're done. I think it best if we look at this as an adventure and face all obstacles with strength and self-assurance."

"This calls for a group hug," I said, opening my arms to the rest of the group. It was just the therapy we needed. Everyone felt better after being held.

"What say we all go down to the zero-gravity room and play a game of space polo?" Adam asked.

"That's a good idea," I added. "I'll stay here and man the bridge while you guys go and get your minds off all our troubles."

•———•

The next day there were 32 dead. The day after that, there were 167. The deaths were evenly distributed around the globe and there were already thousands of people sick. Gilmore was honest and forthcoming in his day-to-day assessments, but there was no sense in him trying to hide anything from us, because we had access to all the world television broadcasts via the internet.

"Things are much worse than we had originally thought," Gilmore explained. "This virus is a much more efficient killer than anyone could have imagined. How it's spreading and the rate at which it is spreading is beyond scientific explanation. All of humanity is locked down with our movement restricted just like the Covid-19 pandemic, but nothing the experts do seems to have any effect on it. After my conversation with Dr.Tucker, from the Global Institute for Infectious Diseases, I think I can safely say that millions, perhaps billions will die."

The word, *billions* echoed throughout the room and shook the foundation of our existence. The entire group feared for their loved ones back on earth.

The television programs depicted a world in panic. People were stocking up on drugs, water, toilet paper, and non-perishable foods. Many were staying in their homes and feared to step outside their doors. The people that dared to venture outside wore surgical masks and gloves in a futile effort to ward off the disease. Some tried to flee the cities in hope of finding refuge in a remote area. Many reverted back to religion; the temple, synagogue and church web sites were swamped with people looking for answers. Thousands were attending virtual religious services online and reaching out for solace. The health care systems were already showing signs of strain. Nothing could have prepared them for an outbreak of this magnitude.

We all took turns talking to our families that day. Up to this point everyone that we knew was safe. I talked to my mom and dad, who were still on the farm back in North Dakota. They were both fine, but my father was unnerved by the death of one of his pigs that morning. Apparently, pigs were dying from the same disease that was killing people. He could not be sure what caused his pig to die, but it definitely had him concerned for his and my mother's lives.

INTERVENTION

I had cancelled any further efforts towards completing our class space project. Not only did it seem of no consequence in light of what was happening on earth, there were now too many variables that would have rendered the experiment inconclusive. Naturally the students were under too much stress to be able to concentrate properly.

The free time that was now available thanks to the termination of the memory project, was used to enrol my students in various on-line university classes. They would now be able to continue with their education without interruption from any further delays in our return to earth. It was imperative that the students were kept busy. I did not want them thinking about the troubles on earth any more than what was inevitable. I used some of my free time to look down at the planet and contemplate its future. How many people would be left alive after the virus had burnt itself out?

By nine o'clock the next morning, NASA time, 2,500 people were dead and hundreds of thousands sick and dying. Morgues were filling up and crematoriums were working overtime to dispose of the bodies. The whole situation was getting seriously frightening for everyone. Captain Dick went about his duties, as if nothing had happened and showed no signs of emotion. We sometimes watched the news reports together; his only reaction was the odd grunt of disapproval and shaking of his head in disbelief. I started calling a meeting once a day so that everyone could talk about what they were feeling and offer spiritual help when it was needed, but the man in command never attended. The students ceased to play in the zero-gravity room or romp in the hallways. They just did their assignments from their universities and sat around talking quietly. Adam and I did our best to keep up morale; we even reverted to telling stories from when we were young. We had one of our typical story times that evening with Adam getting things started.

"Hey, Rock. Remember the time when you and I were just little and we climbed up to the top of the hay stack and dared each other to jump."

"Yes, I still have the scars to prove it."

"You went first as I remember and you made the mistake of jumping with your tongue stuck out."

"Yes, you were always so considerate that way. As you might expect, when I hit the ground I damn near bit my tongue right off. That night, at the supper table, my dad noticed I was chewing funny and asked me to open my mouth. When I stuck out my tongue, there was still a pea lodged in the huge gash where I had bitten halfway through the centre. I had to go to the doctor and get several stitches the next day." Naturally, I had to counter Adam's embarrassing story about me with one of my own about him.

"My parents like to tell a story about when Adam first saw me as a newborn. He must have been three at the time and hadn't quite gotten his colors straight yet. Anyway, I must have had that silly little tongue of mine stuck out again, because Adam took one look at me and said, 'Oh, look at the baby's cute little green tongue.'"

"It's refreshing to hear stories like these. It helps us see our teachers from a different, more personal, perspective," Helena spoke up after everyone had stopped laughing at my last story. "Have you got any more?"

"Tell the kids about the time we all went to the butte."

"That story isn't really funny."

"I'd love to hear you tell it again." Adam looked at me in a way that made it impossible to refuse.

"Adam was constantly getting me in trouble in those days and that particular day was no exception. Adam and his brother were over at my place and there wasn't much to do that day, so Adam got the hair-brained idea that we should walk to the butte. For you city slickers that do not know what a butte is, I will explain. It's a tall hill that's kind of stuck out in the middle of nowhere. Anyway, Adam, his brother, my brother and I walked about two miles to the Butte, climbed it and then came home. It was a grand adventure for a little kid like me and I could not wait to get back to tell my mom the wonderful news.

The problem was, Adam, the oldest kid and the one who should have known better, did not tell our parents where we were going. Naturally, they were worried sick about us. When we finally got home and I ran up to my mother full of pride and exuberance, I wasn't greeted by a woman that was looking forward to hear my story. She grabbed me by the arm and started wailing on me like I had never been wailed on before. I was in a state of shock because I didn't realize I had done anything wrong. I was sent straight to my room, bawling my eyes out and holding on to my aching ass. What I remember most about the incident is how extremely fast I went from the highest emotional high to the lowest low, in just a split second of time."

"Those must have been different times, when you were young. Spanking isn't socially acceptable now."

"It wasn't acceptable then either, Eve Anna. It's just that my mother was so frightened for me, she couldn't contain herself. I have never held it against her; she was always an excellent mother to me."

"I guess I can understand how she must have felt," Helena commented. "It's hell knowing your loved ones' lives could be in jeopardy and you are helpless to do anything to help them."

"All we can do is pray and be there for each other." I was grasping for something more reassuring to say, but nothing would come to mind.

"It's almost time for shift change," Adam announced in an effort to divert our train of thought. "I have to go to the bridge."

"And we should head off for bed,' I added. No one wanted to go to sleep because we knew the morning would only bring more bad news.

The next day there were over 60,000 people on earth dead from the plague and millions sick and destined for the same fate. The most alarming statistic of all was that, as of yet, no one that contracted the disease had survived. The media had nicknamed it *The Grim Reaper*.

Many services had been disrupted. Most essential workers were either afraid to go to work, or chose not to because it did not make any sense under the circumstances. There was panic everywhere.

I was crushed to hear that both my mother and my father were now very ill. Dad's entire swine herd had perished overnight. It did not take a degree in medicine to realize my parents were as good as dead. Randy's mother was dying as well. Most of us on board now had someone that we knew affected by the plague: cousins, aunts, uncles, brothers and sisters. The Grim Reaper was striking close to home and it was devastating for our morale. I was too young to be losing both my parents. How did the children feel?

Since we now had far too much free time on our hands, it was easy to dwell on our problems. The students' online classes had already been disrupted, because no one was showing up for work at the universities to operate and maintain the online systems. We tried to start a chess tournament, but no one could concentrate enough to play with any proficiency. I insisted that we work out at least an hour every day. It was imperative that we stay in shape. Unfortunately, most of our free time was spent in front of the television screen watching the carnage play out on earth.

I tried to keep in touch with some of the HAM radio operators I had made contact with while on board the station. None of them could downplay the severity of what was happening back at home. Fred was doing fine up in northern Canada. He told me he had been fortunate enough to have gotten supplies just before the first case of the plague had been reported. He was sure he could survive comfortably for at least a year and a half. After that he could live off the land almost indefinitely. It was comforting to know that there were a small number of people that would be unaffected by the disaster.

The next day there was an estimated three million dead, my parents included. The whole situation seemed gruesomely surreal. It was a bad nightmare that you tried desperately to wake up from, but could not. I locked myself in the zero-gravity room and cried like a baby for half an hour. It was a shame I was not with them in the end. I should have been there to comfort them and to pray for them. I prayed for them now.

•———•

Society was in a state of chaos. People were so terrified they dragged their loved one's bodies out onto the streets, rather than risk further exposure to the disease from the outside. Many cities had to build massive provisional crematoriums to handle the extra dead that were removed from the hospitals and the streets. Various types of trucks and dumpsters were used to pick up the numerous bodies. There were food shortages in the cities because of interruptions in the supply chain. The biggest problem was the shortage of truckers that were required to deliver food and unprocessed commodities from the country. The truck driving community was especially hard hit by the disease because of the nature of their work. Their constant traveling had increased the odds of them picking up the virus from someone. People were exiting the cities in droves, desperately seeking refuge in the rural areas. The people in the county had guns and they were determined to keep what was rightfully theirs for themselves. Everyone was dedicated to survival at any cost. The Grim Reaper was finding new ways of taking human life. The plague was turning everyone against each other. It was a world gone mad!

Chapter Twelve

THAT NIGHT, AS I WAS stationed at the bridge, I received a call from Commander Gilmore.

"We're scrambling to get the *John Glenn* refurbished and loaded with supplies, so that we can get them to you before it's too late," he said.

"What do you mean, before it's too late?"

"Our staff down here are dropping like flies. I don't know how much longer we can continue to run a viable operation. It is imperative that we get this shipment to you. The fate of the entire human race may depend on us delivering that ship and its contents to you intact."

"I don't understand."

"Dr. Tucker, unfortunately, is dead; but his assistant thinks this plague may have the ability to kill every human on the planet. The President has asked me to assemble a team of doctors and scientists to put together a survival package for you."

I think I heard the words, "My God" struggle from my trembling lips.

"The most important part of the package will be a cache of genetic material, that was put together and sealed long before the outbreak occurred. It consists of sperm collected from prominent men of diverse backgrounds that have one thing in common. Each exemplifies the paragon of an admired human characteristic. Some excel in the arts and are the great painters, actors, musicians and composers of our time. There are also great architects, philosophers, doctors, scientists, astronomers, and physicists; all the great thinkers in the world today. We have also included people who excel in sports and other physical activities: hockey, baseball, soccer, football, gymnastics, dance, wrestling and bodybuilding. Almost every major sport has been represented. So, as you can see, we are sending you an ark that holds all of mankind's hopes and dreams for the future."

"I'm confused, Commander Gilmore. What are we supposed to do with this ark?"

"That's why I'm talking to you, Morris. It's up to you to artificially inseminate all the females on board. That way we can ensure the perpetuation of the human race."

"I know four young men up here that would be more than happy to do the job." I did not want to include Captain Dick in my account, for obvious reasons.

"Their time will come. Naturally you can understand the importance of keeping the genetic backgrounds of such a small initial population as diverse as possible, to avoid interbreeding. That's why we are asking all the females to have a baby, by someone other than the males on board the station, while that option is still available. Of course, we cannot keep the sperm frozen indefinitely. So, it's imperative that you accomplish this task as soon as the ark arrives at the station."

"I would feel extremely uncomfortable performing that duty."

"Unfortunately, you are our only option, other than the captain."

"Okay, I'll do it then." There was no way that pervert was getting anywhere near my girls. "These girls are barely seventeen years old. They're not ready to be mothers yet."

"I'm sorry about that, but it's not a question of being ready. It's a matter of necessity. Besides, girls much younger than them have been having babies for centuries."

"How will we get home? We do not have a full flight crew."

"Captain Dick is quite capable of doing the job alone. Besides, he's just there in case of an emergency. Otherwise, the computers do most of the flying."

"What if something were to happen to him? We'd be screwed."

"Your chances for survival would definitely be put at risk if that were to happen, but it would be possible for you to get home without him. There is a concise manual inside the SSTO that would take you through the entire procedure."

"I did spend one day on the simulator doing re-entry procedures when I was at NASA, but I'm hardly qualified to do the job."

"If you needed to, I believe you could manage."

"But if everyone's dead, how will we be guided down?"

"NASA has three backup systems that are capable of keeping the system running for up to ten years. We have diesel generators, fuel cells and nuclear batteries that are all linked together. At the rate that this pandemic is progressing, you should be able to come down in six months or less."

"That's a lot to think about, Commander Gilmore. And that's a lot of responsibility."

"We have every confidence in you and everyone on board the WSS."

"But we're only talking about a worst-case scenario, am I right?"

"Correct, Morris. I'm convinced that the scientific community will find a way to beat the Grim Reaper before it comes to an apocalypse. There are eight-billion human lives at stake here. It's unfathomable to think that the mighty human race could be brought to extinction by one of the least complex life forms on earth."

The commander's mentioning of the scientific community struck a nerve with me. Most scientists consider themselves to be morally neutral. In the excitement for discovery, mankind has used this moral immunity to disregard important issues that were traditionally accepted as being unethical, taboo or environmentally irresponsible. It was disturbing to think that our fate was controlled by a community that lacked a moral compass. My heart reached out to a more powerful and more dependable leader. Surely God had our best interest in mind.

"Maybe there is a higher power at work here," I said.

"Let's not get into that, shall we. It's all because some asshole doctor, in another part of the world, made a mistake and that's all there is to it."

"That was the mistake of the century." Whoever could have imagined that one individual could have such lack of forethought and such callous indifference to medical protocol, to commit a mistake that would cause the extinction of the entire human race. I thought to myself as I spoke.

"You can tell the others whenever you see fit. There's no sense waking them. They will have several days to adjust. Goodbye Morris, I'm proud to have you on the team."

"Thank you, Sir. I'll try not to let you down."

Since Captain Dick was fussing on the SSTO vehicle and the girls were watching television, I felt free to request that they come to the control room. Rather than me trying to explain the situation, I decided to just play back the digital recording of Commander Gilmore's and my conversation. The girls were flabbergasted to say the least. Dick just sat with a blank stare on his face. Because of my religious background I thought a prayer was in order.

"Why don't we all join hands and pray to God to give us strength."

Everyone stood in a circle with their hands extended, everyone but Dick. In an instant, he jumped from his seat in a fit of rage, screaming in an uncharacteristic tremor of passion.

"There are eight billion screaming souls crying out to Him in agony right now! Do you honestly think He'll hear your pitiful pleas for help?" He glared at us venomously and then stomped out of the room.

His actions and his words were beyond comment. I did not understand why he erupted with so little provocation; and since I could not dispel anything that he said, I kept quiet. I just continued to say a prayer and just like any prayer I just had to trust that God was listening, even though I could understand if He was not.

"Teach, I'm not ready to have a baby," Nicole spoke up after our prayer.

"Let's not think about any of this until we are absolutely positive it has to happen. Nothing is ever going to be the same again. Even if they found a cure tomorrow our life styles would still be dramatically changed. There's too much damage already done. Most of us will not have a family to return to in the end. We will have to create our own new families. It will take years to get the social infrastructures back in order. We will need to learn many new skills to survive. No, Nicole, we aren't going to be prepared for a lot of the shit that we are going to have to put up with from here on in, but we are going to have to face all our new challenges with courage and dignity."

Helena covered her face when I stopped speaking. She was unable to hold back her tears.

"I'm scared," she whimpered into her moist palms.

"What's wrong?" Eve Anna asked.

"I've never had to think about death before. I've always, sort of, avoided the subject." She was still sobbing as she struggled to get out the words.

"Yes, I remember what it was like to be young. You think you're invincible. You take far too many chances, because you think that bad things only happen to other people and not to you. You don't treat your body with the respect it deserves, because being young and vibrant is all you know. It's human nature to avoid the fact that you will grow old and die someday, even though it's as natural a process as life itself. Dying is as natural a progression as being born."

"I'm sorry, but that's just not very reassuring to me," she said, regaining her composure. "My family is probably going to be killed by the plague. And they're most likely going to suffer terribly before they die. Because of this, I can no longer avoid the obvious; I am going to die. I'm afraid the virus will still be around when we get back to earth and I'll die an agonizing death just like the others."

"Are you only afraid of the process of dying or are you also afraid of what comes after." I felt this was as good a time as any to get it all out in the open and discuss the matter.

"Of course, isn't everybody? Death is too final; and no matter how well prepared you are, all too sudden. My life has been so short compared to the eternity I will be dead for."

"Yes, you will be dead for an eternity. However, you were absent throughout several millennia of human history before you were born and I'm sure that doesn't cause you any concern."

"That's different. I didn't have anything to lose before I was born."

"Yes, but all I'm saying is, you shouldn't be concerned that you will be dead forever."

"I once thought that I could live on in the hearts and minds of those that loved me, but now they are all going to be dead. My memory will be lost forever. I also thought that I might achieve or create something in my life that might bring me a semblance of immortality, but any chance of that happening will die along with civilization."

"That's the trouble with trying to gain immortality through such a tenuous means. Time has a way of erasing any mark we try to leave in this world, as easily as the tide washes away footprints in the sand." I tried to lighten up the situation by adding: "A man named Woody Allen once said: 'I don't want to achieve immortality through my work. I want to achieve it through not dying.'" I received a small chuckle for my comic efforts.

Because Helena seemed to be getting frustrated with me, I decided to direct attention away from her by asking, "Does anyone else have fears pertaining to dying?"

"I'm afraid of the unknown," Eve Anna contributed. "What if dying is like falling into a sleep from which I will never awake? It scares me to think that all that will be left is nothingness."

"I'm afraid that I will be punished for my sins," Nicole admitted reluctantly.

"Mankind has feared this day of reckoning throughout the ages. It's a common belief that after death you will be rewarded for doing good in this world and punished for being bad. What greater incentive could we have for doing what we know is right? And what greater incentive could we have for the appreciation of life, but death? The ever presence of death gives life value. We are acutely aware of life, because of an inevitable death. I know I strive to do well with my time here on earth, because I know my time is limited." I paused while I surveyed the blank faces before me. We had dwelt on the negative aspects of death long enough. It was time we moved on to the more positive aspects of dying.

"Eve Anna mentioned the dark nothingness of death. Is there any reason to reject that notion?"

"Life after death." Nicole mentioned timidly.

"Yes of course." I tried to sound encouraging. "Don't you all feel in your hearts that a part of you survives bodily death?"

"I do want to believe," Helena confessed. "But I learned a long time ago, that just because you want something really bad doesn't necessarily mean you'll get it."

"Nicole said before that she feared retribution. Moral law dictates that justice will eventually prevail. As we know, many people live their lives without ever being punished for their wrong doings. Therefore, we must imagine another life in which moral law is ultimately fulfilled."

"I'd like you to show me some encouraging hard evidence."

"Okay, Helena, what about the large number of near-death experiences that have been documented. And what about people that can describe events that happened in a former life while under hypnosis."

"Some clairvoyants claim to be able to talk to the dead," Eve Anna added. "And lots of people have admitted to seeing ghosts."

"I think you have to believe in life after death, otherwise life has no meaning." I tried to sound confident, as I looked into Helena's eyes. "Well, are you just a piece of meat with sophisticated neuron activity, or do you have a soul? Only you can decide."

"I would prefer to think that my life has meaning and that I have a soul."

"Do you believe in God?" I asked.

"Yes, I guess so."

I looked at Nicole and Eve Anna to see if they felt the same. They both nodded, yes; but I think Nicole was only trying to please me with her response.

INTERVENTION

"I can't guarantee that you won't suffer when you die, but you can all rest assured that your soul will go to heaven after your body fails. Trust that death will bring the greatest of all blessings."

Helena stepped forward, put her arms around me and pulled me into her bosom.

"That's what I love about you, Teach," she said. "You're always ready to give us a lesson at the drop of a hat. I'm so glad you are here for us. I need you to protect me and prepare me for what lies ahead."

Before I knew it, I was surrounded by three beautiful girls and almost smothered in firm young breasts. I was 300 kilometres up and the closest to heaven I had ever been in my life. I was glad the girls had not pursued the question of life after death any further, because if they had questioned the existence of God, any argument I could have come up with would have been on shaky ground.

"I hope I can live up to your expectations," I said, not struggling in the least to free myself from their embrace. Now that all hell was breaking loose on earth, I was not so rigid with my relationship with the girls.

The girls released me all too soon and we went about our business on the bridge the same as usual. When Adam and the boys came to relieve us, they took the news just as you might expect. They were in shock and disbelief by the time we left for our turn in the sleep capsules.

It was no surprise to me that I could not sleep that night. The cocoons were great for sleeping in, but terribly confining if you were compelled to toss and turn. I decided to rise and make myself a warm drink in the galley. Before I left, I closed up the capsule to keep the internal conditions optimal for my return. I made myself a mug of warm milk and tried to relax, but of course it was impossible to divert my thoughts from the sick and dying back on earth. I stayed up for half an hour before I realized I would never get to sleep unless I was in my bunk.

When I got back to the cocoon room, I was shocked and outraged by what I found. Our captain had the hatch to Nicole's cocoon open and had both his arms extended inside, right up to his shoulders. Because I was in my sock feet, I was able to sneak up behind him without him knowing. He had one hand over her mouth and the other hand down inside her pyjama bottoms. Poor, sweet Nicole was whimpering beneath his forceful, smothering grasp.

"What in the fucking hell do you think you're doing?" I yelled so forcefully I made myself cringe.

Dick jumped back from the cocoon with an expression on his face that—under any other circumstance—would have made me laugh. He looked as if he had soiled his pants. The captain never said a word. He only started walking backwards towards the doorway, as if he was afraid of what would happen if he turned his back to me. I followed him and was relentless in my reproach.

"If you ever so much as lay a hand on any of my girls again, I will cut off your nuts, boil them up and feed them to you for dinner. Is that understood?"

Dick nodded his head in an unmistakeable confirmation of his new found awareness and continued to slither backwards towards the door.

"I'll kill you, you son of a bitch. I will not hesitate to kill you and toss your body into outer-fucking space."

When Dick got to the threshold, he seemed to regain some courage.

"You can't talk to me that way," he said pitifully as he walked away. "I'm the captain of this outfit and don't you forget it."

"Get out of my sight," I said. "You make me sick."

Nicole was still cowering against the side of the cocoon when I finally came to comfort her. I patted the side of her head and took her trembling hand in mine. Her hair was wet beside her ears from the flood of frightened tears, that ran down her face when he had her pinned to the bed.

"Are you okay?" I was as anxious as I was upset.

"Yes, I'm fine." She spoke between her sobs of terror. "I'm so sorry. I didn't know what to do. I was so scared, I just froze there and cried like a stupid little baby."

"You don't have to apologize for anything. It's not your fault he forced himself on you."

"I should have fought back, instead of just lying there like an idiot."

"Don't beat yourself up. You were jolted from your sleep and trapped inside that tin can. He didn't exactly catch you at your best. That's the way cowardly slime like that work. They try and catch you when you're the most vulnerable."

"He had his grubby fingers inside me."

"I know, I saw him. Why don't you go have a shower? Maybe that will make you feel better."

Nicole climbed from the cocoon and started towards the shower stall. Then she stopped, turned and looked at me with her head tilted.

"You've got quite the potty mouth when you're riled," she teased from behind a warm friendly smile.

"You can't blame a teacher for wanting to protect a special student, can you?"

"I love you for it. But I was surprised you could be so forceful."

"You'd be amazed at what I'm capable of when the wrong buttons are pushed."

"What do you suppose got into that rat-bastard? Look at the way he acted when we tried to pray tonight. Do you think he's losing it?"

"I hope not. As much as I hate the man, we need him to get us home."

"Scary, isn't it?" she added, as she closed the shower door behind her.

Our captain may have lost his mind, but I feared something much worse. What if he believed that mankind was already doomed? That would make him accountable to no one and beyond retribution. He was a wild man out of control; like a nuclear warhead without a guidance system. He could make our lives a living hell. I had to somehow reverse the pecking order. That is when I recalled the old frontier saying that I had attributed to John Wayne, 'God created men; but it was Samuel Colt who made them equal.'

Chapter Thirteen

AS SOON AS I BEGAN my shift on the bridge that morning, I asked to speak to Marty. I then explained the predicament we were in with our Captain Dick.

"How do you want me to help?" Marty asked.

"Is there a master key to the storage lockers where my things are kept?"

"I know the commander has one."

"Can you get it from him?"

"Unfortunately, the commander went home sick. We aren't likely to see him back here again, but I could look through his office if you like."

"Holy shit, is this going to jeopardize the launch of the supply ship?"

"No, everything is on schedule. It should lift off today at eighteen hundred hours."

"I need you to get the key and open up my locker. You'll find a handgun with two loaded magazines inside. I want you to put them in a box, write my name on it and label it as medical supplies. Will you have time to get them on board with the rest of our equipment?"

"I'll do my damnedest."

"Thanks, Marty. I know this is a highly irregular request, but our situation dictates the use of drastic measures."

"I understand completely. Down here on earth, all bets are off and it's a whole new ball game. Things are safe here on the cape because we're surrounded by a thousand troops with tanks and guns, but the rest of the country has gone insane."

"What's the death count?"

"Last I heard it was around two hundred million."

"My God, Marty, when will it end?"

"Maybe it won't, that's the scariest part."

"Anyways, I should let you go. You don't have much time. Thanks for everything."

"Best of luck to you. Over and out."

When my regular duties were complete, I accessed the internet to watch the news. Travel on any of the major highways was impossible. The mass exodus from the cities had caused major traffic jams, which in turn blocked the vital supply chain. There was a mushrooming effect because road blockages held up fuel tanker trucks, which quickly led to gas shortages, which eventually led to countless vehicles dying on the roads forcing all travel to a halt. It was a devastating predicament, that could only expedite the Grim Reaper's rapidly spreading blanket of death. There were wildly contagious human bodies littering the landscape in all areas of the globe. People wandered aimlessly, searching for sanctuary from the disease; lost souls that were thirsty and hungry and in need of any small scrap of encouraging news. Some were shot trying to steal food from farmers and other country dwellers. Many of the people that were driven out of the cities died from exposure, because they possessed no practical survival skills. They had been trained to survive in the dog-eat-dog world of modern urbanism. Most failed miserably when left to contend with the great outdoors. Those that survived were left to the plague.

That evening we watched the John Glenn lift off with our supplies on board. Within two hours we had it docked to the WSS. All we could do for the time being was release the fumigation chemicals inside the SSTO with hopes that they would kill every living organism on board. What was sealed inside the tiny containers, stored in the ark, would be safe from harm.

Marty called me during my shift to say goodbye. He was coughing intermittently while we spoke.

"This is the last you'll be hearing from me," Marty said. It was apparent from his voice that he was overwhelmed by his emotions. "I'm going home to die."

"Surely not."

"There's no sense trying to deny the inevitable, Morris. I only have a couple of days now."

"May God have mercy on your soul."

"The rest of the crew is going to try and hang on here for another day or so. The entire system has been set for your Automatic Computer Controlled Descent. Other than some last-minute double checking, all of our jobs have become redundant. We can't do much more than offer each other moral support from here on in."

"Thanks for everything, Marty. I hope your last days aren't too painful."

"Don't worry about me. You just concentrate on your new mission. There is a lot riding on your successful return to earth. Goodbye." Marty switched off the mike after those words. It was the last I heard from NASA.

I had to search the internet for several minutes before I found a television station that was still broadcasting. The news for the day was grim. Many nuclear power plants had been shut down while there was still enough staff alive to perform the task. Mankind did not need to add a legacy of nuclear disasters to its already overwhelming list of abuse and debauchery.

Governments were powerless to reverse the lack of order. Hospitals had been abandoned, leaving the sick to die alone and in agony. All law enforcement agencies had been disbanded. Women were raped on the streets. Homes and businesses were looted. People were killing each other without provocation. Society, now in a shambles, had collapsed.

The news anchor said that this was his network's last broadcast. They were running on a skeleton crew and he felt that they had ceased to provide a vital service.

"Nothing we do or say will affect the outcome of this catastrophe," he said. "I can only hope that those who survive will rebuild a just society. Not a social order based on fear and domination, but a brave new world free of terror and hate. Goodbye and may good fortune be with you." The camera zoomed in to catch a glimpse of a tear running down his cheek. After that, a test pattern came on. Within fifteen minutes the screen was blank and that was the end. The internet system had collapsed.

We were now totally isolated from Earth. The airwaves were dead at NASA and we were not receiving any radio or television signals. Our only means of communication was by HAM radio.

The only people on the air that day were Stuart, from a remote location in the outback of Australia and Fred, my friend from northern Saskatchewan. They were both as shocked and disturbed as I was over the events of the past few days. Since they both relied on the media for their information, they could not add anything to what I already knew. In most cases I was bringing them up to date on the state of our civilization.

Within a week most of the earth was in the dark. One by one the power stations had to be shut down as safely as possible. What was once a bright network of city lights was now a dark, foreboding landscape. The last indication of mankind's existence was snuffed out like a candle.

We were now able to unload our supplies from the John Glenn. The ark was to remain on board, because its temperature had to be maintained by the liquid nitrogen cooling system, which had been built into the ship. The cockpit had been converted into an infirmary for my convenience. My assignment was clear, but I was reluctant to perform the designated procedures.

Captain Dick had insisted on helping with the unpacking of our supplies which consisted mostly of survival gear, food, water purification containers and a small pharmacy. There was a survival manual in hard copy and a Memory Wafer containing a detailed description of the artificial insemination procedure. Marty had placed my special parcel strategically amongst the other medical supplies, but Captain Dick was intrigued by its heaviness for the size of the box.

"Medical supplies?" he announced with a curious frown. "This is rather heavy for medical supplies." He set the box on the counter and reached for a utility knife that we were using to open packages.

"That has my name on it, if you hadn't noticed." I reached out to take it from him.

"I'm in charge here," he said, pushing me forcefully against the opposite bulkhead. "I have the right to inspect everything that comes on board."

"Give me that." I tried to pull the package from his grasp. "That's my personal property."

He let go this time all right, but only long enough to give me a back hand across the cheek. I was shocked by the unrestrained use of his strength and his brutality. I wanted to take my hand and rub the stinging flesh on my face, but it was imperative I not let go of the package. I struggled for it with all my strength and determination, but he outweighed me by over a hundred pounds.

He tore the package from my fingers and gave me another quick right hand to the face. By the time I had pulled myself from the floor he had the box open and the gun pointed at my chest.

"Well, looky here. What were you planning to do with this?"

"We are going to be in an extreme survival situation when we get back to Earth. I thought it might come in handy."

"Good thinking, Shorty. I'm sure this will come in handy."

"May I have it back now?" I reached out my hand, fully expecting him to give me my property.

"I don't think so."

"But it's my gun. My Grandfather gave it to me just before he died."

"Well, God bless his soul. I sure do appreciate his thoughtfulness." He rotated the gun in his hand to admire its mechanical splendour and its intrinsic gift of power. "As captain of this outfit, I feel it's my duty to take possession of this beauty."

"You have no right."

"I have every right. Besides, who's going to stop me?"

I was appalled by the undeniable truth of his last statement. In my attempt to swing the balance of power, I accidentally tipped the scales in his favour. What a fool I had been.

"You rat-bastard, you'll pay for this someday."

"Now, now, let's not say anything we will regret later, shall we?"

"Fuck off!" I spouted, glaring maliciously into his beady yellow eyes. Because the sight of the smirk on his face sickened me, I turned and stomped away in defeat. The captain wore my firearm defiantly tucked into his pants for the duration of our stay on the World Space Station. It made my blood boil every time I saw it with him.

Chapter Fourteen

THE NEXT DAY I OPENED my fertility clinic. I had three reluctant customers scheduled for that morning. Since teenage girls were unlikely to be in tune with their reproductive cycles, the ark contained enough semen samples to enable each female on board to be inseminated once a day for two months, if necessary.

"Who wants to be first?" I asked through the narrow opening from the SSTO. I was glad to have Nicole put up her hand. Because I was not as sexually attracted to her as I was to the other two girls, I hoped the procedure would be a little less uncomfortable. I also wanted to see how she was doing after her encounter with Captain Dick.

Nicole was undressed from the waist down and positioned on the gurney before I had a chance to initiate a conversation. It was difficult to keep my eyes focused on her face with her slender legs spread wide so provocatively, only inches away.

"How are you doing, Nicole?" She could tell what I was referring to by the tone of my voice.

"As good as can be expected, I guess."

"Are you going to be okay with me poking around down there, after everything that just happened?"

"The fact that it's you doing it doesn't bother me a bit."

"Okay, is there any particular type of male you would like to be impregnated by?" I asked. I was standing before the ark inserting my hands into a pair of surgical gloves.

"What are my choices?"

"Brainy, artistic or athletic."

"Athletic, I believe our children will have to be strong and agile to survive."

"What sport?"

"Hockey."

"Why hockey?"

"Hockey players are about as tough and as manly as you can get."

I selected one of the five available hockey players on board the ark. The semen was already stored in a handy little syringe dispenser. Because of my lack of medical background, NASA had simplified the procedure. The method of application was reduced to its most rudimentary form. The key to the device was a catheter tube encased in a flexible, cigar-shaped, rubber applicator that was about fifteen centimetres long. This was attached to the syringe and then inserted into the vagina. The rest was not exactly rocket science. It had all the high-tech features of a turkey baster.

When the assembly was complete, I applied a lubricant to my fingers and gently applied some internally to provide ease of entry. Luckily the procedure was so quick and simple it was over before I had a chance to become uneasy with its provocative nature.

"That's all there is to it," I said, tilting the gurney in order to invert her body to a head down inclination. "You just have to rest there for a few minutes then you can go."

"That was quite painless," Nicole offered reassurance.

"Well, thanks for volunteering to go first. And thanks for making me feel at ease in what could have been an uncomfortable situation."

"Don't sweat it. I'm just glad you were here to do the job. Can you imagine how icky it would have been for me if Captain Dick was the only adult here?"

My entire body shivered violently at the thought. Then my gorge rose when I realized Captain Dick would be more inclined to donate his own semen, along with his own personal applicator. I shook my head vigorously from side to side, to eliminate that disturbing picture from my mind.

"The fact is, I am here and we don't ever have to think about the alternative again. Right?"

"Right." An amiable smile stretched across her face. It reassured me that all was well.

"You have a beautiful smile, Nicole. It's a shame we don't get to see it more often." I turned toward the ark and made preparations for my next patient.

Helena was a little more self-conscious about undressing in front of me. I had to ask that she remove everything from the waist down. She was even more reluctant to climb onto the gurney. Who could blame her for not wanting to assume such an uncomplimentary pose in front of a very familiar authority figure—her teacher.

"Don't be shy, Helena. This is uncomfortable for me too, but it doesn't have to be that way. It's just an impersonal clinical procedure. There's nothing to be embarrassed about." That was easy for me to say, but a lot harder to apply to the reality of the situation, especially with her shapely legs waving back and forth nervously in the stirrups. She has as close to a perfect body as any woman I had ever met, but for some strange reason, I am not nearly as attracted to her as I am to Eve Anna. Eve Anna has an indescribable sensual quality that overwhelms me and drives me to obsession. Now being distracted, I was able to continue without getting flustered.

Helena picked a nuclear physicist as her first donor. I had the job done and Helena out the door before either of us could become uncomfortable with the proceedings.

Eva Anna was bubbling with confidence as she entered my makeshift medical centre. A quirky, enigmatic smile illuminated her striking features and her eyes sparkled with a mischievous light. Her high-spiritedness and her boldness intimidated me thoroughly. I started to shake in dreaded anticipation. She was soon to let me know that I was rightfully concerned.

"Is something wrong?" she asked, slowly unzipping the front of her orange NASA- issue jumpsuit. "You look as white as a ghost."

"No, everything is fine," I finally choked out after a long hesitation; my eyes riveted to the long, narrow strip of milky-white flesh, that was slowly becoming exposed with each tantalizing release of the zipper's interlocking teeth. The slow, downward motion of her hand magically uncovered the cleavage of her bare breasts. The "V" shaped channel of glisteningly smooth skin widened as her hand extended to reach her tight young tummy. The same moment her belly button came into view, she dropped one of her shoulders, causing a rigid pink nipple to pop out from behind the splitting garment. In an instant, she was standing suggestively still and peering deeply into my overwhelmed eyes. She was unapologetically sensual as her hand rested motionless at the end of her zipper; only partially hiding her dark bush, her kinky locks protruding teasingly through her fingers. And her perky young breasts pointed at me like bullets.

"What happened to your underwear?" I asked.

"No need," she said, slowly rolling the flight suit off her shoulders, allowing the garment to fall to the floor, permitting me to absorb the full impact of her nakedness and her untamed femininity. "Just one more thing to have to take off."

How could I argue with that kind of rationality? Her statement was indisputable. I wanted to be angry with her, but I could not. She was too much of a sweetheart; too much of an angel; too much of a seductress. I was putty in her hands.

"Get up on the table, please." I had to avert my eyes as I spoke. Eve Anna's unclad body made them sting. It was as if I had been too close to a fire and could not stand the heat. I blinked to soothe my sight and calm my mind.

"How about a musician?" she asked. She had obviously been talking to the other girls about the procedure.

I found what she was looking for and made it ready.

I could feel my temperature rising as I approached her with the apparatus. I found her calmness and her willingness unsettling. She sat up with her arms wrapped around her knees. The closer I came towards her, the further she pulled her knees apart. I was like a north pole magnet coming between two south pole limbs. I was dizzied by the treasure that lay so temptingly close to me. Then she reached out and took hold of my right hand. She slid my surgical glove off my fingers with a snap.

"You won't be needing these," she said with a flirtatious wink, guiding my hand between her legs.

"Eve Anna, what do you think you're up to?" My mind was whirling as I spoke.

I am unable to give an accurate account of what happened after that. There are several minutes missing from my memory. My recollections consist of nothing more than fragments of disconnected images—the strangest picture being that of an orchid in bloom.

Sure, I was emotionally distraught; and sure, my faculties were in a frenzy, overdosed with adrenalin. But never before, in my brief history, has any situation caused so much consternation, that I was unable to recall my actions. It was beyond explanation.

I have always been an individual of high moral standing. I have always conducted myself with decency, respectability and a sense of propriety worthy of my profession. I like to think that I behaved in a manner indicative of my disposition. But what if I did not? What if I was naughty?

If I could remember what I did, I could pray to God to ask for His forgiveness and I could apologize to Eve Anna for my indiscretions. As it is, I am at a terrible disadvantage. She knows what happened and she will be smug about it. I cannot ask her, straight out, what happened; it would be too embarrassing. All I can do is continue on with things as they are and hope for the best.

"Are you and I still virgins after yesterday?" Eve Anna asked when she came in for her second round of artificial insemination. A bolt of apprehension traversed the length of my body at the speed of lightning. What was she insinuating by her question? What could I have done in our previous visit to make her think she had lost her virginity?

Eve Anna was wearing a sleeveless red sweater with a short, black, leather skirt. It suited her to perfection, making it hard not to stare. She was dazzling; standing with one hand on the gurney, wide-eyed, child-like, twisting her hair with her free hand, waiting for me to respond to her question.

"Whatever do you mean, Eve Anna?" My heart was pounding hard and fast, representative of my degree of guilt. I hoped that she would volunteer more information.

"It's a fairly straightforward question, isn't it? Are we still virgins or not?" A small smirk made her lips curl, implying that she was only being playful.

"Can you give me any indication why you would think we weren't?" still begging for a scrap of evidence.

"Aha! So, you are a virgin," Eve Anna announced with self-satisfaction. "Just as I suspected."

"So that's what all this is about; you trying to delve into my personal affairs. Really, Eve Anna, I'm disappointed in you." Truthfully, I was relieved.

"Don't be too hard on me, Teach. It's not my fault you blabbed. I honestly wanted to know if I could be pregnant and still be a virgin."

"Haven't you heard of immaculate conception?" I asked.

"You mean, like in the Bible?"

"Yes, Mary conceived as a virgin and had a virgin birth." I was trying to reassure myself as much as Eve Anna.

"Aren't you forgetting something? She wasn't pumped full of semen from a mortal man; her pregnancy was a miracle from God." Eve Anna said in frustration.

"Still, you haven't been intimate with anyone. Have you?" I was still fishing for clues pertaining to the missing few minutes of my memory.

"No, of course not."

"Then, in my mind, you are still as innocent as you ever were and a virgin in the eyes of God."

"Okay, I trust your judgement." Eve Anna seemed happy to dismiss the subject as quickly as it came up. Then she hiked up her skirt and dropped her panties in a blur of motion. She was up on the table with her feet in the stirrups before I knew what hit me.

"How about a doctor of medicine this time?"

I searched through the ark to find her a doctor.

"What kind of man did you pick?" she asked.

"I haven't yet." I was slightly embarrassed to admit that I was dragging my heals.

"How come?"

"I wasn't psychologically prepared yesterday." I took her by the hand and squeezed some lubricant onto her fingers. I was not going to fall into the same trap as yesterday.

"Oh, and the rest of us girls were?" She made herself ready for the insertion as she protested.

"Cut me some slack, Eve Anna. I'll do the job today, I promise."

"How come a woman of your age is still a virgin?" She asked with a smirk.

"You are full of questions today, aren't you?" I inserted the apparatus while she was distracted.

"If it's none of my business, just say the word."

"It's kind of complicated, that's all." I turned and walked back to the counter.

"You're not a lesbian, are you?" Eve Anna was still fishing for some kind of clarity.

"I thought we went through this before? I believe same sex relationships are wrong. No, I am not a lesbian!"

"What is it then? Is it a physical problem?" She continued with her artful interrogation.

I turned and looked over my shoulder with a reproachful glance.

"I'm only asking as a concerned friend. You mean a lot to me you know," she added.

Why was I keeping it a secret? Just like Marty said, 'all bets are off, and it's a whole new ball game'. I may as well tell her. Her imagination would probably fabricate something far worse than the truth.

"Okay, I'll tell you. But only because our relationship has changed; I'm no longer your teacher and you are no longer my student."

"Just a minute," she said, jumping down from the gurney. "Let's go sit over there and be comfortable". She slipped her panties back on and followed me to a piece of equipment that could double as a bench. She placed my hand between her soft fingers and beseeched me to continue with her eyes.

Then, I dropped the bomb: "I'm a man trapped in a woman's body."

Eve Anna never said a word, but her mouth fell open involuntarily. Then her eyes started glistening with sympathetic tears. She was in my arms in an instant.

"Your transgender? Oh, Teach, how awful for you."

"I would prefer that you not call me that. It sounds like I'm a freak and it makes me feel dirty."

"What do you want me to call you then?" It was an innocent request.

"Call me Candy."

"Yes, of course. No one likes to be labelled." She sounded needlessly apologetic.

I took her by the hands and slowly concluded our embrace. It was even more awkward for me now that she knew the truth.

"Now you know my dirty little secret," I said with sorrow. "I can never be with a man, for obvious reasons. And I can never be with a woman, because I do not want to be labelled a lesbian. That's why I'm sworn to celibacy and still a virgin. It's the only way I can keep my sanity. Most people like me commit suicide by the time they're twenty-five."

"This explains so much."

I looked at her inquisitively. "Meaning?"

"I would be embarrassed to say."

"Eve Anna, think. You can't hold out after making *me* spill *my* guts."

"What I was going to say was: now I know why I'm so strangely attracted to you."

"I have always been fond of you too, Eve Anna."

"With your stunning good looks and beautiful body, you must have trouble keeping men at bay?"

"Dealing with men does tend to be a hassle sometimes. My relationship with Adam has been my biggest regret. But I do like the fact that I'm attractive. I have always tried to be the best woman I can be, in spite of my gender dysphoria. I would never subject myself to disfiguration by having a sex change operation. That's just not an option for me."

"Mr. McGinnis has a thing for you?"

"Since we were teenagers. But I'm telling you all of this in the strictest of confidence. No one must know about Adam or about my secret. Promise me you won't tell a single soul." I gripped Eve Anna's hand to beseech her.

"Don't worry. I know how to keep a secret."

"I would die if anyone else knew this." I could not believe that I had just let the cat out of the bag.

"You must feel a little strange, having to get yourself pregnant?" Eve Anna sounded genuinely concerned.

"It's the most unselfish thing I have ever had to do in my life." I admitted.

"Me too." She offered me a timid smile, which alluded to her inner turmoil. "It's great that we will be going through this together."

"In some aspects it might be fun; the four of us being pregnant together."

Will you deliver my baby for me?" Eve Anna's eyes started to moisten as she spoke.

"That would make me proud."

"Well, I guess I had better let you get at it then. You have given me a lot to think about." She turned and headed for the exit.

"Do you really think I'm stunning?" My vanity crept to the forefront while I was susceptible.

"Absolutely... bye." She blew me a kiss and then crawled out the hatch.

I sat frozen in the same spot, immersed in thought, for several minutes. The knowledge of Eve Anna's attraction to me, braced my interest in life. She was a bright and shimmering spark in what had otherwise been a dark and gloomy week. Maybe the four of us expecting at the same time did have the potential to be fun. It was going to be interesting to say the least; trying to raise four little babies in a tough survival situation. It was sure to test my metal. That is exactly how I choose to address the situation, as a challenge; the biggest challenge of my life, but still within my capabilities. I would have to make a new addition to my philosophy on life—make the best of the cards God dealt you. Be the best person, best woman, best mother you can be.

There was only one problem. I had to conceive first. I got up and approached the ark. It was the *who's who* of potential fathers. Which one to pick? I pulled out an architect, only to replace it with an astronomer. Then the astronomer lost out to a lawyer, who lost out to a gymnast. I was racked with indecision, until I discovered a vial that had lost its label. That was the one I chose. It was better not to know. It was best not to burden the child with some preconceived legacy that would be impossible for him or her to live up to. It would be much easier to accept them for who they are.

Chapter Fifteen

I KNOW IT WAS PROBABLY all in my mind, but I felt different the following morning. I felt like I had a better reason to live. There was a spark of life inside that brought new meaning to my existence. It was a rewarding sense of responsibility and giving. Against all reason and against all physical technicalities, I was going to have a baby!

I felt an indescribable urge to look at the earth. The home that man was being forced to abandon by his death. It was a beautiful home—maybe unique in the universe—a delicate ecosystem of intricately balanced and interdependent species all living in relative harmony, except for man. Instead of being satisfied with just fitting into his environment, man choose to try and take control. Look where that got us.

Was there anything the girls and I could do to prevent this sort of thing from happening again? Not likely. Humans have inherent tendencies that always seem to lead them to destruction: improvidence, greed, jealousy, hostility and ascendancy. God even sent us a list of rules to live by and we still could not get it right.

INTERVENTION

Over the last century man had arrogantly turned his back to God, denouncing all for which He stood. Society had become perverse and out of control. Population numbers were soaring unrestrained, placing a burden on the earth that was unmanageable. I could not help but wonder if God had a hand in what was playing out below; a Divine intervention that would cleanse the world from a society gone wrong; a flood of disease that would wash away evil.

There was a pious irony in the method of man's extermination. The human race was succumbing to a tiny organism whose sole purpose was to multiply to unsupportable numbers that were injurious to its host—the center of its universe—until that host could no longer exist. Man was doing essentially the same thing to the center of his universe. The earth was quickly becoming incapable of handling our numbers. Just like a virus, we were altering our environment so negatively, it was losing its ability to support life. I think God was obligated to intervene before we had gone too far.

Now it might be up to Nicole, Helena, Eve Anna and me to repopulate the world. Our descendants would be the future custodians of the earth. We would have to raise them with strong principles that would lead them away from self-destruction. But how many generations would it take to lose sight of what is important?

I sat quietly for over an hour looking down at my home. I could only guess at how much time mankind had left. Those that remained must have been going through a living hell. I felt the urge to make contact. I needed to talk to someone, anyone.

Stuart, in Australia, was the only person I could make contact with today. I would regret having made contact with him before our conversation was over. Apparently, his wife had just succumbed to the disease.

"I just got back from burying my wife. We'd been married for thirty-six years. She was a good woman and I'm sure going to miss her."

"Who was she in contact with?"

"Don't know, that's just it. We haven't left the ranch for over two months."

"Are you sure it was the Grim Reaper?"

"Yeah, it was the plague all right. No mistake about it. The most horrible thing I have ever seen in my life. At least she went quick; she was dead within two days from the time she was bedridden."

"What were her symptoms?"

"She started off with just a nasty cough. Then she started to gurgle inside when she breathed. Within a day her eyes looked like ripe cherries and she started puking and passing blood out of every opening in her body. Her skin broke open everywhere and a smelly clear liquid mixed with blood oozed from every sore. It was downright nasty to watch her die like that."

"You were a good husband to stand by her to the end."

"I just wish I would have had something to ease the pain. She screamed like an animal that was being slaughtered alive. Thank God she was only conscious part of the time. Towards the end her tummy swelled up something fierce and just before she died something popped inside. It made a terrible hollow thud that sounded like you'd hit a sack of flour with a baseball bat. At least I will not have to carry that memory around with me for long. I expect to be gone within a week."

"I'll pray for you." I felt insensitive for asking him to describe the horrible details of her passing.

"I wouldn't waste your breath. If my prayin' couldn't help a God farin' woman like my missus, ain't nothing going to help an old sinner like me."

"Are you going to stay at the ranch, or are you going to head into town and look for help."

"Help! There ain't no need for me to look for help. When the time comes, the only help I'm going to need is an old .303 that I got hangin' out in the shop. I know I'm being a chicken-shit for taking that way out, but I haven't got the guts to face what my wife went through; seeing that would have caused Lucifer himself to run back to the gates of hell with his tail between his legs."

"I guess this is goodbye then."

"You'll have to forgive an old man for running out on you darlin'. I'm going to miss our little chats. You sound like a real sweet gal. Good-luck to you, Candy. You're going to need it."

"Good luck to you too, Stuart."

Shortly after signing off with Stuart, I was reminded of a famous suicide note that was pertinent to his situation. I searched the ships computer files to find the last communication of Charlotte Perkins Gilman: "Human life consists in mutual service. So, grief, pain, misfortune, or 'broken heart' is no excuse for cutting off one's life while any power of service remains. But when all usefulness is over, when one is assured of an unavoidable and imminent death, it's the simplest of human rights to choose a quick and easy death in place of a slow and horrible one."

I called Stuart back at once and read her suicide note to him over the air. He seemed to be mildly comforted by her words.

A week after my first insemination, I tested positive on my pregnancy test. Helena and Nicole were also with child. Eve Anna, however, was not.

"Well that just sucks," Eve Anna announced when I told her the results. "I thought we could all have babies together."

"It probably only means that you're not at the most favourable part of your cycle and nothing more. I find it amazing that three out of the four of us are pregnant already. Having our babies a few weeks apart will mean nothing. In six months' time, you won't be able to tell them apart. Besides you can learn from our mistakes."

"And some of you will need help with your deliveries."

"That's the spirit." I encouraged.

"How are you accepting your new role as mother-to-be?" Eve Anna asked.

"It feels strange, but yet exciting. Just think, Eve Anna, there's a new life growing inside me; a little miracle that will emerge from my body in just nine short months and will rely on me alone for its existence. It will suckle at my swollen breasts and I'll nurture it and protect it from harm. I will teach it right from wrong and I will show it how to survive in, what is bound to be, a hostile world. And then I will have to be physically bred by one of the males in the group, so that my little darling will have a brother or a sister. That will not be an easy task for me. I have a lot of issues that will need to be addressed."

"Who will you pick to be the father of your next child?"

"Adam of course. He's a wonderful friend and he will go out of his way to make it easier for me. Besides, genetically he is just the kind of father I'm looking for: he's good looking, well built, and has a wonderful personality. What about you? Who will you pick?"

"Would you be mad if I picked Adam as well?"

"Not at all, but why are you overlooking the boys your age?"

"Strangely, you strike me as more of a man than any of those three will ever be. I'd pick you if I could, but since that just wouldn't work, Adam is my second choice for basically the same reasons that you gave. He just strikes me as the kind of guy that would take the time to do me right, if you know what I mean."

"I think I know exactly what you mean. It's going to be my first time too. I can't explain what Adam has to offer that the other three would not. His maturity is definitely an asset, but there's more, an intangible something of great worth." I thought for a moment then the answer came to me. "Integrity."

Eve Anna pointed at me for emphasis, her expression validating my words. Then her look changed, depicting a dramatic alteration of thought. "I don't have to do it with Captain Dick, do I? I'd rather see the human race become extinct before I succumb to his advances."

"Relax, Eve Anna. I don't plan on letting that sleaze-ball lay a finger on any one of you girls. I wouldn't dream of asking you to do anything I wasn't willing to do myself. Entertaining thoughts of being intimate with that man makes my flesh crawl."

"I can't tell you how glad I am to hear you say that."

"If the Captain tries anything with you, I want you to kick and scream and do anything in your power to resist. Wet your pants or soil yourself; do whatever it takes to discourage him." I spoke with as much emphasis as I could to drive home my point.

"If that S.O.B. tries anything with me, I won't have to think about wetting my pants, it will just happen naturally." Eve Anna said with a wicked little smirk.

Eve Anna and I laughed in order to eradicate several disturbing images from our minds. At that very moment the devilish subject of our conversation opened the hatch to the SSTO and stepped inside.

"What's so funny," he asked.

"A joke," Eve Anna offered a clumsy, encrypted explanation.

"Are you all done here for today?" He looked at me as he spoke.

"I can be. What do you need?"

"I want to check you out on the MMU."

"You want me to do an EVA?" I was startled at the thought of leaving the safety of the station with only my space suit and jet pack to protect me from the perils of open space. "Why?"

"It's important that someone other than myself is capable of making untethered excursions outside the station. My role in this mission is too crucial to be put at risk."

"Why me?"

"I trust your abilities more than anyone else on board."

"Why, Captain Dick, I'm strangely flattered," I joked with a sarcastic tone.

"Don't let it go to your head, Shorty. I didn't have much to choose from."

"Well, I'm still going to take it as a compliment, as yours are surely few and far between. I take it you wish to start right away?"

"Yes, I have all the equipment ready to go. The girl can help if she wants."

I looked at Eve Anna, then I turned slowly and gave Captain Dick a penetrating glance. The concern on my face must have been clearly evident, because he felt obliged to reassure me.

"Don't worry. I promise not to try anything." He wore his guilt as clearly as a boy with his hand stuck in the cookie jar.

I could not be with all of my girls all of the time. I had to hope that he had learned his lesson. "Okay, let's get started then."

Before I knew it, I was outside tightly grasping a handrail that ran the full length of the cargo bay. My instructions were to push off to the end of my fifty-meter tether; then try to get a feeling for the controls. It was easy to see why the first person to try this lost control of his bowels. I was reminded of my jump from the haystack at an early age. This was the ultimate jump.

I cannot tell you how insignificant I felt compared to the earth below. It seemed to be at its greatest magnificence viewed in this way. I felt as if I could almost reach out and touch the oceans. I was startled to see little anomalies in my vision, but soon realized that it was only tears floating lightly inside my visor. The sight had touched me deeply.

Within half an hour I was dancing with mechanical agility throughout space and felt quite confident in my ability to proceed to a non-tethered flight. However, Captain Dick thought that any more experimentation would be a waste of valuable propellant. I returned to the space station. Eve Anna had already been dismissed. I was ill prepared for Captain Dick's greeting.

"Good job, Morris. You're quite a woman: beauty, brains, manual dexterity. I can hardly wait to breed you."

I felt like I had been shot with a bullet of repulsion.

"You're such a sweet talker, Captain. I suppose you're attracted to me because I can take a punch." I said this with as much sarcasm and spite in my voice as was within my means.

"I don't have to explain why I'm attracted to you. All I know is, I'm going to enjoy having my way with you." He looked at me like a dog eyeing up a porterhouse steak.

"There is no way in hell that's going to happen." I'm sure the disgust I was feeling was clearly evident in my expression.

"It's your duty," he said with a growl.

"And how do you see that?"

"It's your duty to have sex with me to increase the genetic diversity of our tiny population."

Deep down, I knew it was a legitimate request. It was indisputable that genetic diversity would increase the chances of our mission being a success. But at what cost?

Fewer genes would be better than bad genes. Having four women that still had their self-respect would be much more of an asset. I would lose face if I ever allowed that man to have his way with me and I would die before I would let him near my girls. I was too confused to compose a proper response.

"Never! You stay away from me and you stay away from the girls."

"Don't worry, Shorty. I'll have your cherry one way or another." He wore a sneaky grin that seemed to beg me to slap it right off of his face.

His insinuation struck a dreadful chord within, that made me recoil with fear. What if he had somehow overheard my conversation with Eve Anna? I would die of embarrassment if that rat-bastard knew my innermost secrets.

"How do you know I'm a virgin?" I asked in a threatening fashion. I was so furious I was oblivious to my admission. I cannot tell you how uncomfortable I felt at that moment. *What the hell is going on?* I asked myself. *Do I have virgin stamped on my forehead this week, or what?*

"Just a lucky guess." His expression changed from sneaky to smug.

What an idiot! I fell for the same stupid trick twice in the last couple of days. But, if that was the limit of his knowledge, it would change nothing. I was mildly comforted by that notion.

"Don't worry, little lady," he continued. "The Reverend Doctor Dick happens to know that your prognosis is good. Virginity can be cured. All you need is a massive meat injection. And I'm just the man that can give it to you."

"You make me sick. Why am I even having this conversation?"

"Because you know I'm right and there's nothing you can do about it."

"I have the right to say no."

"We'll see about that." He turned his back to me and started stowing away gear as if to say, this is the end of our conversation.

I stomped out of the compartment, aware that I was leaving the confrontation on a losing score. He had beaten me with his fist. He had beaten me with his mind games. He really had a knack for making me feel like a shorty. I left with only one small positive consequence. If Dick was fixated on having sex with me, he would not dare jeopardize his chances by making advances with any of the girls. I could use his interest in me as a tool to buy time for Eve Anna, Helena and Nicole.

I removed myself from the shuttle dock at an angry pace. My pumping legs and swinging arms symbolized my urgency to be alone and to distance myself from my adversary. To my misfortune, I met Adam in the corridor on my way to the zero-gravity room. I could tell he was alarmed by my obvious distress.

"Rock, what's wrong?" He grabbed me by the arm to arrest my attempt at marching right on past.

"Please, Adam. Just leave me alone, okay." I turned my head away to conceal my rage. I had deliberately withheld the truth about Captain Dick from him in the past in order to keep peace on board the station. Such provocation would have driven Adam to violence. And of course, violence against Captain Dick was not an option. Fearfully, we needed him to get us home to earth.

"Rock, come on. Don't push me away like this." He immobilized my hands despite my vicious struggling. "I only want to help."

"You can't help me. No one can," I said, surrendering to his strength.

"Please try me. Don't deny our friendship." The agony of his concern was clearly evident. He looked like a man that had just seen his mother drive over a cliff in his new corvette.

"Take me to the hub." It would be cruel to reject him now. I was incapable of such heartlessness. "We need to be alone."

Once inside the hub, Adam and I arrested our movement and faced each other. I painted an ugly, but truthful portrait of our Captain Dick. I left nothing out: the first meeting, the fist in the face, Nicole, the verbal sexual harassment, everything. His brow furrowed, his teeth clenched and his eyes smouldered with hate as I itemized the captain's blatant misdemeanours.

"I'll kill the son-of-a-bitch!"

"Now, Adam. This is precisely why I didn't tell you in the first place."

"I don't care. If that asshole so much as touches you again, he's a dead man."

"No! You promised not to do anything rash." I cradled his face in my hands, looked him directly in the eyes and commanded: "You will not betray my trust."

Adam hesitated before he begrudgingly nodded his head in obedience.

"You can't stop me from watching him like a hawk."

"I'd be disappointed if you didn't."

Adam's strong arms enveloped me and I drifted without resistance into the sanctuary of his embrace. I was instantly at peace. He moaned with unexpected pleasure as I buried my face into his masculine chest. I did not feel like a man holding another man or a female in the clutches of a male; instead, I felt like a little child being held by their father. For a moment nothing else mattered, because I was safe in the blanket of Adam's love. My mind drifted sweetly back to the days of my youth. I remembered the security of my father's adoring hugs. My acute sentimentality, governed by my feminine chemistry, squeezed tears from my eyes. How was I to carry on without my father and my mother? In the past, when I was faced with an extreme situation, I could count on them both for advice and moral support. Now I was on my own. I was totally isolated in every respect. It was terrifying to think I and I alone was accountable for the repercussions of my actions and decisions, with no one to fall back on. For the first time in my life, the buck stopped here with me.

I lifted my wet cheeks from Adam's chest to see who was entering the room. My sight was blurred because my eyes were moist and my eyelids puffy, but Eve Anna's confusion was unmistakable.

"I'm sorry." Her startled face paled with awkwardness and bewilderment when she saw me wrapped in Adam's arms. She backed out of the enclosure clumsily, turning her head to hide her bruised feelings and resentful tears.

"It's okay, Eve Anna," I called out after her. "Please come back."

The sound of her running footsteps in retreat was her only answer.

"What was that all about?" Adam asked.

"She has had to deal with so much lately. Seeing two of her authority figures being intimate was probably the last straw."

"Is that what we were doing, being intimate?" Adam's eyes sparkled with optimism.

"In a non-sexual way, yes."

Adam's hopefulness was replaced by a familiar disappointment. His expression was similar to how a football player's might appear after the winning touchdown was disallowed because there was a penalty on the play. The warmth of his embrace chilled and he released me unceremoniously.

"I should go to her," I said, kissing Adam on the cheek to cheer him up a little.

"There's nothing to explain. We are two consenting adults. It doesn't concern her."

"It's complicated." I squeezed his hand and used his mass to push myself off towards the entrance. I was glad that he was understanding enough to leave it at that.

I found Eve Anna in the lounge with the rest of her peers. She seemed to be unaffected by the events that she stumbled upon in the hub. Being careful not to cause suspicion, I asked her to step out into the corridor.

"Is everything okay?"

"Everything's cool. Why do you ask?" If she was upset, she was cleverly hiding her feelings.

"Adam and I just had some things we were trying to work out."

"That's none of my business," she said with detachment. "You're a grownup; you can do whatever you want."

"You seemed a little upset when you left, that's all."

"I caught my teacher making out; it just took me by surprise."

"We weren't making out."

"Yeah, sure, whatever. Like I said before, everything's cool."

"If you change your mind and you feel like talking, just let me know."

"Sure, Teach." She turned and headed back to the lounge, effectively closing the conversation.

"It's Candy, remember."

She turned her head and nodded, nothing more. I resolved to dismiss the situation altogether.

Chapter Sixteen

THE NEXT MORNING, I SEARCHED for survivors with the HAM radio. Fred was the only one I could find. He too, had not talked to anyone else in several days. The absence of humanity was a very disturbing picture for both of us. Somewhere in the conversation, I was reminded of an unresolved issue I had discussed with Adam. It seemed appropriate that I confront my colleague, from a different era, with the problem.

"Ah, yes, the loss of artistic genius in our time. I have pondered on that same question many times." Fred admitted.

"Adam and I wondered if it was us as teachers that were to blame."

"Some people would probably like to point their finger at us, but I hardly think we are to blame."

"Where does the blame lie then?" I was eager to hear Fred's opinion.

"Why does anyone cease to devote attention towards what they truly want or value? Distraction. Temptation. Pressure. Stress. Fear."

"Can you expand on that?"

"Take the distraction of television for instance," he continued. "Not only is it a colossal misuse of time, I firmly believe that children who watch too much of it acquire a mild form of attention deficit disorder. Their minds are so accustomed to taking on information in short rapid bursts, they are no longer able to focus on a subject for any duration. Years ago, young men and women probably spent a lot of their free time in thought; not lying on the couch, soaking up the sauce of TV as it pours over them."

"You've got that right," I said, feeling Fred was onto something. "In my day, kids also had video games as a diversion and now they have virtual reality games. But don't you think Beethoven was faced with distractions and temptations in his day as well?"

"To a much lesser extent, yes." Fred stopped to collect his thoughts, then carried on. "My other theory has to do with value. Take education for instance; now everyone gets it for nothing, so it doesn't have the same value as it once had. Years ago, only the very privileged were able to attain knowledge. Then there's The Arts. Modern society just doesn't put enough value on the finer things in life any more. Most people would rather sit through a boring baseball game than go to a stimulating art show. All people want nowadays is a quick, cheap rush; mostly in the form of mindless entertainment.

"It's complicated, isn't it?" I hoped that my question would prolong the discussion.

"Yes, there are so many variables; it's hard to put your finger on where the problem lies. Throughout history, man's greatest achievements blossomed in the midst of passion or pain; maybe we have evolved into a species insensitive to our surroundings and our fellow man." Fred said this with regret then added: "But don't blame yourself. We teachers, as a whole, are not to blame. We have just been caught in a shift of social order, nothing more.

The fact that you even worry about this subject tells me loads about you as a teacher."

"Well, I guess it doesn't matter now anyway, does it?" I said with a sigh. "Centuries of human genius will be lost with the end of civilization. So much of our legacy is stored on the mainframe computer. Thousands of years of accumulated knowledge will be lost in a single collapsing electromagnetic pulse. All the backup systems will be just a bunch of technological clutter. Unfortunately, our existing books are made with modern paper filled with acid, that will cause them to self-destruct and turn to ashes in less than a century."

"That only emphasizes the importance of our role as survivors. It's up to people like you and me to assure that the human race does not regress to the stone ages."

"That's one hell of a responsibility." My voice rose with frustration.

"No one said it was going to be easy."

I thanked Fred for his opinion on the subject and signed off for the day. Even though Fred had redirected blame away from teachers, I could not help but feel guilty for the times I scolded a child for daydreaming in class, or subtracted marks for opinions that diverted away from what would be considered a normal point of view. Today's children had to learn so much, on such a broad range of subjects, just to survive in today's hectic society. Since the system was designed to cram in as much information as possible, over a short period of time, there were not enough allowances made for stimulating the brain.

I decided to make my rounds and check on how everyone else was doing. Adam and his crew were sleeping. Captain Dick was on shift in the control room. The girls were moping about in the lounge. All the long faces signalled a definite need for some positive reinforcement.

"Why so glum?" I asked unnecessarily.

"What do we have to be happy about?" Nicole responded coldly. "Our families are all dead and civilization is in a shambles."

"I'll never meet the man of my dreams, or land that special job and I won't get my nice home in the suburbs," Helena added. "My whole life is screwed."

I suddenly felt my temperature rising and the hair on the back of my neck bristle. I felt strangely agitated by their self-pity. I had to set things straight.

"You guys are the lucky ones!" I lashed out with my fists clenched and my body ridged.

"How do you see that?" Nicole made the mistake of asking.

"There are billions down on earth dying in agony, while you sit here in comfort and good health. Sure, your parents and siblings are dead, but at least you'll have a chance to start your own families. You three have been chosen out of all those left to die, for the serious undertaking of rebuilding society. You have been granted stewardship over the earth and all its living things. This is not a situation to enter into lightly or negatively. Please stop feeling sorry for yourselves and divert that energy into developing a constructive and optimistic strategy for the future. You can be the victims of destiny, or the tools, it's your choice. Someday, many years from now, our story will be the stuff legends are made of. Your ancestors will sit around a camp fire and sing your praises. Don't you see what a great privilege you've been granted? We all have the ability to become folk heroes."

At first the girls' expressions were of stunned disbelief. I had never had the occasion to lash out at them before. As soon as they had gotten over the initial shock of seeing me angry and had absorbed what I was trying to get across, small grins remoulded the shape of their lips.

"Wow," Helena said, now softer and more respectful. "I never thought of it that way."

INTERVENTION

"Just think of it, you guys," Eve Anna added. "A small band of six teenagers and three adults take a world left in ruins and slowly rebuild it into a paradise."

"It's not going to be easy," I cautioned. "But the possibilities are endless."

"We can do it. I know we can." Nicole pounded her fist against the arm of her chair to emphasize her statement.

"That's the spirit everyone." I motioned towards them with my arms extended as I spoke. Before I knew it, we were in each other's arms and making brave plans for the future. The girls talked about how, initially, we could make use of the existing infrastructures. There would still be homes left standing. Non-perishable food would still be stockpiled in many places. We would have several years to prepare for self-sufficiency. The next few hours sped by as we mapped out the blueprints for our bold new world.

The next day I felt good about myself and it must have shown, because Captain Dick made a snide comment after entering the control room. He was there to relieve me of my post.

"How come you're so frickin' happy today? Did one of the boys beat me to you last night?"

"No, Captain, you can rest assured that I'm just as pure as I ever was. You know I'm saving myself for you." I added sarcastically, playfully messing with his brain. Because he appeared confused, I decided to get serious. "*There is no greater satisfaction for a just and well-meaning person than the knowledge that he has devoted his best energies to the service of the good cause.* Albert Einstein once said those words."

"Well, la-de-da. Who made you an expert on happiness?" It was an acerbic reaction typical of his nature.

"I have never felt such a profound sense of purpose as I feel today. Sure, being a teacher and developing the minds of our youth was an important contribution to society and very rewarding, but that was nothing compared to what I'm feeling now."

Captain Dick seemed surprised that I was opening up to him. I was surprised at myself, but I was so full of good spirit I felt I had to pass it on. And for sure I was not going to let his cynicism spoil my new found exuberance.

"I have a new life inside me, Captain. I'm not just excited about being a mother, I'm excited about being the mother of the next chapter of the human race. I firmly believe that happiness is not derived from material wealth or personal pleasure, but requires participation in something that brings fulfillment, like being involved in a worthy enterprise. What could be more worthy than our new mission?"

"Well, since you're a member of the team, it's good to see you focused on the mission, but I would argue with you that wealth won't bring happiness."

"You can achieve security by accumulating wealth, but rarely will it bring you happiness. This misconception has been the downfall of many an individual, because we've been programmed by corporate advertising to believe it is true." I thought for a moment trying to recall some of the things I had written down in my journal that I had touched upon previously with Helena. "The situation they have put us in reminds me of long ago when they used to hang a carrot out in front of a donkey to keep him running a treadmill. Now, most of us are trudging along on occupational treadmills. We are helplessly trying to catch that unattainable carrot of happiness that's constantly eluding us through change, because of technical advancement, or moving farther away through increase in value."

"You've obviously given this a lot of thought. But I don't give a shit what you say; give me a hundred million and I'd be happy as a clam." The captain seemed unmoved by my speech, because he nervously fondled the handle of my handgun in a blatant show of authority as he spoke. He clearly did not know how to deal with my openness and recoiled from it coldly and with suspicion.

"Anyway, have a nice day," I said as I got up from my seat and left the control room.

"I'm sure it will be just ducky." I heard him—true to form—mumbling to himself as I crossed the threshold, on my way to join the others.

It was that part of our twenty-four-hour period where Adam's shift and my shift overlapped. The teens were talking and doing various activities. Adam was eating a chocolate bar and reading a book on his electronic text reader.

I approached him and asked what he was reading. He looked up and smiled in a special way that could not help but make a person's day. I sat down across from him and awaited his answer.

"*A Tale of Two Cities.*"

"Good choice; I'm a huge Dickens fan. The opening line is one of the best in literature. *It was the best of times; it was the worst of times.*"

"It kind of hits home, doesn't it?"

I just nodded my head in agreement; then changed the subject. I did not want to brew over our situation; I wanted to take charge of it. "It's great to see the kids together, isn't it? I was hoping we might see some pairing up by now."

"What if that's not the best way to go?"

"What do you mean?"

"We need to formulate the optimum mating strategy for the mission. If we choose to go with multiple partners, it may turn out to be a problem if two of them fall in love. If they make a marriage-like commitment to each other, the idea of multiple sexual partners, for the good of the group, may not be agreeable to them." He offered me some of his bar as he spoke.

"Thanks, my blood chocolate was getting low." Adam and I shared a laugh over my self-diagnosed blood analysis and then I added: "I have to agree with you that it could become a problem, but we can't discourage them from falling in love, just for that reason. I'm sure God wouldn't want it that way."

"Shouldn't we map out a game plan now, before the problem arises?" Adam asked.

"Sounds like you have given this some thought. What do you think?" I skillfully tried to avoid the issue.

"I didn't come to any concrete solutions."

"Well, first and foremost, we have to look at ourselves as a community." I realized it was up to me to start the discussion. "And inside that community, we should have families with a man and woman, bound together as the head of those families, just as God intended. But sometimes families may need to intermingle for the good of the community."

"The problem with having multiple partners is, how will we keep track of all those half brothers and sisters?" Adam rightfully asked.

"I suppose we will have to keep records for the first few generations; after that it won't matter."

"What do you think would be the best situation?" Now Adam had turned the tables with his shrewd questioning.

"I would like to see us stay with one other person, if possible. Like I said before, that's the way God intended it to be. Each family unit will keep the name of the father to set them apart from the other three families. That will eliminate confusion, as well as any jealousy that is bound to develop if we choose an, anything goes, kind of system."

"I was leaning in that direction as well. I worked it out on the computer. If we choose that scenario, some of our children will actually have one more choice of possible non-related mates."

"Perfect."

"What if one of us men is infertile?"

"I have a feeling we won't have to worry about that. I'm sure we have all been chosen to be here for one reason or another and I can't see sterility being one of them."

"There's one other variable we haven't addressed. Where does Captain Dick fit into this scenario?" Adam addressed a question I was trying hard to forget.

"He doesn't." I stated with resolve. "The girls and I are of the same mind. Being with Captain Dick, in a sexual way—as a clinical procedure or otherwise—is not an option."

"I don't think he's going to agree to that."

"He shouldn't have been such an asshole then." There was no need for me to sugar coat my feelings.

"I agree one hundred percent, but we can't deny the fact that it's going to create a problem."

"We will have to cross that bridge when we come to it."

"I suppose you're right."

"Adam," I made sure our eyes met before I continued. "I want you to be my partner."

If we had not been in the common area, I think Adam would have tackled me to the floor and smothered me with hugs and kisses. As it was, he had to make due with a huge boisterous grin.

"This is a dream come true, Rock. I know we will be very happy together."

"We have always been good together." I reached out and squeezed his hand. "If I have to take on the role of a wife, I can't think of any man I'd rather do it with."

Adam's eyes became glazed with tears and he could not help but take me in his arms and hold me tight, even though everyone in the room was watching.

"You, Candy Mary Morris, have made me a very happy man," he whispered into my ear.

"Ditto," I answered.

Chapter Seventeen

ADAM AND I WERE NOT in each other's arms very long when we realized that everyone else in the room was standing close and encircling us. We released each other slowly and made eye contact with those nearby.

"Is there something going on here that we should know about?" Frankie's dark-skinned face became taut and glistened with his smile. Eve Anna was the only one of the teens that was not grinning from ear to ear. They were either happy for us or amused by our unsuspected display of affection.

"I suppose we have some explaining to do," Adam said to the group.

"Why don't we all sit down," I added. "We need to have a team meeting." Everyone sat in accordance to my wishes.

Adam and I took turns explaining our newly resolved plan for the perpetuation of the human race. The teens sat attentively, hanging on our every word. Their intermittent comments showed that they had given the situation a lot of thought; they were apprehensive about their role in the grand scheme of things and seemed very happy to be getting some answers.

"So, what do you think of our plan?" I asked.

"I like it," Helena admitted. "I wasn't looking forward to loosely sharing intimate situations with every man on board. I think it would have created an uncomfortable and stressful atmosphere in the group."

"The simplest situation is usually the best," Nicole volunteered. "Why over complicate our lives if we don't have to?"

"My dream has always been, to find a nice girl, settle down and raise a family. I'm glad that your plan won't interfere with my plans."

"That's great, Randy." I was glad to hear him contribute to the conversation. "Is there anything about this arrangement that you disagree with, or think could be improved upon."

"If it ain't broke don't fix it, right?" Frankie summed it up for us.

We all took turns hugging each other before we disbanded for the purpose of completing our separate duties. Eve Anna and I headed towards the fertility clinic for her daily insemination.

She seemed rather distant as we walked down the hall together. I tried to strike up a conversation several times, but she would not take the bait. After we entered the clinic, she took off her clothes unceremoniously and jumped up on the gurney. We were both becoming accustomed to the routine. We were now to the point where I would acquire a semen tube randomly, because Eve Anna was getting tired of making that decision. I put on my surgical gloves, loaded the applicator, and approached her as usual.

This time things went differently than before. As soon as I got close, Eve Anna pulled the applicator from my hands and said:

"I can do this part myself, thank you very much." Her glaring eyes told me to keep my distance.

"Are you angry with me for some reason?"

"What do you think?" Hardy flowers would have wilted from the chilling temperament of her voice.

"Judging by your tone, I'd say yes. Do you want to talk about it?"

"You promised me Adam could be my first." She confided after a lengthy pause. "What am I to do now that you two are hooked up?"

"I'm sure Adam would still be willing."

"It wasn't Adam I was worried about. Now that you two are *in love* wouldn't it be a little awkward for you."

"Adam and I love each other as friends, but I wouldn't classify us as being in love." A tiny glint formed in Eve Anna's eyes when she heard my last statement.

"What was with all the goings-on in the hub then?"

"We were just settling some issues. I told you that. Adam just happens to be the most logical choice for me as a mate. We're friends and he's the only male here my age. How could you perceive it being any other way?"

"I suppose you're right. I don't know why it bothered me so much. I'm sorry, but it just seemed to rub my fur the wrong way." She handed the applicator back to me with a gentle touch and then smiled as she added, "No pun intended."

Her allowing me to finish the job was a gesture of forgiveness. I set the device on the counter and removed my gloves. She sat up on the edge of the bed and reached out to grab my hand. Her warm submissive eyes beseeched me to come near. How vulnerable she looked as I moved in close to her and how transparent her need for a tender moment together. I cringed as she wrapped her bare legs around my hips and pulled me toward her. A reassuring grin dispelled my instinct to bolt. Then, her doting arms quickly pulled our bodies even more tightly together in an implosion of hungry flesh. As she pushed her pelvis into mine, my raw desires triumphed over common sense. I willingly aided in the strength of our embrace and stroked my cheek against her soft flowing hair. Just when I was destined to purr like a pampered kitten in her arms; just when her seduction was complete; she released me, tersely and without shame.

"Thanks, I needed a good hug." She glanced up at me shyly, straightening her hair; seemingly oblivious to the fact that she was still naked from the waist down. Was that all that was to her, a good hug? What the hell would I do if she decided to get serious? I was relieved to think that I had misinterpreted her intentions, but I was still very much confused. She had a special aptitude for complicating my life. I had no alternative but to forgive her.

"I think it was mutually agreeable."

"Well, I guess I had better run along now." She slipped on her clothes as she spoke. "I know you have work to do."

"Don't forget to do your preg tests every morning." She promised me that she would remember as she went out the door.

While I was doing some rearranging, I heard a knock at the entrance. It was Randy.

"Candy, could I have a moment of your time?"

I welcomed him freely. Nervously, he ran his hands through his hair and shuffled his feet from side to side as he watched me clean up the counter top. I tried to give him a reassuring smile and asked him how I could help.

"Adam told me I should talk to you," he said, still shuffling and twitching. "It has to do with your strategy of joining us into family units."

"Have you had second thoughts?"

"No, I think it's the right thing to do; that's why I'm here. I want to ask Nicole to be my mate, but I don't know what to say."

"Great, I'm happy for you. Nicole is quiet and mysterious, but she has a big heart and has a good head on her shoulders."

"I'm very taken with her and I can't see myself with anyone else in the group, but I can't exactly say that I love her yet, if you know what I mean. I would feel awkward and presumptuous asking her to marry me, but yet I don't want one of the other guys to beat me to her."

"Yes, I can see your dilemma." Randy waited patiently while I thought for a moment. "I think you just plain and simply have to somehow convey to her how you feel. Couldn't you just tell her you think she's a very special girl and you would be honoured if she would consider you for her mate? Nicole is an intelligent young woman, who is fully aware of the present situation. I'm sure she'll understand that your courtship will have to be abbreviated for the sake of the mission. Trust me, I'm sure she will appreciate where you are coming from. Besides, I have seen the way she looks at you; I'm convinced that you'd be her first pick as well."

"Thanks so much, Candy." He reached out and gave me a tentative, A-frame hug. "You're much better at this sort of thing than Adam."

"Feel free to speak to me any time. And good luck with Nicole. I'm sure you two will make a great couple."

There was another knock at the docking-door. I gave whoever it was the go-ahead to enter. Blaine stumbled through the door with absence of grace. When he realized that Randy was already with me, he volunteered to come back a little later; but was happy to stay when Randy assured him that he was just about to leave. Randy thanked me again for my advice and left Blaine and I alone.

"Let me guess. Adam sent you, right?"

Sounds like I'm not the first." He was able to establish that he was not from my shaking head. There was a short moment of awkward silence before he continued. "I'm here because I have a thing for Helena and I don't know what to do about it. I find her beauty very intimidating."

"You shouldn't let that stop you."

"Look at me, Candy. I'm not exactly a babe magnet. She's way out of my league."

"Listen to me, Blaine. If you are genuinely attracted to her and feel that she's the woman of your dreams, for God's sake, don't let anything stand in your way. You must overcome your shyness, your insecurity and your fear of rejection. He who hesitates is lost."

"I suppose you're right, but..."

"No buts!" I felt compelled to interrupt. "If there's one thing I've learned in life, Blaine, it's that you have to take advantage of an opportunity when it presents itself, because there's an excellent chance it won't come again. Now gather your courage and go find Helena. Ask her if she would like to go for a walk around the station. Then ask her some questions about herself; let her know you're interested. Appeal to her vanity by telling her how pretty she looks. Once she senses your readiness to make a connection, she'll know what to do."

Blaine looked confused by my last statement and asked, "And how is that?"

"She will send you signals, Blaine. Try to pick up on them. Helena is a very nice girl; if she is not interested, she will let you down easy. If she likes you, I'm sure it'll be quite obvious. Now run along. If you don't do this and someone else wins her affection, you will regret it for the rest of your life."

"You've been a big help, Candy. I feel a lot more confident, thanks to you."

"I've had to do a lot of impromptu student counselling over the years. Don't hesitate to come and see me any time. I'd be happy to try and help you."

"I'm sure I'll have lots more questions. I'm not very experienced around girls."

"So why the sense of urgency? Was it the team meeting in the lounge?"

"Yea, pretty much. You and Adam getting together kind of emphasized the need to find a mate. And since I had been thinking about Helena for quite some time, I figured: why wait?"

"Okay, enough talk. Get out there and knock Helena off her feet." I slapped him on the back and ushered him out the door. He seemed surprisingly self-assured.

"Well," I thought to myself after Blaine was gone. "Isn't this a strange turn of events."

If things worked out for Blaine and Randy, that would leave Eve Anna and Frankie unattached and limited to each other. I'm sure that would not be a problem for Frankie; after all, Eve Anna is a very vibrant and beautiful young woman. Who wouldn't want to be with someone like her? I know I would. To say I was a little jealous of Frankie would be an understatement.

But how would Eve Anna feel about being paired with a black man. I do not think there is a prejudiced bone in her body, but just because you show no prejudice towards a different race, that does not mean you are inclined to be bed partners. This whole situation would be interesting to say the least. Personally, I have always had mixed feelings about inter-racial marriages. I'm not against them. I am just not sure I would be able to adapt to the differences. At first you are both young and beautiful in your own way, but as you age, I think the differences in facial features are exaggerated and maybe that physical attraction you had in your youth would diminish. Maybe I am just being too superficial. I am sure, if two people love each other enough, those differences would become insignificant.

INTERVENTION

The next morning as I was making preparations in the clinic, Eve Anna hurried in showing signs of excitement. She rushed over and drew me into a big bear hug. She spun me around and jumped up and down while she embraced me, all the time laughing and squealing.

"I'm pregnant!" she finally blurted out amongst her giggles. "At long last, I'm pregnant."

"That's wonderful," I said, as I put pressure on her shoulders to try and cease her joyful bouncing.

Eve Anna's exuberant behaviour came to an end all too abruptly and her smile transformed into a look of stunned disbelief. She stood looking at me strangely for quite a while before she spoke.

"You're disappointed, aren't you?" Her eyes seemed to penetrate right through me.

"No, not at all. I'm happy for you."

"Ya, right, you bastard," she said with no hint of animosity or disrespect; her bewildered expression flip-flopping back to a suggestive smirk. "You were enjoying having to stick that thing into me, weren't you?"

"No, Eve Anna. What gave you... ?" I am sure I was not very convincing as my words came with great hesitation. Luckily, she was considerate enough to interrupt me.

"It's okay, I'm not mad at you." Her arms were still around me and her eyes were just inches away, riveted to mine. "You're a man at heart, why shouldn't you be fascinated with my body."

"I've had access to the same body parts since birth." I still felt the need to plead innocence, even though I knew Eve Anna was not buying into my efforts.

"Lying doesn't become you." She leaned closer and gave me a peck on the lips. "Now enough of this; I came to celebrate my conceiving."

"Then celebrate we shall," I said, knowing that she understood. Deep down in my heart I was truly happy for her. I went to one of the medical cabinets and got out a bottle of ethyl alcohol and mixed us a cocktail by adding some distilled water and orange drink crystals.

"A Screwdriver, how fitting," she said, as I handed her the concoction in a beaker highball glass. We both laughed lightheartedly; then we clinked our beakers together. I proposed a toast.

"Here's to future motherhood." I still held my beaker high as I spoke.

"Is it okay for us to be drinking now that we are pregnant?" She rightfully asked.

"I only pored a few drops in each glass. Just a symbolic gesture, that's all.

"Strangely, I have no misgivings about being a mother at this early stage of my life," Eve Anna confided. "The fact that there is so much at stake places much more significance to the whole process. It truly is a miracle, isn't it?"

"Yes, a human life is a miracle. I too, am looking forward to bringing another life into the world." I studied her splendid young face as I spoke. Eve Anna is an atypical beauty, possessing a passive loveliness that allows her inner beauty to shin through. She does not have the classic lines that Helena possesses, but her large bright eyes and warm, disarming smile endow her with a charm which is much more intriguing than just another pretty face. If each one of her features was studied individually, they could be sighted as being imperfect. But when they are brought together, each one compliments the other in a way that is inexplicable; adding character to the whole package. Every facet being unified by her deliciously flawless skin, whose ultra-smooth surface temptingly shimmers, even in the most subdued light.

"What is it?" Eve Anna tilted her head in reaction to my blank, dream like stare.

"Have you given any thought as to who you would eventually like to have for a mate?" I blurted out hastily in an effort to divert attention away from my staring.

"It's been the furthest thing from my mind. Why?" She took a big drink from her glass, inadvertently signifying that she was uncomfortable with the subject.

"Oh, just curious. That's all." It would have been inappropriate to tell her what Randy and Blaine had shared with me. "Is there any one of the boys who is definitely not an option?"

"No, I like them all about the same." She seemed disinterested, but was artful enough to leave me unacquainted with her inner most feelings.

"Have you noticed any budding romances happening with the other teens?"

"I haven't paid much attention." She took another uneasy sip then added: "How did we get on this subject in the first place? I came here to talk about having a child."

"It sounds like you're up for it. Do you have any questions?"

"Tons... what about you, are you up for it?"

"Yes, I'm surprisingly ready to meet the challenge. In spite of the fact that I'm living proof that God has a warped sense of humour."

"You think God deliberately plays tricks on us?"

"I've suspected it for some time."

"Give me another example, other than the whole gender dysfunction thing."

"Why did He choose to make some men go bald early in life, while others are able to keep their hair well into old age? What good could ever come from losing the hair on top of your head? None that I can think of, other than providing a subject for people to joke about." ·

"I see what you mean." Eve Anna paused a moment in thought. Then she contributed with: "What about acne? Why did God choose to curse us with acne, right at that one time in our lives when we are so intensely conscience of our appearance? If that isn't the mark of a warped sense of humour, I'm not sure what is."

"And these same guys that have to face the indignity of losing all the hair from the top of their heads, later in life suddenly start to sprout great gobs of hair in other places like their ears, back, and the inside of their nose. What's up with that? It doesn't serve any purpose."

"Something that I have always been curious about, is the 'ugly duckling' sibling." Eve Anna obviously assumed my inability to grasp what she was saying from my blank expression. "You know, when one sister is really pretty and the other one is uglier than a stick. It has got to be hard on that ugly sister, knowing her sibling used up all the best genes and left her with all the nasty ones. You know what I mean?"

"I know exactly what you mean." I said, wanting to share. "Have you ever met Helena's sister?"

"That's a perfect example," Eve Anna admitted." Helena could be a model, but her sister looks like she stepped out of the shallow end of the gene pool. She is short, fat and uglier than sin. How fair is that?"

"Now do you believe me when I say that God has a weird sense of humour?" I did not mention one other example that was on my mind at the time—having to endure the unspeakable agony that comes from being trapped in a one-sided love affair. The callous, absurd hilarity of being hopelessly in love with someone that can never, or will never, return your love; ironically making them as inaccessible as east is to west. How could God have given human emotion precedence over common logic?

"Yes, I do tend to agree with you." Then, mercifully, she changed the subject back to babies, effectively taking my mind off of a restless craving. "Do we have any information about raising children on file in the station's computer banks?"

"Actually, I downloaded heaps of information on the subject just before the internet collapsed. Since no one on board has any experience in this area, I was sure we could use all the help we could get."

"Would you like to go with me to check it out?"

"I'll accompany you to the control room, but I'm long overdue to try and make radio contact with earth. Would you mind if I do that while you do your research?"

"As long as you are there to keep me company and answer any questions, I don't mind." She finished her drink and set it on the counter behind me. Then she motioned her hand towards the exit and said, "Shall we?"

Captain Dick was in the control room when we arrived, but he was just as content to ignore us as we were to ignore him. Eve Anna went right to work reading files and I sent message after message out over the air waves. I used many different frequencies, as my search to reach any living soul down on earth became much more desperate with each unsuccessful try. I was ready to give up for the day, when I got an answer back from Fred.

"Thank God you're still with us. I was afraid when you didn't respond."

"Sorry, Candy. I just got back from a fishing trip. It's a stroke of luck you got me at all."

"So how was fishing?"

"Great, thanks. There's one good thing resulting from this pandemic—it's damned the size restrictions and to hell with the bag limits." We both had a good chuckle over this. "I caught about fifty nice walleyes and two big northern pike about twenty-five pounds each. I plan on cleaning them and hanging the meat out to sun dry this afternoon. The weather has been wonderful this fall. The only drawback has been the mosquitoes; they damn near ate me alive while I was out in the boat. I'm almost looking forward to the first frost."

"I can't tell you how envious I am. I gave up my annual summer fishing excursion for the NASA training trip, so it's been a whole year since I've been out. What else have you been up to?"

"I've been fishing and hunting quite a bit lately. I'm trying to get stocked up for the winter, while the getting is good. My canning jars are full of moose meat and I have a big crock of homemade sauerkraut brewing in the root cellar."

"You're quite the survivalist, Fred. You'll have to share your recipes when we get back to earth."

"It's funny you should say that, because I was going to suggest that we try and get together sometime this spring after you land. My plane is all fuelled up and ready to go. As soon as I receive your coordinates I can be in the air. I presume you will be landing in Florida, so hopefully I can find fuel along the way."

"You'd be a great asset to our team. We would be happy to have you join us."

"The pleasure would be all mine, Candy. I'm afraid you guys are going to be my only hope of not having to live out the rest of my life in solitude. I haven't been able to reach a single soul on the radio for days now."

"I haven't had any luck either. I guess civilization, as we know it, has ended."

"Surely there are other people like me who live in a secluded spot, insulated from the disease."

"All we can do is hope, but I'm facing our situation as a worst-case scenario—that our small band of human beings holds the last four females left in the universe."

"That has a rather ominous ring to it, does it not?"

"No argument here."

"Well, Candy, I hate to run off, but I have to get those fish cleaned. From now on I'll try and check in with you every day. If I am going to be gone on any extended trips, I'll be sure to let you know so that you don't worry."

"May God be with you and protect you, Fred."

"Same to you and yours, Candy. Over and out."

"We could commandeer a small commuter jet and meet him at the Minot Air Force Base or maybe at some airport in Canada," Captain Dick suggested. He had obviously been listening in on our conversation. "I'm more than qualified to fly that type of plane."

"I'm sure Fred would be delighted to hear that, Captain. I will mention it to him tomorrow." I got up from my seat and checked to see what Eve Anna was doing.

She was studying the birthing process and what has to happen during delivery.

"Study hard, Eve Anna. Remember, I'm picking you to deliver my baby."

"How hard can it be?" she said with a facetious smile.

"Come, it's time for a break. Let's take a walk." She was more than willing.

When we got to the lounge, everyone else was there. Adam was making use of a script reader, but the teens were flopped slovenly over the furniture like lizards basking in the desert sun. Because we barely warranted a sleepy glance upon entering the room, Eve Anna and I decided not to disturb them and turned to leave.

"No, wait!" Nicole pleaded. "We are all bored to tears here. Couldn't you think of one of your childhood stories to keep us amused?"

"I don't think so," I protested. "How about if we save a few stories for another time? Or even better, why don't one of you teens contribute with a story of your own."

"For some reason none of us can think of any humorous anecdotes to amuse each other with," Blaine said. "I guess we didn't have as colourful a childhood as you two did.

"Well, Adam and I created our own fun and didn't spend much time in front of the TV."

"I miss television," Randy contributed with a mournful voice.

"I miss television too," Blaine empathized. "And I miss my virtual reality games."

Then the dam broke and we were flooded with an inundation of things that we all missed. Everyone felt the need to contribute. I longed to have beer, cheese and homemade bread. The others yearned for hamburgers, pizza and soft drinks. The list became quite extensive before we were finished. It was sad to think that we might not ever get to sample any of these things again.

Chapter Eighteen

WEEKS LATER, WE EXPERIENCED A minor problem. A small piece of space debris eluded the stations defence system and blasted a small hole through the bulkhead. It looked exactly like we had been shot with a thirty calibre, high-powered rifle. It was scary to think that someone could have been killed if they had been standing in that spot at the time.

To prevent air from escaping, Captain Dick used a special adhesive to plug the opening from the inside. I had to do an EVA later in the day, so that a more permanent repair could be made to the station's outer shell. It felt good to find something productive to occupy my time and it was enjoyable to be able to leave the confines of the space station. Everyone had been feeling a little claustrophobic lately. Months in space was starting to take its toll.

Adam was minding the control room while I was out, but everyone else was there to congratulate me on a job well done upon my return to the ship. I received lots of thankful handshakes and hugs from the crew. Even Captain Dick seemed somewhat appreciative.

"Good work, Morris. I never would have thought that a woman could be so handy."

"Try not to strain anything while doling out the flattery, Captain." Because he seemed unappreciative of my sarcasm, I changed the subject. "How come we didn't see that piece of junk coming?"

"It was too small for the station's detection system. If NASA was fully operational, we would have been notified well enough in advance to have gotten out of the way. Most of the outer shell is capable of stopping a marble sized projectile. This chunk of shit just happened to hit us in one of our vulnerable spots."

"What are the odds of us being hit again?" Naturally, I was concerned.

"Probably a thousand to one. We're unlucky enough to be in the middle of a meteor shower right now."

"Those are good odds in a poker game, but I'm not sure I like them when you're gambling with somebody's life."

"I've turned the station, so that our smallest profile is presented towards outer space. That, and staying vigilant, is all we can do."

"Rock!" Adam burst into the chamber with a fretful look on his face. "You had better come to the control room right away. It's your friend, Fred."

"What about Fred?" I struggled to get by all the others in the room as I inched my way to the exit.

"Just come," Adam insisted, full of anxiety. He grabbed me by the hand and led me to the control room at a very brisk pace.

"Fred, what's wrong?" I gasped into the HAM radio microphone when we reached our destination.

"I'm afraid I have bad news." Fred seemed to struggle for breath as he spoke. "The worst kind of news... I've caught the plague."

"No!" I shouted out involuntarily. "It can't be. You live hundreds of miles from civilization. How could this happen?"

"I'm not one-hundred percent sure, but..."

"Are you sure it isn't just a cold or the flu or something?" I interrupted, grasping for some simpler more benign explanation.

"I have all the dreaded initial symptoms of the Grim Reaper," he insisted begrudgingly, still labouring for each breath.

"But you would have had to have come into contact with someone."

"I was in denial for quite some time, because of that assumption." Fred coughed in painful sounding heaves away from his microphone. He then had trouble resuming his speech, but struggled on bravely. "I had forgotten about the... the damn mosquitoes!"

"Of course, the mosquitoes." I admitted with much regret.

"Like I told you the other day, we've had above normal temperatures here lately; the winds being predominantly from the south. Obviously, I was unlucky enough to have been bitten by one of those little bastards that was carrying the plague."

"I can't tell you how sorry I am to hear this, Fred." Tears trickled down my cheeks as I spoke. "I'm going to miss you."

"Don't be too upset for me, Love. I'm an old man. I've lived a full life." Fred had to stop again for more hacking and coughing. "I would have loved to have helped out with your mission; but alas, I'm going to a better place."

"I still can't believe this is happening."

"I can't talk any longer. I'm sorry, but the pain is just too strong."

Goodbye, Fred. God bless you."

"Goodbye, Candy. It's been nice knowing you. Over and out."

Everyone except the captain was in the control room with me now. He was stowing away my gear from the EVA. At first everyone was stunned and unable to speak. Finally, Adam put his arm around me and expressed his condolences. The others were quick to follow. They all closed in around me, smothering me in sympathy. I have never been able to deal with people feeling sorry for me. Suddenly, I felt a warmth building up inside me and the air seemed to grow thin in my lungs. Perspiration flowed uncontrollably from every pore in my body and I started to gasp for breath. The room appeared to be spinning. I knew people were talking, but I could not understand what they were saying. I could feel tears swelling in my eyes and a lump formed in my throat. Everything was a blur, except for the sheer panic that was erupting inside me.

"Please, everyone. Leave me alone!" I screamed, jumping up from my chair. I pushed everyone aside discourteously and charged towards the doorway.

"Just let her go," I heard Adam say as I pushed through the soft barricade of intermingled bodies. All the while, my hardened tears melted from the intensity of my grief and gushed in streams down my burning cheeks. Confusion ruled my mind. I was unable to understand why the death of a stranger could have such an overpowering effect on me. He was just a man I met on the air waves, yet I suffered as if he was the closest of kin. Then it hit me. He was not just a man; he was the last man! I felt helpless, because there was nothing I could have done to save him. Like many men whose plans were crushed in the past, our only mistake was being caught in the unravelling stream of history.

I was almost to the doorway when I heard Nicole speak.

"This is the work of the devil."

This proclamation stopped my feet in their tracks. I raised my arms and caught hold of the door frame, because I felt light headed. I stood in the doorway, braced in a wide stance for several seconds, aware of the many eyes that were focused upon me. I turned slowly to face Nicole and the rest of the students. I wiped the tears from my eyes without embarrassment and tried to regain my composure.

I cleared my throat and asked, "What did you say, Nicole?"

"Just as it has been prophesied, the anti-Christ has taken over the world and there is nothing we can do about it."

"Even if that were true, and I'm convinced it isn't, the Bible says: 'the people who know God will display strength and take action.' Those few of us standing in this room are the people, and we are obligated to do something about it; otherwise, the entire population of the earth will have died in vain."

"Then who is to blame for all this, Candy?" Nicole asked.

"We are. Man is to blame for his own demise."

"But how could any merciful God stand by while all this is taking place."

"In the beginning, God chose to limit his sovereignty over the world, so that man could have free will. God established universal laws allowing man to make choices, that can have far reaching effects on our lives; the results of which can be both good and bad. God does not cause them to happen. They happen as a result of God's laws. When people oppose God, the natural result is that bad things happen. Because mankind has largely rejected its Creator, God allows these natural consequences to take their toll. God is not responsible for evil. Evil is the natural result of man's inappropriate choices.

"In the physical realm, if you jump off of a haystack for instance, you will fall and get injured. God did not hurt me on purpose all those years ago on the farm. It was gravity, God's physical law that must be obeyed by all physical matter. Gravity couldn't make an exception for me, because I made the wrong dumb choice. It's the same with man's rebellion against God's spiritual laws. When we choose to break the law, the consequences can be devastating. And these consequences can accumulate over several generations, compounding even after the original offender is dead and gone. I'm sure this, along with prayer, gives God reason to intervene on occasion. Sometimes God intervenes in what seems like a cruel or unproductive way, but always with a divine purpose meant to arrest the accumulative negative effects caused by generation after generation of disobedience. The kind of blatant disobedience that corrupts entire civilizations. As you know, in the time of Noah, God wiped out the entire population of the world, choosing only eight people out of the masses to repopulate the earth."

"That kind of sounds familiar, doesn't it?" Eve Anna announced.

"It does indeed." I said, as Nicole stepped forward in order to take my hand. "Now don't try and feed me any of that devil nonsense, ever again."

"I'll try not to." She glanced with timid eyes as she spoke.

I recalled a quote from the Bible. "Remember, Nicole. *God is light, and in Him is no darkness at all.*"

"God, there is no fucking God." Captain Dick trumpeted as he entered the room, obviously having caught my last statement. We all looked at each other in disbelief; the captain's uncouth behaviour not failing to amaze us.

"Now Captain, you don't really believe that do you?" I asked, in as condescending a tone as possible.

"I can't think of one good reason to believe He exists." His eyes looked empty, resembling those of a lost child, as he tried to stare me down unsuccessfully. "Nowadays people kneel before—or bend over, as the case may be—and give reverence to a greater power: the Almighty Dollar."

"I'm not in the mood to argue this matter with the likes of you." I was mentally drained after hearing of Fred's imminent death and I felt I had done enough preaching for one day.

"I understand," he returned with a sneer, preparing to throw down the gauntlet. "You realize you don't have a case to prove that God exists, so you are taking the coward's way out."

"I can't prove God's existence beyond a shadow of a doubt, but I think I can make a strong case on His behalf."

"Well, let's hear it then, Shorty. I've nothing better to do that listen to your ramblings."

"The rest of you don't have to sit through this if you don't want to," I said, realizing that convincing the captain could take a while. "You are free to leave."

"No way." Eve Anna piped up with a strong voice. "I wouldn't miss this for the world."

Everyone else seemed to be of the same mind. I am sure they were more interested in observing a confrontation between the captain and me than listening to what I had to say about God.

"I guess we might as well sit down and get comfortable then. This could take a while." The captain sat at the computer terminal and the rest of us formed a circle using him as part of the perimeter.

Once again everyone was looking at me expecting an answer. It is in times like these that all those years of teaching experience really come in handy.

"Why, Captain Dick, do you suppose there is something, rather than nothing?"

The captain merely shrugged his shoulders in a disinterested fashion.

"Don't you think that the existence of our accidental universe needs an explanation?"

"You've never heard of the Big Bang?"

"Where did the primordial atom come from? Even that needs an explanation."

"I suppose."

"I think you would have to agree that the existence of something is capable of being understood only if it has an explanation."

"That's pretty much a no-brainer."

"Okay, then. The existence of the universe is either incapable of being understood, or it has an explanation. Which is it?"

"Of course, it has to have an explanation."

"Any rational person would have to accept that the universe needs and has an explanation. Does everyone concur?"

Everyone else was in agreement.

"There are only three ways of explaining anything: it either has a scientific explanation, a personal explanation, or it is an undisputedly essential entity." I looked around the circle to see if everyone was with me. Since there were no blank faces, I continued. "We talked earlier about the primordial atom; the singularity that burst in the beginning of time, creating what physicists now call the Big Bang—the subsequent birth of the universe. Most physicists would agree that if the conditions of the Big Bang had been even slightly different than what occurred, very different results would have ensued. By that, I suggest that stars and galaxies may have failed to materialize and the universe could easily have consisted only of widely dispersed gasses. It's only natural to suppose that if every large object in the universe could have failed to exist, then why couldn't the sum of all its parts have also failed to exist—the universe itself. It's easy to imagine nothing ever existing in the physical realm; therefore, the universe is not the sort of thing that is undisputedly necessary or essential. I think it is safe to say that we must look elsewhere for an explanation of the universe's existence."

"There has to be a scientific explanation," Captain Dick insisted.

"I think that everyone here would agree that the accepted scientific explanation is that the Primordial Atom exploded in a cataclysmic phenomenon known as the Big Bang, creating an expanding array of objects that we now know as the physical universe." Everyone including the captain nodded their heads. "But the problem is... where did that singularity and the governing laws that caused it to explode come from? This is the question science cannot answer."

"Ah, if I can interrupt here Rock. I know a Stephen Hawking quote that should substantiate what you are trying to say."

"I can use all the help I can get, Adam. Please go ahead."

"As all my students know, Stephen Hawking was one of the greatest minds to ever study the cosmos and the natural laws of physics. He wrote several books on the subject concluding that: 'the usual approach of science of constructing a mathematical model cannot answer the questions of why there should be a universe for the model to describe. Why does the universe go to all the bother of existing'?"

"Thank you, Adam. I think we have proven that the universe is not an essential entity and has no scientific explanation; therefore, by the process of elimination, a rational person must conclude that it has a personal explanation. Remember that we said there were only three methods of explanation: essential, scientific and personal. Does everyone see where I'm headed here?"

There were just blank stares looking back at me.

"No personal agent but God could have created the entire universe; therefore, any rational person should believe that there is a God."

"Then how do you explain God's existence?" The captain asked slyly. "By following the same line of reasoning, one could argue that in order to explain God one would have to believe He exists only through the personal activity of a greater-god. And that greater-god could only be explained by a super-god. And so on, and so on, until infinity."

"Would you agree, Captain, that man's idea of God is: an absolutely perfect being lacking nothing."

"I suppose."

"If an absolutely perfect being did not exist, then it would lack existence. Therefore, as it's clear that an absolutely perfect being cannot lack existence, the being must exist. God *can not* fail to exist. God exists necessarily. It is God's essential nature to exist. God, unlike the universe, is essential."

"Words," the captain remarked with agitation. "Just a bunch of fancy words that mean nothing."

"Words that make a lot of sense…" Eve Anna came to my defense, but was cut short by a malicious glance from the captain.

"One other thing." The captain pounced at me again. "How come you believe in God if you accept the scientific explanation for creation instead of the Bible's?"

"I believe in both."

"That's impossible. The Bible says that the universe, the earth, and everything in it were built in six days."

"How could anyone who lives on earth consider its existence as being a mere fluke?" I insisted. "When you take into account all the beauty, diversity and complex interdependencies of the natural world, you have to believe it is the work of a super-intelligence; a supreme being—our God. Sure, the Bible says that God only took six days to complete Heaven and Earth, but no one said they had to be earth days. Why couldn't they have been cosmic days or days of some special galactic calendar? It's only reasonable that a supreme being should work on a different timetable than us mortal individuals."

"You're grasping at straws."

"Maybe," I admitted. "Smarter men than me have been grappling with this question since the beginning of time. No one has ever been able to come up with a clear-cut answer. But why has man always had the notion that there is a God? Why have we always felt His spiritual presence and sensed His unseen guidance in favour of moral order? Maybe that's the strongest evidence in

God's support. How can I believe there is no God, when I know He exists in my heart?"

"The problem lies in your heart all right," the captain answered. "Love is the crux of the problem. Love is the bane of man's inexistence."

"Whatever do you mean?" I was astounded by his strange, but oddly confiding remarks.

"What is love?" He continued on the same peculiar path. His question was met with stunned expressions from everyone. "None of the great scholars managed to answer that age old question. For over five thousand years now, the greatest human minds have only produced conflicting definitions. Terence, for instance, said: 'It is in love's power to change a person beyond recognition.' But Plato was known to have thought that: 'Only love is capable to make you truly yourself'. Does everyone here agree that love has never been properly defined?"

We all agreed, even though we knew—deep down inside—we were sure to regret our decision.

"If you will allow me, I would like to try and shed some light on the subject." The captain sat back in his chair and crossed his arms. His body language appeared boastful and defiant.

"It seems amusing to me that you would consider yourself an expert on the subject, Captain," I said, smiling wide. "But if I can use your own words. I've nothing better to do than listen to your ramblings."

"What is love associated with?" He looked around the room smugly, doing mirrored spider push ups with his fingers. "Chekhov said: 'What a great happiness is to love and be loved'. And Hugo was in agreement when he said: 'The biggest happiness in life is to be sure that you are loved'. Of course, love's everlasting companion has to be happiness. But what is happiness itself?"

I wanted to express my opinion, but was afraid of being the brunt of one of the captain's smart-assed remarks.

"Morris, you and I touched on this subject briefly." His sharp eyes stabbed directly into mine. "You thought that it had to do with an aim or a way of life. Or is it an emotion, a process or an aspiration? Happiness dwells in various domains and escapes definition. But what I do know for sure is that wishes are our driving force in our pursuit of happiness. And the harder our wish is to fulfill, the stronger our will works to achieve it. The source of this pursuit of happiness is a complicated instrument at work in our soul and I will give it the name—Satra. With the help of man's revving hormones, Satra paints a pretty picture filled with anticipation and wonder. Satra is an amazing factory, converting unrefined mega-wishes into the anticipation of fantasy. Satra explains the world of love."

"Wow!" I said in amazement. "You surprise me, Captain. I had no idea you were such a deep thinker. I'm not sure I understand a lot of what you are saying, but I can't help being curious about where you are headed with this. Please continue."

"Love is the process of Satra focusing. The keys by which the mechanism aims the striving to happiness and holds it in focus are inseparably linked to love. These keys are hope and faith.

"Hope adheres to the object's ideal qualities and focuses Satra. Faith holds the focus, preventing it from straying to greener pastures. Hope ensues from the introduction of the pretty picture, the promise. Faith, however, needs reinforcement via dynamic imitation of the Satra environment by means of pleasure, comfortable surroundings, gifts, offerings and miracles. But what happens when the object tires of maintaining the imitation. After all, generating the ideal reality takes a lot of effort. Soon faith falters and focus shifts, but optimal hormonal balance is reluctant to let go, hope strains to maintain the façade; clutching at any ghost or mirage which helps it stay on course and retain focus.

INTERVENTION

When the last mirage fades, focus is totally lost and love comes to an end. Hope ceases to hold on, as the soul sees that the object of love has lost all of its Satra qualities. Faith is dead. Hope to achieve happiness is smothered. Then the human entity decays into a pathetic state; unable to focus, unable to find direction in the universe, burdened by the many stresses of a fast-paced world. When man reaches out to others for assistance he is only met with rejection." The captain's face grew solemn as he spoke and his posture failed as he sank in his chair. Everyone in the room was extremely uncomfortable as he paused in silence.

"What is the point of all this, Captain?" I asked in an effort to shock him back into the moment. "This all sounds very fascinating, but you need to clarify what you are trying to say."

The captain lifted his head and continued. "When a man reaches this pitiful state, Satra transforms our wishes—which are incapable of being brought to fruition in the here and now—into dreams of a self-serving world, where there is no judgment and negativity. Where constant pleasure is the norm, happiness and amusement never subside and all our wishes come true. What have I just described? Supreme happiness that can only be provided by a Supreme Being—God. God is a fabrication of Satra."

"Just a minute, Captain." I said angrily. "Love is Satra or God is Satra; which is it?"

"The difference lies in our existence," he said with conviction. "If Satra is faced with an existential problem, such as the meaning of life and what happens after death, then existence tends to alter the equation in such a way that it becomes possible to believe in anything. God equals Satra plus existence. That is the simple and clear equation of God. One has to admire the universal mechanism of Satra, which can find a specific way of consolation for any problem. Basic intellectual existence wishes to find the reason for all the universe. This wish evolved from the cause-and-consequence structure of human thinking, as well as the need for wisdom and reliability of cognition. Basic ontological existence is dread of death and wish of eternal life. God is an absolute, designed to console both of our existences. God is the skill to be happy in misfortune."

"Did you come up with this bullshit yourself?" I asked with heated breath.

"I admit that my claims are based on my own loose interpretation of someone else's work. Most of my argument has been borrowed from one of the greatest thinkers of our time, Vadim Kirpichev; just as most of your arguments were stolen from great minds that preceded you. My primary objective was to disprove the existence of God; I didn't think I had to do it with originality of thought. Do you have a problem with that?"

"No, not at all. I was just wondering where you came up with such an outlandish hypothesis."

"May I continue?" he said bluntly. He did not wait for an answer as he entered seamlessly into the final piece of his argument. "There is no God outside the existential Satra. God is a fabrication of your soul. In science, Occam's razor states: 'entities must not be multiplied beyond what is necessary'. Therefore, God does not exist."

"This is just a bunch of bullshit!" I protested.

"The truth hurts sometimes," he added with a self-satisfied grin.

"If God doesn't exist, then who is responsible for the creation of the universe?" I was determined to disprove his bone headed theory.

"In order to disprove the necessity for God, we need only build a model where a universe can develop out of nothing. Current scientific thinking believes that universes can indeed spring into existence as a quantum fluctuation of nothing. Many astrophysicists think that our universe, along with many other parallel universes, sprang from tiny bubbles in the time-space continuum. This is because positive energy found in matter is balanced against the negative energy of gravity; therefore, the total energy required is zero. Since it takes no energy to create a universe, no outside help was required to cause their creation; thus, eliminating the need for a God."

I looked towards Adam for some reassurances. I knew that science was leaning towards the existences of parallel universes, but I never really thought about how that would impact the theory of creation until now. Adam just shrugged his shoulders as if to say, "he's right and there is nothing I can say to disprove what was said." Finally, after a lot of intense concentration, Adam offered an alternative case for God's existence.

"I can't disprove your parallel universe theory, Captain; but wouldn't you agree that as we model the laws that govern our universe more accurately, we find that certain basic forces, like the stability of subatomic particles and the longevity of stars, are inexplicably specific and sensitive, in some cases to the third decimal place. The recipe for a universe that contains a life supporting environment has very tight parameters. Any slight changes would short circuit the development of such a universe and render it sterile. Doesn't this sound like an argument for intelligent design?"

"Not really," the captain replied. "Most current theories support the existence of billions of these self-causing universes contained in what they call a multiverse. All possible arrangements of matter must exist out there somewhere. We just happen to be lucky enough to be on the one that is able to support life. Let's use the analogy of a million monkeys with typewriters eventually hammering out all of Shakespeare's plays. Our universe was randomly acquired only through coincidence."

I looked at Adam again. This time he appeared hopeless, as he shrugged and raised his palms in defeat. Then I slowly turned my head in order to check out the captain. He could not have looked more self-righteous. I wanted desperately to be able to disprove everything that he said, but my mind was confused and in shock. I could see that the teens were looking out to me and expecting guidance; I felt ashamed that I could not deliver. A feeling of panic was arising inside me at an alarming rate.

"I'm sorry to disappoint you, Shorty, but your all-important God does not exist. Man has expended boundless energies through the ages, worshiping and fighting over a false idol. Just think of all the millions of lives lost in the religious wars throughout history. Think of all the needless hate in the world, all because of differences in our religious beliefs. If man had been of the same mind, there's no telling how far we would have gone. Instead of putting all our faith and energy into the fantasy of an idealistic utopia after death, we should have strived to create our own paradise here on earth."

My head was spinning by this time, as my whole system was teaming with high anxiety. All I could think of was distancing myself from my aggressor—the destroyer of dreams. I would rather he run a sword through my heart, than have him steal God from its boundaries. I lifted myself out of my chair and spoke in a stuttering, semi-coherent fashion.

I—have--to go--now." I almost ran out of the room after that, having to restrain myself from bolting. How dare he attack my faith so callously? The unmitigated nerve of that man. But where was I to run to? When I arrived at the opposite end of the station I simply paced back and forth, cursing obscenities with great profusion. That son-of-a-bitch beat me again. No matter how hard I try, that man always seems to get the upper hand.

Sometime later a peace keeping force, consisting of Adam and Eve Anna, came to check on me. They approached me tentatively trying to get a sense of my mood before invading my personal space.

"It's okay," I assured them. "I was just blowing off a little steam, that's all."

"None of us believes any of that crap he was trying to feed us." Eve Anna hugged me and tried to console me.

"I feel better now. I just needed to vent my hostilities in private. I'm tired; I've had a very stressful day. First, I find out Fred is dying and now this. This is the last fricking thing I needed. I just want to go to sleep."

"We'll walk you to your cocoon." Adam put his arm around me and led me back to the sleeping area. Not a word was spoken, other than to say goodnight.

I lay in my enclosure for some time, all the while thinking about the captain's allegations. Of all the audacity, saying that love was the bane of man's existence. I knew that love was not what he said it was, but I did not have a concrete definition to oppose his theory. I was sure, however, that the emotion of love was unique to man. No other species uses love as a focusing mechanism—as the captain so boldly called it. What was it intended for? Was it solely for the purpose of attaching oneself to a mate or did it serve another function. It was too obscure an entity to have been a product of evolution. It was left here on purpose. Of course, that was it! God does not equal Satra plus existence. God equals love. That is why the captain is unable to grasp the concept of God. The answer was in the Bible all along. John 4:7-13— "He that loveth not, knoweth not God: for God is Love". That is the simple and clear equation of God. God = love.

Now I was upset for a different reason. Why did I not think of that in the midst of the debate with the captain? It frustrates me when I think of a good rebuttal long after the confrontation is over. At least I know that I was right; that is the important thing. I would tell Adam and the others my thoughts when I wake up. As to Captain Dick, he may as well continue to think he won another battle, for it would be impossible to convince him otherwise.

I drifted off to sleep thinking about my friend down on earth. He was losing a more crucial, high-stakes battle. He was fighting for his life.

Chapter Nineteen

I FELT SURPRISINGLY RESTED WHEN I awoke from my sleep. I had hit rock bottom the day before and today I felt I had nowhere to go but up. Naturally, it is easier to recover from a hardship if you feel the worst is over.

I decided to celebrate this fresh start with a shower and a change of attire. When I went to my locker to find some different clothes, I was shocked to see that someone had been snooping in my underwear drawer. I shivered uncontrollably and gasped when I realized who the culprit had been. I had heard of women selling their seasoned panties over the internet and wondered what kind of sick, demented pervert would be interested in purchasing such an item. Captain Dick was just that type of person.

My first reaction was to march down to the control room and give him a piece of my mind, but then I realized it would be a waste of time and energy. The captain was incorrigible. I reminded myself that as long as the captain was focused on me, the other girls were safe from his advances. It was better for him to centre his silly little fetishes around me, than Eve Anna and the others. Besides, it was rather comical in a way. What would the captain's reaction be if he knew he was fondling a transgender's underwear? As it was, I had the last laugh.

I was not laughing for long, however, because an emergency alarm sounded on board and I could feel the stations manoeuvring engines shove us harshly in a sideways motion. I was almost jolted from my feet.

"What the hell's going on!" Helena screamed, after being roused from her sleep. All three girls sprang from their beds in dazed confusion. Red lights were flashing and the station was still shuttering with motion.

"Get dressed!" I shouted over the deafening alarm systems and the firing of rocket propulsion engines.

I paused while putting on my jumpsuit to recollect who was in charge. This was Adam's shift at the helm. I finished dressing in a flash and abandoned the girls to see if I could help at the controls. I was almost to the control room when something terrible happened. There was a dreadful, crashing explosion and the station buckled from the concussion, throwing me against the bulkhead.

"You fucking moron!" I heard the captain hollering in anger form the control room. "Now look what the fuck you've done."

I recovered my balance and dashed into the room.

"What is it?" I shouted above the confusion.

"We've been hit by a piece of space debris," the captain barked as he looked up from the controls, pointing towards the starboard side of the station. "See if there is anything you can do, Morris. I'll be there as soon as I can."

I turned and looked down the hallway in the direction of the impact. There was a thick cloud of dust and smoke billowing towards me. I had to consciously move one foot and then the other towards the threatening sound of rushing air.

"Morris, whatever you do, don't get sucked out the opening!" I heard the captain shouting out orders behind me.

INTERVENTION

The smoke started to clear naturally as I approached the place of impact. It was all getting drawn out into space with the rest of our internal atmosphere. I would have to work fast to save the station and all those on board.

The sound reminded me of when an excavation crew struck a natural gas line outside my apartment in Boston and we had to evacuate the building; it was ear piercing. Pieces of complicated electronic circuitry and high-tech gadgetry littered the hallway. It was telltale evidence of extreme damage to the ship. When I could finally see the damaged bulkhead, I was amazed at the smallness of the hole. It was about three inches in diameter and strangely, my first thoughts were of relief, because I was too fat to get sucked through the opening.

I scanned the rubble frantically for something to plug up the aperture. Since nothing seemed suitable, I undressed and jammed my NASA issue flight suit into the breach. It slowed the release of atmosphere to a minimum. When I looked for an exit hole, I was shocked to realize that the projectile had struck the carbon dioxide scrubber. It had absorbed the full impact of the collision and was totally destroyed. I stepped back from the rubble when I heard the sound of footsteps clamouring down the metal framework of the station.

"Good work, Morris." I heard Captain Dick remark as he jumped in front of me to examine the puncture. "That was thinking on your feet," he added, as he examined my makeshift patch. Then he glanced over his shoulder at me slowly, sporting a covetous grin.

That is when I realized I was standing there braless, with nothing on but my panties. I had not had time to get completely dressed because of the incident.

"Nice tits, by the way."

"Just concentrate on stopping the air loss, Asshole," I snapped at him, self-consciously covering my breasts and backing away.

"I can repair the hole, no problem," he said. "That's the least of our problems. The CO_2 scrubber is a write-off. Without that we're screwed."

"Define screwed?" I asked in apprehension, conscious of my stark nakedness and my timorous shivering.

"Never mind that now. You run along and get dressed while I make a better patch for this bulkhead breach. I'll need you to do an outside repair as soon as possible."

Since I heard more footsteps coming from the direction I came, I decided to return to my locker the long way around to avoid being seen without my clothes by the rest of the crew.

"That's the last thing I needed to be doing," I thought. "Adding more fuel to Captain Dick's flaming desires." It was not hard to interpret from his remarks and his hungry looks that the captain liked what he saw. It gave me the chills just thinking about what was going through his tainted mind while he was caressing me with his eyes. But I had to put all these thoughts aside and focus on the problem at hand.

•———•

"We need a team meeting," the captain said to me, as he was helping me off with my space suit and MMU.

"Aren't you going to ask me about the repairs?"

"As long as it'll hold for a week," he said bluntly.

"What do you mean, a week?"

"I'll tell everyone at the meeting. Come along."

Everyone was waiting for us when we arrived at the control room. Captain Dick motioned for us to sit down and then took a position of authority by sitting on part of the control panel.

"The situation is grim," he started. "As most of you know, thanks to the incompetence of team member McGinnis, the station has been struck by a meteorite and the main carbon dioxide scrubber has been totally destroyed."

"Just a minute," Adam spoke in his own defence. "I came and got you as soon as the object was detected by the computer."

"You should have called for immediate evasive action, Asshole. By the time you came running to me, with your tail between your legs, it was too late to do anything."

"That's not fair Captain," I challenged. "Adam is not a trained astronaut. How can you expect him to know the correct procedures?"

"That's bullshit and you know it!" He said with a malicious glare. "I have stressed the proper protocol several times, but dodo here was too incompetent to get it right."

"You know we had a slim chance of getting out of the way without advanced warning from NASA. There's a good chance we could have been struck no matter who was at the controls," I stressed.

"We'll never know that now, will we?" The captain stared fiercely at Adam as he spoke.

"There's no sense laying blame." I decided to fashion a new theme for the conversation. "What's the status of the mission?"

"Unfortunately, the main carbon dioxide scrubber is totally bitched. With nine of us exhaling CO2 inside the station the internal atmosphere will become toxic in a matter of days. I have employed a small backup scrubber that will buy us only enough time to get the SSTO ready for our return to earth."

"But that's at least two months sooner than the authorities suggested." I blurted out in spite of the fact I knew the captain and everyone else did not need to be reminded. "The plague may not have run its course."

"I know it sucks, but it's just a chance we're going to have to take." The captain raised his palms in defeat. "We are damned if we do and damned if we don't."

"What about the unit on board the John Glenn?" I asked. "Couldn't we cannibalize the ship to supplement the small unit on board the station?"

"Good thinking, Morris." The captain rubbed the stubble on his chin as he pondered my suggestion. "No wait... that would only buy us a few days at the expense of an important backup vehicle. I can't see any way out of this. We have to return to earth as soon as possible."

"Well, that settles it then. What do we need to do to get ready?" I asked.

"I'll look after the ship," the captain volunteered. "Morris, I'm putting you in charge of everything else."

"Right." I accepted readily. "Can you give me a brief breakdown?"

"We'll need food supplies for a week and water for two. Transfer all the survival gear and medical supplies over from the Glenn. Download all pertinent information off of the main computer and store it on memory wafers. Make sure you have all your personal things and anything else you can think of that doesn't weigh a lot. From now on we only take time out to eat and sleep. Now let's get to work."

I asked Adam and his team to look after the food, water and survival gear, while the girls and I packed up the medical supplies. NASA had sent a broad spectrum of pharmaceuticals and first aid supplies. All we had to do was organize them before we stowed them away. While we were sorting through the boxes some of the girls expressed their feelings.

"Do you think Adam screwed up?" Nicole asked tentatively.

"I'm honestly not sure, Nicole." I was uncomfortable with her question. "If he made a mistake, I'm not going to hold it against him."

"Besides, you always tell us there is no mistake so bad that you can't recover from it through hard work and strong determination," Eve Anna piped up.

"Unless it kills you," I said involuntarily, under my breath.

"What was that?" Nicole asked.

"Nothing," I answered quickly, being angry with myself for letting those words slip out of my mouth. "I was just being stupid."

Because the girls were scared, just like I was, I had no business making things worse. Luckily Eve Anna found something to divert our attention.

"Orgasmax!" She exclaimed holding up a bottle of pills. "What the hell did NASA expect we needed these for?"

"Where did you find those?" I asked, grabbing the bottle from her hand.

"In this box marked 'Attention: Captain Dick'."

"That was rather presumptuous of him, wasn't it? Little does he know, he doesn't stand a chance of making it with any of us." My hair bristled on the back of my neck when I thought about the captain's expectations. "Give me that box of things that are all ready to go. I'll pay the captain a little visit."

I put the pill bottle in my pocket and proceeded to the SSTO vehicle. The captain was in his cockpit when I arrived. I stowed my supplies and then stepped into the front of the ship.

"What are you up to?" I asked in a nonchalant manner.

"Doing a systems analysis," he grunted. "Haven't you got better things to do?"

"I found something in the medical supplies that belongs to you," I said; digging the pills out of my pocket and shoving them into his face. The captain's complexion instantly turned a bright hue of red and he started to stutter.

"Ah... well—yeah—I—guess those are mine." He tore the bottle from my hands.

"What are those for, by the way?" I was feigning ignorance, playfully increasing the pressure.

"You know damn well what they're for!" he said, with a burst of anger.

"You might as well chuck those things in the garbage right…" I did not finish my sentence because I was interrupted by a loud alarm inside the cockpit.

"What the fuck?" The captain tossed the pills aside and started frantically pushing buttons and fiddling with knobs. The alarm quit after about five seconds. "Holy shit, that scared the crap out of me."

"What is it?"

"I lost the descent beacon for a few seconds."

"That's a bad thing, right?"

"It's how NASA is supposed to guide us home; you know that. Without that beacon, I will have to fly by the seat of my pants."

"Can anything else go frickin' wrong?" Naturally I was getting very frustrated.

"It's probably nothing; just a minor glitch. Everything seems fine now."

"Let's hope it stays that way. There's nobody left on the ground to get it back on line." I stated the obvious.

"I'll set up a diagnostic to check this end. If there's a problem with the ship, I'll find it."

"I'll leave all this in your capable hands." I knew I was holding him up for no good reason. Just before I exited the ship, I heard the familiar sound of pills rattling in their bottle. I turned around to see the captain with a big, fat, stupid grin on his face, shaking the container.

"You and me, Baby. You and me."

It was a display unworthy of a reply. I turned smartly and exited the vehicle.

INTERVENTION

I met Adam and the boys in the hallway. Adam barely looked at me when I greeted them. He was obviously feeling guilty about the incident with the space junk. I made a mental note to speak to him alone as soon as possible.

The rest of the day went well. The girls and I organized all the medical supplies and had them stowed away before our evening meal. In a show of courtesy, we waited for half an hour for Adam and the boys to complete their duties before we started preparing the food. We were sitting and eating already when Captain Dick entered the galley.

"I see you guys waited for me, like one pig waits on another."

Everyone chose to ignore his remark.

"How's the preparation coming?" I asked. "Any more glitches?"

"So far so good. What about you guys?"

"We have everything transferred from the Glenn."

"Great. Next you can start downloading information from the computer. McGinnis, you're in charge of all the scientific knowledge from the invention of the wheel until present day. Morris, it's up to you to decide what literature is to be saved and what's to be left behind. We only have limited storage capacity. That should keep you both busy until just before departure. We'll put our personal things together a few hours before we leave."

"How long do we have?" Adam asked.

"A week for sure. Maybe ten days. I'll be monitoring the CO_2 levels constantly."

The rest of the conversations at the table consisted of idle chit-chat, because everyone chose to ignore the problems at hand. I asked the teens to clean up when we were done, so that I could take Adam aside and talk to him about the meteor incident.

"Don't let it bother you," I encouraged. "Even if the captain had been sitting at the controls when the alarm sounded, he would not likely have been able to get out of the way."

"We don't know that for sure. I still feel responsible."

"I still trust you," I said, giving him a kiss on the lips. That seemed to cheer him up a bit.

"I'll make it up to you, you'll see."

"Don't sweat it." I gave him a hug and then took him by the hand and led him off to the control room to download files. It was difficult deciding what to keep and what to toss. Shakespeare was a given, so was Dickens, Tolstoy, Pascal, Plato, Aristotle, Nabokov and so many more. It was hard to not put too much pressure on myself; it was important that I make the right decisions. It was sad to think that the bulk of five thousand years of human thought could be lost forever.

Chapter Twenty

THE NEXT DAY THE GIRLS and I were working in the control room when we heard the captain screaming all the way from the SSTO vehicle.

"Son of a bitch!" He was obviously severely annoyed about something. I had to go and investigate.

"What's wrong?" I asked as soon as I stepped through the opening into the ship. The high-pitched alarm sounding from the cockpit was an ominous clue to the answer.

"I've lost the fucking signal again!" he shouted in distress.

"How long has it been off?"

The captain looked at his watch. "It's been almost a minute."

"Now what?" I asked in a meek, helpless tone. I sat down in the co-pilot's seat adjacent to him and could only stare at the red light flashing on the control panel. Then the alarm stopped and the light turned from red to green.

"Thank God," the captain sighed.

"Thank who?"

"It's just an expression. Don't read anything into it," he growled.

"What do you think is going on?"

"I wish I knew. It's not at this end, that's for sure."

I got up out of my chair and left. There was nothing more to be said. If the beacon failed on re-entry, we would fly off course. I am not a rocket scientist, but I know enough to realize the SSTO vehicle has special landing strip requirements. You can't set this baby down just anywhere.

"Wait," the captain said as I was ready to step outside the vehicle. "I've been meaning to talk to you. I want you to be my co-pilot for the trip home."

"I'm not really qualified." I did not know what else to say.

"You've got more balls than anyone else on board. That's all I'm worried about. Will you do it or not?"

"Oh, I'll do it if you want me too; anything for the good of the mission."

"That's the spirit, Honey. Show up here at six-hundred hours tomorrow and I'll take you through the flight plan."

"Okay." I tried to ignore the fact that he had just called me, 'honey'.

•———•

Nine days after we were struck with space debris, we climbed aboard the Herald of Democracy with hopes of returning safely home to earth. The captain had checked me out at my role as co-pilot, which he had basically reduced to calling out instrument readings and administering moral support. All our equipment and personal things were packed and as much information was downloaded from the computer as was possible within the restraints of time and transportable memory space.

"McGinnis, you can close the front hatch and prepare for separation from the station." There was a small clunk below, as Adam performed his duty.

"Ready for separation," Adam confirmed. "Everyone is strapped in and ready for our descent."

The captain fired the manoeuvring thrusters. We slowly moved away from the station that had been our home for almost four months. I was having mixed emotions, because of the uncertainties on earth. Hopefully we would not be greeted by the 'Grim Reaper' when we arrived. We would have to orbit the earth once before re-entry, to stabilize our trajectory. Half way around the world the alarm went off to indicate we had lost our descent beacon one more time. I expected the captain to have another fit; but instead, he casually reached over and switched off the alarm as if it was nothing. I looked into his eyes for some sign of what he was thinking, but his cool demeanour told me nothing. He was going about his business as if nothing had happened. The red flashing light that continued to blink on the instrument panel told otherwise.

Finally, he switched on the mike and made an announcement: "Everyone, this is your captain speaking. We are experiencing a small technical difficulty. I'm going to make another orbit to buy me enough time to correct the problem. Just relax and I'll have you home in no time."

I had to give the man credit for keeping his cool. I would have expected something more along the lines of: "Oh shit, we're all going to die!" I sat in my seat silently for about ten minutes. By now I had pretty much figured out that the beacon was not coming back on.

"Now what?" I asked, after I had flipped the switch which restricted the conversation to just us two.

"We're going in blind." He said with a hint of regret.

"I don't like the sound of that."

"It might not be pretty," he said looking me straight in the face. It was the first time I had seen terror in his eyes. "If we go in too shallow, we'll skip off the atmosphere and bounce into outer space. If we go in too steep, we will burn up in the atmosphere. We have a very narrow window of opportunity to hit the continent of North America let alone land at the cape. We will need a very long, very flat area to land safely."

"What are our chances?"

"We have no global positioning systems and no flight line beacon. If you were flying with anyone else but me, I would say, a snowball's chance in hell. Luckily, I have gone through this descent sequence dozens of times. I'm giving us a twenty percent chance for survival."

"At least that's something." I choked out after having to swallow my spit. "Good luck, Captain."

"We're coming up to our window," the captain said. "There's the Indian Ocean coming up to your left."

"Roger that, Captain."

The captain switched on the mike and spoke to the rest of the crew. "Everyone, we are set for re-entry in just a few minutes. We should be on the ground in about an hour."

He fired the manoeuvring thrusters to rotate the vehicle 180 degrees so that we were flying backwards. Then there was a shuttering jolt and an explosive roar, as the main engines were fired in what the captain called the re-entry burn.

"We're orbiting at twenty-eight thousand kilometres per hour and we need to slow down to twenty-four thousand, so that we can fall out of orbit," he reminded me.

The re-entry burn lasted for about three minutes. A little while later the captain righted the vehicle; flipping it over so that its tiled surface would be facing the earth.

"We're now set to enter the atmosphere at a forty-degree angle. Morris, hit the switch to jettison the fuel."

I pushed the switch to start the fuel release sequence.

"There's no turning back now," he added.

Within moments a soft red glow was coming off the tip of the vehicle's nose. This was an indication that heat was beginning to build up, because of friction with the Earth's atmosphere. It was ironic to think that something we could not live without might end up being our undoing.

Captain Dick switched the mike back on. "Hang on everyone, this could get rough."

Right about now I was wishing I had given everyone a big hug before we left. We had to survive. I was convinced that we were part of God's master plan. What good would we be to Him if we were dead?

The heat gradually built up until eventually there was a horrifying buildup of flames licking at the windows. We were encased in a fire ball of hot ionized gases and hurling towards earth at almost 20,000 miles per hour. My heart was pounding like a five-pound hammer and I was wet with perspiration. I had to fight strenuously to ward off the onset of full-blown panic.

"We're going in too steep!" I screamed, in spite of all my efforts to stay calm. "We're going to burn up."

"Shut up!" the captain shouted back, frantically checking the controls. "Everything is fine. We just have to trust that the computer knows what it's doing. The hull temperature is only about sixteen-hundred degrees Celsius. Nothing to worry about."

I'm glad he was not worried, because I was ready to soil my flight suit. The ship was starting to roll from side to side now, as the computer was steering the ship in a series of s-curves in an effort to slow us down.

"From now until we hit Mach One it's just a waiting game," the captain added.

It was hell knowing what I knew about our chances for survival. How lucky the others were, seated comfortably behind and below us, totally oblivious to the dangers that we were facing.

"If you don't mind," I addressed the captain. "I'm going to close my eyes and say a little prayer. Let me know if you need me."

"It can't hurt, Honey. Pray away."

My eyes were closed for about ten minutes—partly to pray and partly to shield myself from reality. I do not have to give an account of what I was praying for, that of course is self-evident. I woke from my trance like state because of the terrific G-forces that were being thrust upon me and the panic-stricken sound of the captain's voice calling out my name.

"Candy! Candy, wake up." I knew there was something dreadfully wrong, because he had never had the courtesy to call me by my proper name before.

I opened my eyes and was going to ask what was wrong, but I stopped in mid-sentence. I could see the problem spread out beneath us.

"We're way off course." He was blunt and to the point. "We're right above the Rocky Mountains."

"Can you get us over the top?"

"I'm doing everything I can to buy us as much hang time as possible. It's hard to tell at this distance, with no navigational readings. We have no power and I'm steering a flying brick. My options are limited to say the least."

"Just do the best you can." I reached out and touched his arm with reassurance. He glanced down quickly at my hand on his arm and then just as quickly our eyes met. He seemed appreciative of my understanding and my physical presence. He continued his flight manoeuvres with even more determination. I looked down at the flight speed indicator. It was reading about 600 miles an hour. If we slammed into one of those rocky peaks at that speed we would disintegrate on impact.

"If I bring the nose up any more, we'll stall out," the captain shouted. The last range of tall peaks was directly in front of us. I feared the end was near. We seemed terribly close and we were falling at an alarming rate. I closed my eyes for the second time and said one last prayer.

"I think we're going to make it," he said with excitement.

I opened my eyes again in time to see a jagged slab of rock slip silently beneath our wing.

"Yeee-ha!" the captain screamed into the mike. "I did it. I frickin' well did it."

"Thank God," I said in inexplicable relief.

"This might not be all that bad," he added.

"What do you mean?"

"Look out there, Shorty. That's the Great Plains in our sights. We might actually find a patch of ground flat enough to set this sucker down in one piece." He held up his gloved hand in expectation of a high-five. I was more than willing to accommodate him.

"Has anyone ever done anything like this before?"

"We'll be the first. Our chances are still less than fifty-fifty."

"At least the odds are getting better." I had an overwhelming feeling of confidence; deep down inside I was sure we were going to land safely.

The captain did not reply, because he was focusing on the task at hand. On a positive note, the topography was getting flatter and less rugged as we glided forward. When we were over some of the flattest farmlands I had ever seen in my life, the captain made an extreme banking turn to slow us down to our optimum landing speed. We seemed exceptionally low to the ground now, but yet our speed was tremendously fast. The ground below was rushing past in a blur of motion. It must have rained recently because water was lying between the furrows.

"Aren't we landing awfully fast?" I needed reassurance from the captain.

"We'll be traveling about two-hundred miles an hour when we touch down. That's as slow as I can go and still retain altitude. Like I said, we're going to need a lot of luck on our side."

"Should I notify the rest of the crew?"

"That's your call."

"Attention crew, we have flown off course and are forced to make an emergency landing. Brace yourselves for the worst. God have mercy on us all." I did not think there was any sense of sugar coating our situation for them.

We were only about a hundred feet in the air when a farm yard rushed into view and just as quickly breezed underneath us in a streak of motion. Within seconds our landing gear was deployed and the well-groomed farmland was just inches away. I had flipped the safety cover and my fingers were positioned near the switch that released the braking parachutes, just as I had been instructed in our pre-flight plan. As soon as I felt the landing gear touch the ground, I popped the chutes. It was terribly rough, but the captain seemed to be managing to keep things together. Just when things started to become hopeful, the captain derailed my enthusiasm.

"Ah shit, look at that," he said pointing ahead.

My heart sank when I realized what was causing him concern. There was a gravel road directly in front of us, running perpendicular to our path. Before I could react, we dropped into the ditch and glanced off the shoulder of the road. We were all slammed forward as the landing gear and some of the fuselage was torn out from under us.

"Son of a bitch!" the captain yelled as we bounced off the opposite side of the ditch causing us to spin out of control. Thankfully we had just enough momentum to skip over the obstacle; if the nose would have dug in, we would have been finished. Mud sprayed up and covered the windows as the craft spun around and around like a top. The whole ordeal seemed like an eternity. Finally, we skidded to an abrupt stop with warning alarms and red lights flashing everywhere. Within seconds the cockpit was filled with smoke, adding to the sense of urgency.

"Let's get the fuck out of here!" the captain yelled for everyone to hear.

I knew that it was my job to open the upper exit. I released my restraint system and found my way to the door by feeling the way with my hands. I popped the hatch and deployed the inflatable slide that stretched to the ground below. I leaned out to see if the crew below were able to get out. To my horror, the lower exit was buried in mud.

"Captain," I hollered into the smoke and confusion. "The front hatch is blocked. I have to go down and help the others."

That's my job," he yelled back from the far end of the ship, hidden in smoke. I leaned out of the opening again, so that I was able to see well enough to help the others slide down the chute. Everyone was accounted for except the captain, Eve Anna and Adam. My heart sank and a lump formed in my throat when I noticed a fire burning towards the rear of the vehicle. I knew it would be foolish to go back in after them. I had to trust that the captain had the situation under control.

"Get away from the ship," I yelled to the others already on the ground. "It's going to blow!"

I should have jumped down myself, but I needed to know that everyone was okay.

Several minutes had elapsed, but I had heard nothing from the others. The fire was twice the size that it was before.

"Morris, I need help." The captain's voice rang out from below.

I got down on my knees in hopes of being able to see under the smoke and worked my way towards the lower compartment opening. As I fumbled beneath the haze, I was shocked to find a limp body placed awkwardly half way through the lower threshold. I put one hand under each armpit and pulled for everything I was worth. Whoever was in the suit was dead weight and I could barely move him. I had to jerk the person along one heave at a time until I got to the exit. I turned the body around and pushed him down the chute feet first. I did not see who it was until the face slid past me in the light. It was Adam. That meant the captain and Eve Anna were still down below. My heart almost exploded in dreaded anticipation. If Eve Anna was dead, I would be crushed.

All hope was renewed, however, when the captain emerged from the smoke, assisting Eve Anna with one arm around her waist. I was relieved to see that she was upright and able to carry most of her own weight. The captain plopped her down on the ramp feet first while I straddled her with my legs and put my arms around her waist. Randy and Frankie had come back to assist Adam; they were already walking away from the vehicle carrying him with one arm around each of their shoulders. He was conscious now and partially supporting himself. The captain pushed Eve Anna and me down the ramp and then slid down behind us. When we got to the bottom, we raised Eve Anna to her feet and moved her in the same fashion that Randy and Frankie carried Adam.

We were walking at the bottom of the trench, that was gouged in the farmer's field by the SSTO vehicle while it was skidding to its resting place. There was muck everywhere. It stuck to our large space boots and made walking extremely difficult. When we finally reached the others, I set Eve Anna down and opened the visor of her helmet.

"How are you feeling?" the captain asked.

"I've felt better, but I'm sure I'll be fine in a few minutes. That was one hell of a rough ride down there."

I wrapped my arms around her neck and gave her a big hug saying: "Oh, Eve Anna, I'm so glad you're all right. I was worried sick about you." I doted over her for several minutes, until it must have gotten to the point where Frankie could not stand it anymore.

"Aren't you worried about your fiancé?" He said motioning towards Adam who was sitting on the ground looking rather bedraggled. Everyone in the group was looking at me strangely. They were unable to comprehend why I was fussing over my young student, when my future husband was in even more distress. I walked over to Adam and tried to make amends. He was fine; just a little shaken up the same as the rest of us.

After everyone was presumed safe and sound, we all turned around to watch the Herald of Democracy burn. The ship did not explode; partly thanks to the fact that we had jettisoned the fuel to prevent such a contingency. It did, however, slowly burn until nothing was left except a charred skeleton of what was once a proud ship.

Everyone in the group looked pale and distraught. Most of us had tears in our eyes. We were all sad to lose everything on board and we were concerned for our future.

"Well," the captain announced. "Any landing that you can walk away from is a good one."

I did not argue with him, because I knew, deep down inside, that nobody else could have accomplished what he had done; and—in spite of all his shortcomings—we were lucky to have had him for a pilot.

"What now?" I asked with uneasy breath.

"I think our best bet is to walk over to the farm yard that we buzzed just before we touched down. Hopefully we'll find shelter there. Is everyone able to travel?"

Adam and Eve Anna both raised themselves to signify their readiness.

"All right then," the captain said, removing his head gear and placing it under his arm. "Let's head out."

Randy and Frankie assisted Adam for the first few hundred meters, while the captain and Blaine helped Eve Anna. It was a long and arduous journey, traipsing through the mud in our bulky space suits. Every few feet we would have to stop and shake the mud off our boots. We were all totally spent by the time we reached our destination. Being in 45 percent gravity for an extended period had made us weak on earth. It was a small, but well-kept farm yard. There was a quaint little farm house, a hip roofed barn and several out buildings. Everything was surrounded by a large shelter belt, made up of a wide variety of trees. Five large grain bins made up part of the perimeter of the yard.

"Everyone stay here," the captain announced. "I'm going into the barn to investigate. Morris, you can come along if you like." I was behind him in an instant.

When we slid the large barn door open, several chickens flew past our heads and ran between our feet. There were six clean stalls and a ladder up to the loft. At the rear of the barn was a manual water-well pump, which fed a trough that ran to each of the stalls. I was impressed with the slick set up the farmer had invented, so that he could water his stock in the barn; but, most importantly, I was glad to see we had a water supply close at hand. The loft was three-quarters full of hay and wheat straw, which was perfect for what the captain and I had in mind.

"I think we should spend the night here, don't you?" I asked. "I think it would be a mistake to enter the house right away. There could be bodies with the virus still in there."

"Right, that's exactly what I was thinking. Let's go get the others."

When we got outside everyone else was down by the steel grain bins. Adam and the boys had climbed the existing ladders to see what was inside.

"They're all right full," Adam called out in excitement. "There's enough corn and wheat here to last us a lifetime."

"That's great," I hollered back, waving at them to return.

The captain and I informed everyone of our plans and then we all went back to the barn. We found a cup hanging on a nail by the pump; this made it easy for us to all have a big drink of cold, clean, delicious water. The sun was sinking below the horizon and the temperature was dropping well below the comfort range. We needed to get up in the loft and bury ourselves in the straw as soon as possible. Adam had other, more creative plans; he was going from stall to stall collecting all the eggs that the chickens had laid there previously.

"We won't be able to eat those,' the captain said with disgust, realizing we had no way of knowing how long they had been there.

"Yes, but if we get rid of these," Adam reminded. "We'll have nothing but fresh new ones in the morning."

"Let's all get upstairs and get warm." The captain found it convenient to change the subject.

We closed the barn door and climbed the stairs. It was fun tucking each other into bed in the straw and we were all as warm as toast in no time. We got ourselves situated in the nick of time, because it was dark shortly after we finally got settled. It was comforting to have a safe and peaceful spot to spend the night. We were all very tired from our ordeal, but everyone was too excited to go to sleep right away. We lay in our beds of straw and talked for quite some time.

"Where do you think we are?" Helena asked, initiating the conversation.

"There's no way to tell," the captain said unprompted. "We're somewhere in the midwestern United States. That's all I can say."

"How long are we going to have to stay in the barn?" a timid female voice said in the darkness.

"We still have our space suits," the captain explained. "In the morning Morris and I will suit up and go into the house to investigate. We'll breathe our own oxygen and look for some kind of household disinfectant while we're in the house. Then we'll be able to kill any of the viruses before we return."

"What if there are bodies in the house?" I asked.

"That could complicate things," the captain admitted. "Let's just wait and see what tomorrow brings. We'll cross that bridge when we come to it."

We had many more questions about what was in store for us in the future and the gravity of what we had lost in the fire, but most of all we counted our blessings and then drifted off to sleep.

Chapter Twenty-One

WHEN I AWOKE IN THE morning, I was surprised to find that Adam was already up and no longer in the loft. Because there was no sense waking the others, I crept silently down the ladder to look for him. The sun was peaking over the ruler-straight line that made up the horizon and it had the makings of a beautiful day. The ground had frozen overnight and there was a light skiff of snow on the ground, that showed the imprint of Adam's steps. I followed his tracks to the back side of the house, but I could have easily found him even if they had not been there; he was making a lot of noise that would have easily led me to him. When I rounded the corner, I found him fussing with a gas barbeque that was sitting on the back porch.

"Look what I found," Adam said with a big grin on his face. "If we can find some aluminium foil in the house, we can cook breakfast."

"Great," I said, giving him a big hug. "Let's carry it over to the barn."

By the time we arrived at the barn, everyone else was up and waiting for us. The captain seemed happy with our discovery, but was more concerned about investigating what was in the house. We had to put our space suits back on and check them out carefully to make sure there was no damage after everything that had happened the day before. When the captain was satisfied that everything was in order, we proceeded to the front door of the house.

There was a small entrance that contained a clothes closet and a place for the owners' footwear. From there we entered a kitchen-dining area that was clean, neat and appeared to be well organized. There were plenty of nicely finished oak cabinets for storage, as well as all the modern conveniences you would hope to find in a family kitchen. The counter tops were clear and there were no dishes in the sink, but there was a dirty frying pan on the electric stove and two used place settings at the large oak dining table. It appeared as if two people may have had their last meal there.

The next room down from the kitchen was the living area. There was the usual home entertainment system and living room furniture, along with a normal amount of personal clutter that gave the room a lived-in appearance. So far there was nothing that could be viewed as out of the ordinary.

To my profound relief, the two bedrooms that made up the rest of the house were empty and unsoiled. The clothes closets were still full and even the beds were made. It was as if the residents had left in a hurry and never returned. Overall, I was very impressed with the home and was looking forward to being able to make the move from the barn. It was a little small for the nine of us, but I was sure we would make do quite comfortably.

The captain found the door to the basement, but we had to rummage around in several drawers and closets until we found a small flashlight before we could head downstairs. There was no longer any electricity in the house to work the lights.

INTERVENTION

The cellar turned out to be a treasure trove of items that were key to our survival. The cold room held several sacks of potatoes, turnips, carrots and squash. The farm wife had obviously been a good gardener. There were many jars of home canned pickles, fruits, jams and jellies, as well as many other interesting preserves, including some canned meats. There were also several bottles of what looked like homemade wine, as well as numerous small brown flip-tops, which I hoped might contain beer. I grabbed a couple of cans of store-bought canned ham and a box of beer and proceeded to check out the rest of the downstairs.

In one corner, there was an electric water and sewer system that serviced the home. There was also a fuel-oil furnace, an electric water heater and a washer and dryer. There was one finished room in the basement that looked as if it had previously been used as a spare bedroom. Now it was used to store the former residents' home brewing supplies. There were three large fifteen-gallon kettles, two portable propane burners, a grain milling machine and five, six-gallon glass carboys; three of which contained beer that had finished fermenting and appeared to be ready to bottle. The captain and I were both grinning like school kids at recess when we went back up the stairs.

The captain grabbed a can opener, a spatula, a large frying pan and some household bleach out of the kitchen, before we stepped outside. Adam already had the five-gallon plastic pail full of water that we required sitting beside the front door. All we had to do was pour in some bleach and rub it all over our suits and everything else we were taking back to the barn. I used a dish towel I found in the kitchen to rub the disinfectant into every crevice of my flight suit. I washed the back of the captain's suit and he reciprocated by washing mine. I tried to ignore the fact that he acted as if there was an excessively large colony of viruses on my behind.

The captain and I could not wait to reveal what we had found in the house. We described the interior of the house to the others and itemized everything we had seen inside. Everyone was extremely excited about our findings. Adam was especially glad to hear about the hand operated grain mill.

"That's wonderful," Adam pointed out, as he readied the barbeque to cook our breakfast. "We can use the mill to grind up wheat and corn, so that we can boil it for grits."

"That would be great," I said while opening the ham with the can opener. Adam sliced it into chunks with the spatula and started to fry it up in the pan. As soon as some fat had rendered out of the ham, he started cracking in the fresh eggs he had found under the chickens that morning. The teens had already fashioned seats and a table out of square bales that they had found in the barn.

"It was Adam's idea," they admitted, as we sat down for our meal.

Adam set the frying pan in the middle of our makeshift table and I passed around the brown bottles for our beverage. The girls and I shared one bottle between us, just to get a taste. It turned out to be a delicious English-style ale that everyone enjoyed. Beer was a little out of the ordinary for a morning meal, but we were all in the mood to celebrate. We clinked our bottles together and made a toast to our continued success in the future. As soon as our meal was sufficiently cooled, we all ate with our hands. There was lots of light hearted laughing and joking as we devoured the delicious food that Adam had prepared. Every one of us was glad to be alive and thankful to be back on Earth. We were very appreciative of our many blessings.

"So, Captain, what's our next step?" I asked when we were finished eating.

"We have no way of knowing if the people who lived here were sick when they left. There could still be living plague viruses somewhere in the house. I'm not sure if we should camp out in the barn until any threat of an infection is over, or move into the house right away after we've had a chance to disinfect it. What do you think?"

"This is a new virus," I pointed out. "We don't know how resilient it can be. We could wait out here for days and still not be safe. I'd like to move in as soon as possible. Let's give the place a good scrub down with disinfectant and then hope for the best. Why don't we put it to a vote? We're all in this together."

Moving into the house as soon as possible was the unanimous choice. We readied ourselves for the clean-up bee immediately. All of us except Adam put our space suits back on and went into the house. Adam asked if he could stay outside, so that he could do a more thorough investigation of the farm yard. Since there were already going to be eight of us in the house, we all agreed that exploring would be a better use of his time.

We brought a five-gallon pail of bleach water with us and we found lots of cleaning supplies underneath the kitchen sink. One important find was a gallon jug of a strong spray-type cleanser that claimed to kill HIV-1 in three seconds. I assumed that the farmer liked to keep some of this on hand to protect himself from the Hantavirus, which is spread by deer mice that live in farm buildings and machinery. My father always had us spray down the cab of his grain truck with the same chemical every spring, because the mice would build nests in the heater ducts over the winter.

Before we could start cleaning, we had to bring up one of the propane cookers and one of the large kettles from downstairs. Our plan was to position them outside, so that we could heat our water. When the water was up to temperature, we attacked the kitchen. We scrubbed everything in the room, including the walls and ceiling. After that, we emptied the cabinets and scoured their interiors. The dishes and kitchenware that we removed from the cupboards were washed and then replaced in an organized fashion.

By noon the kitchen was sparkling clean and hopefully virus free. Since it would have been too much of a hassle to stop for dinner, we all agreed to keep going until mid-afternoon and then eat before it got dark. I set out a note for Adam, along with some home canned chicken, homemade sauerkraut and potatoes for roasting. He fired up the barbeque and had everything ready for us at the same time we were getting too tired and hungry to continue with the house cleaning. This time we brought place settings from the house and had a more civilized meal than we were able to arrange that morning.

"Good news," Adam informed everyone during our meal. "I found a small, gas- powered generator in the tool shed. It should be powerful enough to handle one or two appliances at a time. If someone gives me a hand to carry it, I'll splice it into the electrical box first thing in the morning."

"That's wonderful, Adam," I said. "We can use it to wash the bed covers in the morning. What else did you find?"

"I checked all the levels in the farm fuel tanks. We're in real good shape for the winter. The heating fuel looks like it was just filled and we must have at least two-hundred and fifty gallons of gasoline. The diesel tank for the tractor is about three-quarters full, but we shouldn't need that until spring."

"By spring we should start heading south to move to a warmer climate," the captain announced.

"But that's right about the time we'll be expecting our babies," I protested.

"I like this place. I think we should stay here," Adam stated.

"We'll discuss it when the time comes." The captain sidestepped the issue.

"I don't suppose that little generator will run the kitchen stove?" I decided to switch back to a safer topic.

"No, sorry." Adam shook his head.

"What are we going to cook on then? We're going to run out of propane within a week." This was a problem I had been wondering about for most of the day.

"I found an old wood-fired cook stove in one of the abandoned granaries. It's rusty and covered in bird shit, but I'm sure we could get it working again with a little elbow grease. And there's lots of wood in the shelter belt surrounding the farmyard."

"As soon as we get the house finished, we'll give you a hand with the stove," the captain said. "We'll have this place shipshape in no time."

"I find it fascinating that people still live like this," Frankie admitted. "It's kind of neat, the way they were so self-sufficient."

"Farm families are usually very resourceful people," I said. "They have to be in order to survive."

"Isn't it lucky for us that they were industrious enough to provide us with all these great things?" Helena pointed out. "By the way, Adam, this is an awesome supper you cooked for us this evening."

We were all quick to praise Adam's culinary efforts. Lately, he had become a very handy guy to have around. He even built us a provisional His and Hers bathroom facility out of aptly stacked bales, in one of the mangers.

The dishes were put in a pile until morning and we were all in favour of going to bed as soon as possible. We had been busy all day and the additional gravitational pull of earth was taking its toll on all of us. Our weights had more than doubled in comparison to that on board the station. The pre-bedtime chatter was kept to a minimum and we were all asleep within a few minutes.

The next morning Adam got the generator hooked up to the electrical system as he promised. The men hauled water from the barn, heated it and carried it downstairs, so that the girls could do the washing. They also lugged the wet clothes up the stairs and hung them outside on the line to dry. We had an inside team that still wore their space suits and an outside team that were free to dress normally. Adam put his suit back on, so that he could explore for a spot to put the wood stove. He ended up finding a patch in the plaster where the chimney was hidden in the wall. It was an indication that the stove pipe had entered there in the past. Adam's next step was to knock a hole in the wall where the patch had been. He was happy to discover that the stove could easily be re-attached and went back outside to look for all the proper hardware. Luckily, everything we needed was still with the stove.

By that afternoon we had all the clothing and bed linens washed and hung outside. The rest of the house had been washed and disinfected by the time we were ready for supper. When all the others had gone outside, I started spraying down the interior one last time. I started in the basement; worked my way upstairs and systematically covered the entire house before I closed the door. There was nothing more we could do. We had all decided to take the gamble and hope that the Grim Reaper had left the building.

Everyone was waiting for me at our hay-bale table when I got back to the barn. Adam had our meal already prepared when I arrived. He was featuring potatoes, carrots and onions roasted in a foil bag. It was all devoured within minutes.

"Tomorrow morning, we can have breakfast in our new home," I announced to everyone's delight.

"I ground up some corn meal this afternoon," Adam said with pride. "We can boil it up to make mush."

INTERVENTION

We all applauded Adam's efforts, but Captain Dick squirmed in his seat. He seemed to be jealous of all the accolades Adam was receiving lately. His hand reached out and touched my hand gun, stroking it in a display of appreciation. He was now in the habit of setting the gun beside his plate as a show of authority. I wished that I had quick hands so I could rip it from his grasp.

• — •

The next morning, Adam was up early again in hopes of being able to start the furnace. With luck, the furnace's fan was well within the generator's capabilities and we were all delighted to have a warm home to move into. It was a great comfort to us all to be able to sit around a nice table, in our warm new home and dine on a delicious breakfast of coffee, fried eggs and corn meal mush. Since everyone seemed so happy and content, I was surprised when Helena started to cry.

"I'm sorry," she said between her sobs. "I feel happy and sad all at the same time. I just let my emotions get the best of me, that's all."

Most of us knew exactly how she was feeling. We had come far since our lowest point, but we had given up so much along the way; and there would be many more obstacles for us to cross in the years that lay ahead.

"I think we could all use a day off," Adam suggested. "Why don't we just kick back and goof off for the rest of the day?"

There was no argument from the rest of the group. Some of the teens had a nap in a real bed and some played with a deck of cards that we had painstakingly disinfected. By noon everyone was restless again and ready to get back to work. Captain Dick went for a walk to check out the SSTO vehicle and the rest of us decided to tackle the wood stove. It was a huge cast iron monstrosity that took eight of us to carry into the farmer's machine shop. We used sandpaper and steel wool to clean up the cooking surfaces and the oven. By evening we had a serviceable kitchen stove.

On our way back to the house, we discovered that Captain Dick was returning from his excursion to the space ship. He was carrying a long, familiar looking object that captured our curiosity. We decided to wait until he caught up to us before going back to the house. As he edged closer, we realized he was carrying a soot-covered, aluminium baseball bat.

"Where the hell did you find that?" I asked as soon as he was within ear shot.

"It was in the things that NASA sent for us," Adam admitted. "I packed it myself."

"Only a bunch of Americans would consider a baseball bat as an essential piece of survival gear," the captain joked, making fun of our heritage. "Unfortunately, it's the only thing I found that didn't burn up in the fire."

"That's a real shame." I did not know what else to say. I turned and motioned for everyone else to follow.

We had a simple supper of fried, leftover corn meal mush, drizzled with maple syrup. After the dishes were washed, we discussed the sleeping arrangements. Captain Dick volunteered to take the couch and Adam and I decided to sleep in the spare bedroom downstairs. That would leave one bedroom for the boys and one for the girls. They would either have to sleep three in a bed or take turns having one person sleep on the floor.

Adam's intentions were very transparent when we finally got into bed. He cuddled in close and started touching me in places that made me feel uncomfortable. I squirmed away and gently slapped his hand.

"Not tonight, okay."

"When then?" he asked in frustration.

"I'm not sure. Whenever I feel more comfortable about it."

"Do you honestly think that's ever going to happen?" He sounded bitter.

"You knew going in, this relationship was not going to be easy."

"We could have the captain marry us first thing in the morning."

"That's not the problem and you know it."

"Shit," he said before rolling over and going to sleep.

Chapter Twenty-Two

"**WHAT KIND OF SHOT ARE** you with that gun of yours, Richard?" Adam asked the captain at breakfast the next morning.

"That's Captain Dick to you," he said almost choking on his eggs.

"Things have changed. The way I see it, we're all on the same level playing field," Adam insisted, pointing his fork at the captain to drive home his point of view. "I should be able to address you as an equal."

"That's horse shit! I'm still in charge here and don't you forget it."

"Well Captain, heaven forbid that I should ever damage your sensitive ego," Adam said in bold defiance.

"Listen here you son of a bitch!" The captain grabbed the handgun from beside his plate and jumped to his feet. "You had better show me some respect, or I'll show you what kind of shot I am with this here gun."

The girls screamed and scrambled from the table. I made an effort to keep the peace. "Captain, for shit sake put the gun away and act your age. You two are acting like a couple of four-year-olds."

Surprisingly, the captain set down his gun timidly and went back to eating his meal.

"I was just curious if he knew how to shoot," Adam said in his own defence, not willing to let the issue die. "I saw a cow and calf out in the trees this morning. I was wondering if the captain would be able to hit one at about fifty yards or so."

"I'm pretty sure I could hit one." The captain was getting a little less feisty, now that he had visions of fresh veal steaks on his mind.

"I've seen Candy hit a skunk at fifty yards with that same forty-five." Adam informed the captain.

"I'm the one with the gun," he insisted. "I'll take a crack at the calf after we're done eating."

"It's a nice day," Adam stated. "I think I can start the tractor so we can lift the carcass."

―――•―――

I watched out the window as the captain and Adam approached the cattle that were hiding in the shelter of the trees. The captain raised the handgun and carefully aimed. His hand kicked back and smoke burst from the muzzle a second before I heard the shot. The cattle bolted sideways then turned and looked back at the two hunters. They were accustomed to being around people; it should have been as easy as shooting fish in a barrel. Adam was waving for the captain to get closer. He was about thirty yards away when he took his second shot. The calf jumped straight up in the air and then headed for open country. It fell dead before it reached the edge of the yard. Adam and the captain ran to the downed animal as quickly as they could. At its side, Adam started waving his arms and prancing around with agitation. He seemed to be angry with the captain, because he kicked the ground and then stomped off to get the tractor.

"You boys had better get dressed and get out there before they kill each other." I said jokingly. "They're surely going to need a hand with the carcass."

While Adam was starting the tractor, the captain started to eviscerate the calf. By the time he had made an incision up to the animal's brisket he had to turn away and throw up.

When Adam and the boys returned with the tractor, he tied the calf's hind feet to the bucket of the front-end loader and raised it up. That made it easier to finish the gutting, skinning and butchering. It took most of the day to get the carcass ready for hanging. They hoisted it up in the machine shed to age and to keep any predators from stealing our meat. The flesh would have to cool down before it would be suitable for us to eat.

"He gut shot the son of a bitch," Adam said with disgust when he came through the door.

"That's what took you so long," "I noted.

"I think I liked it better when I didn't know where my food came from," Frankie said.

"Frankie just about lost his cookies when he saw all that blood and guts," Randy was quick to point out.

"If nothing else, this situation should give you a better appreciation of what it takes to put food on the table." I was not surprised that the slaughtering process had made the boys a little squeamish. They would soon find out that farm life was not an easy one.

The captain was the last one to return to the house. He was quiet all through supper. Then he sat by himself in the living room and polished his baseball bat. Adam apologized for the distraction and promised to install the kitchen stove first thing in the morning. That night we were able to have one small light on besides running the furnace. We were able to stay up a few hours after dark and play cards before we had to shut down the generator. While we were sitting around the table, the boys took pride in explaining to the girls, every gory detail that happened that afternoon.

We were all excited to have fresh meat roasted in a wood stove as soon as Adam could make it happen. He promised to have the stove installed as soon as he could.

The next morning Adam had the generator started and the house warm before he came to wake the rest of us. He made sure we were all out of bed in good time, because he wanted to get an early start with the wood stove. Even though it was earlier than most of us would have liked, it was a real treat being able to dress in comfort.

We carried the stove into the house before we did anything else. The girls and I made breakfast while Adam and the boys went back out for the stove pipes and tools. The captain was content to sit at the kitchen table, sip coffee and recondition his baseball bat while everyone else went about their business. That afternoon he lounged on the couch while Adam installed the stove. It was fairly clear that Adam was quickly becoming the most valuable member of our team, with his stock rising bullishly. The captain's stock, however, had been in a precipitous curve downward ever since we landed back on earth. He was noticeably dissatisfied with his situation and his animosity heightened as the merit gap between him and his nemesis widened. Adam was in his niche; but conversely, the captain was like a fish out of water.

The installation of the stove was completed in time to prepare a late supper. The teens had been gathering deadfall from our wood lot ever since the morning meal. They had at least a week's supply stacked in a wood pile beside the house before they stopped for the day. Much to our disappointment, the stove stunk so badly when we first started the fire, we had to postpone using it for cooking until it had become seasoned and the harsh fumes had been burnt off.

Adam saved the day, however, by cooking our meal outside on the barbecue. The meal was wonderful. The roast was done to perfection and everyone was delighted to have the first fresh meat we had tasted in months. Each of us gorged ourselves so severely that we could hardly move when we left the table. We put off doing the dishes until morning, collapsing in the living room with conflicting feelings of misery and content.

•———•

In the days that followed, Adam was able to eke out a pleasant existence for us all, with only limited resources. The captain's inability to contribute to the group continued to reduce his self-worth. He seemed content to lie around the house all day, barking out demands for the others. Our patience for him was wearing thin.

The relationship dynamics were beginning to heat up on two out of three fronts. Blaine and Helena were becoming very close, but had not progressed beyond holding hands and snuggling on the couch. Randy and Nicole were at the opposite end of the dating spectrum: they could not keep their hands off each other. I had caught them making out on several occasions. Two weeks after we moved into the house, I walked in on them while they were making love downstairs in Adam's and my bed.

My first reaction was that of embarrassment, but my awkwardness soon turned to anger. Primarily, I was upset that they were having sex in the first place; my other complaint was that they were doing it in my bed.

"What's going on in here?" I asked, not knowing where to direct my eyes.

"Nicole and I were just expressing our love for each other." His jerky speech suggested his nervousness and inner turmoil.

"Good answer," I replied, unable to hold back a smile. His straightforward description had cracked me up. How could I be mad at two people that were so much in love and had nothing to lose by following through with their emotions? Nicole was already pregnant and they were totally devoted to each other. They had nothing to lose. I quickly realized that I should be happy for them and give them my blessing.

"I'm okay with what you're doing," I added. "Only next time, warn me when you decide to use my bedroom.

"Sorry," Nicole said. "It's the only private place in the house."

"Fine," I said, backing out of the room and laughing. "Continue expressing yourselves."

On the way up the stairs I thought, "why not have a wedding? Why not sanctify their union in the eyes of the Lord?"

That night at meal time I made the suggestion. Randy and Nicole thought it was a great idea and were enthusiastic about being married at as soon as possible. My idea captured Adam's imagination as well. He expressed that he and I should make it a double wedding. I was hesitant to agree, because I knew that Adam was primarily looking ahead to the wedding night. It was against my better judgement, but in the end, I caved in due to pressure from the others. After supper, while Adam and I were doing the dishes, I dispelled any intentions he might have had about our honeymoon.

"Adam, I love you and I will happily agree to marry you, but you need to know that I do not plan on consummating our marriage any day soon."

"Rock, you know that you owe it to society to eventually have sex with me and have my child. What's the sense in putting off the inevitable?"

"I don't know. I can't explain why I feel this way. All I know is, I just want to wait until after I have this child. Then I promise that things will be different. I will surrender to you willingly."

"If you feel that strongly, I suppose I can accept those conditions." He put down his dish cloth and gave me a big hug. "But I've had second thoughts about the whole double wedding thing. It wouldn't be fair to steal those young love birds' thunder. Why don't we get married another day, so we can give up our downstairs bedroom for their special night?"

I was in total agreement. Adam and I decided to put off our wedding plans for several days. While we were postponing our own nuptials, I remembered an old wedding dress that had been hanging in the closet. We had washed it as a preventative measure before we had moved into the house. We had also laundered a man's suit. It was grossly out of style, but would be far more appropriate than the orange NASA-issue flight suit that made up Randy's entire wardrobe.

Randy and Nicole's wedding was just what we needed to break the everyday monotony of a Midwestern winter. I was asked to be the maid of honour, but declined for obvious reasons. My phoney justification being that I was obliged to prepare the celebratory feast. As it turned out, Frankie and Eve Anna stood up at the wedding. Adam gave Nicole away and the captain begrudgingly performed a Christian ceremony. Randy and Nicole made a beautiful couple and the whole service could not have been more special.

The wedding supper I provided was also a huge success; everyone raved about my dumplings and gravy. After the meal we had a small dance, liquor from the root cellar being provided for the boys. We had to dance by candle light and turn down the thermostat, so that the generator could handle the stereo. The married couple got the dance under way; then, in adherence to custom, the best man and maid of honour shared the floor.

Eve Anna seemed distracted during the dance and noticeably avoided eye contact with her partner. Frankie turned out to be very smooth on his feet and made every effort to make the experience an enjoyable one for Eve Anna. I could see that he was trying hard to strike up a conversation, but Eve Anna was reluctant to reciprocate. After my obligatory dance with Adam, I singled out Frankie in an effort to boost his spirits. I also had a hidden agenda.

"How are things going with you and Eve Anna?" I whispered in his ear.

"I'm glad you asked," Frankie sighed. "What am I doing wrong? Every time I try and get close to her, I strike out."

"Don't blame yourself." I looked to make sure Eve Anna was not listening. "Just be patient. I'm sure she'll warm up to you eventually."

"I sure hope you're right."

"Relax, Nicole and Helena have eliminated your only competition."

"I'm not so sure." His eyes met mine in a suggestive glance.

"Surely you don't mean the captain," I said in disgust after doing the math.

"Of course not. I give her a lot more credit than that."

"Then who are... ?"

"Just forget about the whole thing," he interrupted. "I like Eve Anna a lot and she is my only hope for a mate. I'm not giving up for lack of trying."

"Let's crank this party up a bit," Adam shouted from across the room. He popped a livelier tune into the entertainment centre, which set the mood for dancing in a group. Since there were no set partners for this style of dancing, everyone including the captain was able to participate. We danced this way, for all we were worth, until the generator ran out of gas. That is when we noticed Nicole and Randy were no longer upstairs. The guys had one more drink to toast the wedding couples' night together and then retired for the evening. I slept in the girl's room and Adam with the boys. I thought it would be nice for the newlyweds if we used this sleeping arrangement at least once a week. Of course, they could always sneak downstairs in the middle of the day. I was envious of their situation. They were desperately in love and able to act upon their out-of-control sexual desires without fear of shame and degradation.

•———•

The next day Blaine and Helena surprised everyone by announcing their engagement. Sometime the previous evening—with the excitement of Randy and Nicole's wedding and a few drinks for fortification—Blaine got up the nerve to pop the question. We were all very happy that they had taken the plunge.

"We're not going to get married right away," Helena announced. "I would like to wait until just before the baby is born. Blaine and I need more time to get to know one another."

We all approved of their decision.

After lunch it was customary for the kids to leave the house and go for a walk or pick firewood. Today I strategically asked Eve Anna to stay behind to help me with the dishes.

"Eve Anna, don't you like Frankie?"

"I like him fine. What gave you the idea I didn't?" She seemed uncomfortable with my question.

"He's trying so hard to win your heart and you don't seem very receptive."

"I don't see what's the rush."

"Even if you gave him the tiniest bit of encouragement."

"It's my life; let me live it as I see fit."

"Fine, why don't you run along outside and join the others." I decided to leave well enough alone.

INTERVENTION

As soon as Eve Anna slammed the door behind her, Captain Dick staggered into the kitchen. He had a wine bottle in his hand and roguish twinkle in his eye.

"Ah," he said with a contented grin. "We're alone at last."

"Don't get any funny ideas." I voiced my opposition strongly and started for the door.

The captain hurried to cut me off, but stumbled and fell because of his drunkenness. As his body lunged forward, he clipped me from behind and threw me to the floor. I struggled to get away, but he had hold of my legs. Even though I thrashed about wildly and screamed like a rabbit in a trap, it was easy for the captain to pin me down. He was at least twice my size and as strong as a rampant bull.

"Relax, Honey. This won't hurt a bit."

My arms were buried under his and rendered useless. He reeked of hot, stale sweat and cheap wine. It was agonizing to be so defenceless, knowing he was about to force his slobbering lips on mine. I tried to collect a good wad of saliva in my mouth and then spit in his face when he tried to come near. He only laughed devilishly, as the dribble ran down his face. Then his lips pounced once more towards mine.

"Get away from me, you bastard!" I screamed helplessly, as I turned my face sideways to shun him.

I was filled with nausea when his lips unavoidably met mine. I wanted to vomit in his face, but could only manage another smothered scream while on my back. My calls were muffled by his dry lips and stubbly cheeks. I choked on his fowl breath, that reeked of yeast and sour grapes. Then he raised himself briefly in order to rip open my blouse. While he was occupied with this, my left arm came free just long enough to strike him across his chin with my fist.

"You're a feisty little bitch, aren't you?" he said, quickly restraining my free hand and dropping his head towards my chest. I writhed and quivered beneath him as he rooted like a hog at my breasts.

Then there was a loud crack as the front door burst open and Adam charged into the room.

"Get you're stinking hands off her, you filthy bastard!" Adam yelled, kicking him in the guts.

The captain groaned in agony and rolled off to the side. I scrambled backwards on my hands and feet to distance myself from my attacker. Adam lunged at the captain again; but, to my horror, the brute was able to recover in time to draw his gun. I tried to scream, but my efforts were drowned out by a deafening concussion. I was splattered with blood as the speeding bullet cut through Adam's leg like a chainsaw through Jell-O.

When the smoke cleared, Adam was moaning and squirming convulsively on the floor. The ominous silhouette of the captain stood over him; his hands and my gun quivering at the sight of his dastardly misdeed.

"Now look what you've done, you crazy son of a bitch!" I hurried to Adam's side. My guts heaved when I saw the gruesome extent of his wound. A good chunk of his right thigh had been blown away.

"Help me get him up on the table," I demanded in a tone that would not tolerate no for an answer.

The children dashed into the room excitedly. They had heard the gunshot and were legitimately concerned for our well-being. They were naturally shocked and appalled when it was clear what the captain had done. The boys helped hoist Adam atop the table, while I did up my blouse on the way to the cupboard to find a knife.

"It was his own fault," the captain insisted for his own benefit; jabbering quietly to himself at the edge of the table and nervously prancing from side to side. "He shouldn't have come at me. It was in self-defence."

"Shut up, asshole," I said while slowly cutting off Adam's pants. "If you hadn't tried to rape me none of this would have happened."

The others gasped in disgust when they heard the truth, forcing the captain to retreat to the living room to remove himself from their reproachful stares. He still had my gun hanging loosely at his side when he escaped our view.

Adam's leg was a ghastly mess. Luckily the bullet had not hit any major arteries. We stopped the bleeding and cleaned the wound up as best we could. I bandaged his hip with a ripped sheet that we had doused in disinfectant.

"How bad is it, Rock?" His face was as white as snow and his eyes moist with tears.

"It could have been a lot worse. Luckily for you the captain's a lousy shot."

"Will I be able to walk again?"

"If we can keep your leg from getting infected, you'll be able to dance at our wedding."

"What about you? Did he hurt you?" He reached out to take my hand.

"No, I'm fine. Just a little grossed out, that's all. Nothing some strong soap and a good mouthwash can't fix." I forced out a laugh to put Adam more at ease.

"Well, I'm just glad I got here when I did."

"Not half as glad as I am." I bent over and gave him a big hug of appreciation.

"Adam can have our bed." Frankie volunteered. "We can sleep in the basement."

"Thanks boys. Help me get him settled then."

I hardly got a wink of sleep that night because Adam was tossing and turning in pain, and I was haunted by the memories of Captain Psycho's traumatizing attack. The captain's ambition of robbing me of my virginity had come frighteningly too close for comfort.

Chapter Twenty-Three

"CANDY, COME INTO THE BATHROOM, quick." Eve Anna's distress was unmistakeable.

"What on earth's the matter?" I asked, dashing into the room.

"Is that what I think it is?" She pointed a shivering finger towards the toilet with a look of sheer terror in her eyes.

I examined the contents of the bowl and was struck with remorse when I realized what was inside. I reached out and took Eve Anna into my arms and held her close. We both shed many tears over the loss of her child. She felt like a fallen angel, standing half naked against me and quivering in my arms. Her breasts were noticeably larger, pressing firmly against mine. I kissed her forehead and I kissed her cheeks in hopes of showing her how much I cared. I kissed the tears away from her eyes until my thoughts strayed away to places that men fear to admit exist. I had to pull away before I reached the point of no return.

"Don't take this to heart, Eve Anna. It's not uncommon for this sort of thing to happen," I said holding her by the shoulders at arm's length.

"But I was so looking forward to having a baby."

"You're young. You'll have more babies than me before you're done."

"I never thought of it that way." She seemed to be regaining her spirits.

"We'll get you pregnant again as soon as possible."

"But it won't be so impersonal this time. I'll have to actually *do it* with a man."

"And the problem with that is... ?"

"Oh, I'm ready and willing. But Adam is hurt. I'd feel uncomfortable doing it with anyone else."

"Frankie will be crushed if you don't ask him."

"He doesn't have to know. I'll feel a lot more comfortable about sex when our relationship has had a chance to develop."

"I'll talk to Adam when the time is right. If you are careful, I'm sure he can make it happen. There's more than one way to skin a cat you know."

I backed out of the bathroom and went to see Adam. Eve Anna had called me out of bed before I was able to check on him. First, I talked to him about Eve Anna's request and then I directed my focus to his leg. When I removed the bandage, the area around the wound was red and sore. I sterilized another length of sheet and changed the dressing. I cursed the fact that we had lost all our medical supplies in the fire. If he did not get some kind of antibiotic quickly, he was sure to get an infection. I made up my mind to take immediate action before the situation became critical.

"Adam, I'm going to have to go away for a while." I announced in a casual manner, so as not to alarm him.

"What for?"

"You're going to need some antibiotics. I have to see if I can find some."

"Couldn't you send the captain? He's just dead weight around here anyway."

"Think about it Adam. He'd bring back strychnine if he thought it was for you."

"You're right, the bastard can't be trusted. But you will be careful, won't you?"

"Don't worry; I can look after myself." I bent over and gave him a long lingering kiss as if it was our last. "I'll see you in a few days."

I started putting together a survival kit right away. I found a small backpack that a student would have used to carry books to school and filled it with my provisions. I took a hunting knife, a flashlight, matches, some canned goods and last nights' homemade biscuits. I was also lucky enough to find some particle masks that the farmer had used for handling dusty grain. I had to dress warmly because I was unsure of how far I would have to walk before I reached a town large enough to have a pharmacy. I found winter boots that were two sizes too big, but I was able to make use of them by wearing three pairs of socks. All the other winter clothing that I found was baggy on me. It was a relief to no longer be a slave to fashion. I was warm and comfortable; that is all that was important.

I gave the captain an ultimatum to behave himself while I was away and said my goodbyes to the others. Eve Anna was upset that I was leaving her so soon after her miscarriage.

"Get dressed. You can walk the first couple miles with me," I insisted. She was quick to obey.

The road that intersected with the farmer's lane headed east and west. Since the Rocky Mountains were to the west, I headed east. The road seemed to stretch out forever towards the flat horizon. It was an ominous and intimidating picture that gave no hint of what lay ahead, or of the distances I would have to travel.

"Did you talk to Adam?" she asked, trudging through the newly fallen snow.

"Yes, but you should at least wait until you have your first period before trying to get pregnant again. I'll be back long before then."

"What about Captain Dick? What if he goes berserk again?"

"Never leave him alone and always make sure there's at least one boy with every girl. Frankie's a big guy. He'll be glad to protect you."

"I'd feel safer if you were there."

"And keep the captain away from the booze. He was harmless until he got bent out of shape on homemade wine."

"I'm going to miss you." She stopped walking and waited for me to turn around. She had tears in her eyes and was self-consciously slapping her hands together.

I told her I would miss her as well, and gave her a big hug. It was not very gratifying with all the winter clothing in the way. I insisted that the miscarriage was not her fault and that there was nothing she could have done. I also reminded her that most women experience at least one lost pregnancy in their lifetime.

Because I sensed that it was too emotionally painful for Eve Anna to carry on, I turned my back to her and continued on my journey. I walked a quarter mile before I looked behind me. She was still standing on the same spot, waving good-bye. Now it was my turn to cry.

After walking for about a mile and a half, I came across a snow covered pickup parked in the middle of the road. I stepped around to the driver's side window and swept the snow away with my sleeve. There was a partially freeze-dried body inside the cab. Even though I was prepared for the worst, the spectre behind the wheel gave me a considerable start. Luckily this ghastly image was partially shrouded by the fur lined hood of its parka. I put on one of my particle masks and opened the door to the truck. It took all the courage I could muster to pull the rigid body out of the seat and drag it into the ditch. There was another body crumpled up next to the first, but I wanted to see if the truck would start before it had to be disturbed. It felt creepy sliding onto the seat next to the body in order to see if the engine would start. Unfortunately, the battery was dead. I slammed the door shut and moved on to the next vehicle. It was a car that was just two hundred feet ahead.

I opened the door, grabbed the frozen shell of a body from within and tossed it out onto the ground. I was careful not to have to look the body in the face. Luck was not with me, because the car was a fuel-cell powered unit that was out of hydrogen. I went through ten vehicles and traveled five miles before I found one that would run. It was a full-sized Chevy that was three-quarters full of gas; the only problem was, it was full of dead people. I struggled for fifteen minutes and sacrificed my breakfast before I had everyone out of the car. The smell of death was so bad inside the car I had to drive with my head stuck out the open window like an old-style, railroad engineer. The first junction I came to read: "Dodge City, fifteen miles". I turned and headed for Dodge.

The closer I got to the city the more trouble I had navigating the highways. Every lane was littered with derelict vehicles. About half a mile from the city I had to abandon my death car and strike out on foot. I had to squeeze past hundreds of coffins on wheels that were standing bumper to bumper.

When I reached the outskirts of town, I stopped at a small motel and looked for a place to spend the night. It was already becoming very late in the day. I went into the office and helped myself to all the keys that were hung on a numbered board. I was able to use the first room I tried. Apparently, there was not much call for motel accommodation towards the end. I took off my boots and my backpack so I could crawl into bed. I was chilled to the bone and too tired to get undressed. I removed my mask and drifted off to sleep. There was no way of preventing some element of exposure to the virus if it was still viable. I decided to wear the mask only when I was around dead bodies; everything else would have to be an unavoidable risk.

The next morning, I awoke to the sound of water running off the roof. The temperature had risen considerably overnight and the sun was shining brilliantly. A lot of the snow that was on the ground had already melted away. I removed a can of stew from my backpack, opened it with my knife and had breakfast. I was not looking forward to my mission for the day. I went to the bathroom two doors down, because I had planned on returning to the same room. Since the toilets were no longer working, I did not want to soil my own nest.

Because it was such a glorious day, I was able to venture out with only my NASA jumpsuit and winter underwear. The streets were clogged with vehicles, but the sidewalks were navigable. I only had to step around five bodies within two blocks. My first point of interest was a small convenience store and gas station. Several of the windows were knocked out and the front door was open. I was disappointed to see that nothing of value was left behind; the shelves had been stripped bare.

Two doors down, there was a hardware store. There was still plenty of merchandise left behind, but everything that had not been stolen got tossed on the floors or smashed by vandals. I found no survival equipment, no bottled water and no disinfectants. I did find a carpenter's gooseneck pry bar, that I claimed for my own. I thought I might need it to force open doors and medicine cabinets.

I walked for another six blocks before I came across a drug store. The insides had been totally decimated. Nothing that resembled a drug had been overlooked. I cursed at the top of my lungs and kicked the rubble at my feet. I was becoming very worried that my mission was bound for failure. I did not want to fail Adam by returning empty handed.

"Failure is not an option." I exercised the luxury of being able to talk to myself out loud without anyone else hearing.

I walked all day and only found three drugstores, but the number did not matter; if I had found twenty, they would have all been in the same barren condition. Every business in town had been affected by the aftermath of a society gone mad. I had to return to my motel room with nothing to show for my efforts. Before going to sleep, I placed the room's ice bucket under the rain gutter to catch some melt water. In the morning I would be able to wash up and fill my canteen.

The weather on my second day in the city was even nicer than the first. The only visible snow was in drifts on the north side of buildings. My assignment for today was finding a hospital. That was my next available option, because all the drugstores in town seemed to have been wiped clean.

I did not find the hospital until the sun was at its zenith. When I stepped onto the grounds, a chilling scene lay before me. Partly concealed in the overgrown lawn grass were many desiccated, taught-skinned shells of what were once human beings. Their twisted forms were set permanently, indicating the position in which they took their last torturous breath. Most had assumed the fetal position. The skin on their faces was shrunk by the sun and the cold. As the flesh around the lips contracted, the tension drew them apart exposing the teeth—forcing a wide smile, that came laughing from the depths of hell.

All the vegetation within two feet of the decaying remains was not the usual brown of winter dormancy, but was charred black with death, as if sprayed with herbicide. Apparently, the rotting human flesh was toxic to the plants and was responsible for their seemingly sympathetic demise.

The stench of death was overpowering. I gagged repeatedly when I saw that maggots had punched holes in the leathery hide and black, pointy-tailed beetles lay quiescent in the sockets where crying eyes had once been.

I suddenly got the impression that the body closest to me was grimacing, "Why?" It shook me to the core. They were obviously hospital patients that had been abandoned towards the end and had crawled out onto the front lawn, crying for help and for the mercy of God.

Gaining entrance to the hospital was only a matter of walking through the front door. The atmosphere within those dank walls was more like a morgue than that of a place of healing. The furore of death was everywhere. I removed the flashlight from my backpack and followed the signs to the dispensary. The total drug inventory had been pilfered from the storage shelves. I fell back against the pharmacy walls and slid down it helplessly into a crouch of anger and self-pity.

"Now what the hell am I supposed to do?" My words echoed through the emptiness. I reminded myself that failure was not an option. I would not go back without Adam's medication. Then I had a thought that made me want to holler, "Eureka". The pills I was looking for did not just disappear in a cloud of smoke; they were being transported out of town in the trunks and dash compartments of all those vehicles that were stuck in traffic.

Since most of the cars on the road were abandoned or had the driver die at the wheel, all I had to do was remove the keys from the ignition and help myself to the contents of the trunk. The first car I inspected had a case of bottled water and some groceries. I stuffed two litres of water into my pack and then found some baker's yeast and a can of baking soda. These would be invaluable for baking breads when I got back home.

My spirits were lifted as I went from car to car. I was finding all sorts of wonderful things that were encouraging to me. I knew it was only a matter of time before I found my drug of choice.

My next great discovery was behind the seat of a dilapidated old pickup truck. My eyes just about popped out of their sockets when I hinged the back of the seat forward. I had uncovered an antique SKS assault rifle and a 500-round case of 7.62x39 ammunition. I had hit the jackpot! This one little discovery would shift the balance of power. My fingers scrambled to load the thirty-shot magazine and close the breach. I then fired the entire contents of the magazine into the back of the car in front of me as fast as humanly possible. I was now standing with the biggest grin on my face since my return to earth. I felt empowered and ready to even the score. I reloaded the magazine and packed away one hundred additional rounds.

The next vehicle I inspected conjured up a broad range of emotions. To my delight, the trunk was a treasure chest of pharmaceuticals. I filled my pack with several broad-spectrum antibiotics, acetaminophen, codeine, cough syrup and many more useful drugs. There were also medical disinfectants, sterile dressings, pre-packaged scalpels, sutures, and other surgical instruments. But, the disturbing content of the car was that of the driver. Her throat had been slit and her pants pulled down to reveal a ghastly sight that almost made me lose my lunch. The poor woman had been killed and slaughtered for the meat on her behind. There were two large chunks of flesh carved from her buttocks. She had been a collateral victim of the Grim Reaper's brief reign of death. My fellow man had stooped to one of the lowest points in his lengthy history. It was an image I would not soon forget.

Now that I had reached my goal of attaining Adam's medication, I was anxious to return home, but there were a few other necessities that I needed to acquire. Since a half-ton truck would be the most suitable for hauling a large amount of goods, I tried to find one full of gas close to the end of the traffic pile-up. I was fortunate to find one about ten cars away from the open road.

INTERVENTION

Because I was afraid I might get stuck if I pulled down into the ditch, I cramped the wheels of the vehicle in front to the extreme right and pushed it off the road. My idea worked perfectly. One by one I emptied anything of value out of the next car's trunk and then forced it into the ditch. By the time I had broken free of derelict vehicles, I had a truck box full of items that were key to our survival. And the best part was that this truck had not served as someone's last resting place. I could roll up the window and cruise home with the heater running. The interior was as fresh as the day it was built.

It was dark by the time I was able to get out onto the highway, but I was determined to get back as soon as I could manage. The longer Adam went without antibiotics, the greater his chances for a severe infection. Even though I had to drive slowly in order to avoid the many cars littering the road, I was still home within a few hours.

I coasted the last few feet of the driveway with the engine off, so as not to disturb everyone in the house. The generator had been shut down for the night and everyone was surely in their beds. I walked around to that part of the house where the girl's room was situated and knocked at the window. As soon as someone started opening the window, I jumped back several steps.

"Eve Anna, is that you?" I whispered in the darkness.

"Candy, I'm so glad you're back." She stuck her entire upper body through the window with her arms stretched out towards me. Her invitation for an embrace was a sweet temptation that was difficult to decline.

"I'm sorry. I can't come near you. There's a slim chance I might be infected."

"Where will you sleep tonight?" she asked, dropping her outstretched arms in disappointment.

"How's Adam?" I changed the conversation to a subject more important to me.

"Not great, I'm afraid. I've changed his dressing twice a day, but his wound is starting to smell funny and is oozing pus."

"How does he feel?"

"He seems to be in good spirits, but I'm sure he's worried about his leg."

"Okay, listen carefully. I'm going to leave some disinfectant, some sterile dressings and some antibiotics on the front step. Wipe the packages with that spray disinfectant that we keep under the kitchen sink and then scrub your hands thoroughly before opening them. Wake Adam and give him four pills now, and two every six hours after that. Cleanse his wound with the special disinfectant and then apply one of the sterile dressings. I'll talk to you again in the morning."

"Will you be sleeping in the barn then?"

"Yes, good night, Eve Anna."

I took my rifle, my back pack and a sleeping bag out of the back of the truck and headed for the barn. I was dead tired and hoping I would be able to get right to sleep. I had a lot of things on my mind and did not want to be distracted by them. Luckily, I drifted off shortly after making myself comfortable in the loft. The sound of Eve Anna's angelic voice woke me up the following morning.

"Candy, I left some food on our old straw table for your breakfast. You might want to get up while it's still hot."

"I'll be right down. Thanks for thinking of me." I was out of my bed roll in a flash, because I was starving. I was looking forward to a warm meal instead of something ice cold that came straight from the can. I was also anxious to see if there was any change in Adam's condition.

I was served a hearty meal of veal steak, eggs and corn meal mush. I was also treated to a cup of fresh brewed coffee. It was a breakfast fit for a king. I said a little prayer to thank God for all our blessings and to ask Him to help heal Adam's wound. As soon as I felt ready, I picked up my gun, slung it over my shoulder, and strode off to the house. I wanted Captain Dick to see that I was in possession of a weapon.

"Hello in the house," I hollered at about twenty feet from the front step.

Everyone was out on the deck in short order. They were all smiles and happy to see me. Captain Dick, however, was wearing a big frown that quickly transformed into a belligerent scowl when he noticed I was carrying a firearm. The look of stunned disbelief on his face was unforgettable. I am not sure what he was thinking, but his frustration and hostility were as clear as the pointy nose on his face. We all said our greetings; then I continued directly to the focus of my concern.

"How is Adam this morning?" I looked straight at the captain as I spoke. I wanted him to feel uncomfortable. I wanted him to feel judged as he squirmed in the mire of his own guilt.

"Worse," Eve Anna said in a timid voice, her troubled emotions were marked by a flood of tears. "I can see the infection working up the veins in his leg."

My heart seemed to stop when I heard the news. I wanted to rush into his room and somehow make him better. I had to gather all my will to keep my feet from running to his side. In the midst of all my internal confusion, I was able to recall an incident from my youth. I was scratched by a pet rabbit and contracted blood poisoning when I was about six years old. My mother cured me by applying hot compresses.

"Eve Anna, dry your eyes and pay attention." I continued when she appeared to be ready. "Put some water and some face cloths in a pot on the stove and boil it for fifteen minutes. Remove the cloths with some metal tongs, one at a time and allow them to cool only to the point where you can barely handle them without burning yourself. You have to place them on the infected area, as hot as Adam can stand. This is very important. Keep applying these hot compresses until all the poison has been drawn from his wound. Then apply some disinfectant and redress the injury. Do you think you can handle that?"

"I'll start right away. Pray that this works." Her sense of urgency toward the need for prayer was duly noted, but I had already put in a request on Adam's behalf.

I paced outside the house for half an hour before I heard the screams. I knew the pain from his leg was going to be unbearable. Adam cursed and growled to help fight the anguish. I felt badly that he was going through so much pain on my account. Part of me wished that I had made love to him when we had the chance, but a little voice inside was telling me to wait until after I had given birth to my baby. For some reason that I cannot explain, it was important to me to remain a virgin until after the baby's delivery.

I decided to go for a walk, because I did not want to listen to him suffer. I slung the rifle over my back and started walking towards the SSTO vehicle. When I was almost out of the yard, I heard the captain leave the house in a hurry and turned to see him walking briskly towards the machine shop. I assumed that his conscience was bothering him because it was his fault that Adam was ill and suffering.

When I arrived at the skeletal remains of the Orbiter, I was happy to discover several rabbits taking shelter within the framework. Five took off running at full speed, but I was lucky enough to bring down two before they were out of range. It seemed odd that the ship was still being of use to us. I tied my game around my belt and headed back to the farm. We could make hasenpfeffer for supper. I called Eve Anna to come outside upon my return.

INTERVENTION

"It seemed to go well," she assured me. "We had to keep the hot cloths coming for over an hour before I was convinced that we had drawn out all the poison. It was quite an ordeal for Adam. He was very brave, but the pain eventually wore him out. He's sleeping peacefully now."

"That sounds encouraging. Thanks for all you've done for him."

"I can't take any of the credit. It's only through your heroics that Adam still has a chance at life. Now I know why he calls you The Rock."

"I've never told you why he gave me that nickname, have I? It has nothing to do with me having any strong and resilient, rock-like qualities."

"I find that hard to believe."

"I was always his rock candy, nothing more."

"You will always be his rock-solid friend and he knows how big a sacrifice you've made to try and save his life. We had lots of time to talk while you were gone. He told me about your history together and how much you mean to him."

"I hope you are the only one he told."

"You know I can keep a secret," she said reaching out her hand. "Are those for supper?"

"Yes," I said throwing the brace of rabbits at her feet. "Sorry I didn't clean them. I was afraid of transferring viruses onto their moist flesh."

"I'll get one of the boys to do it. That should be good for a laugh." She picked up the mounds of fur, smiled sweetly and took leave of me with a wave.

Later that night she brought me my meal of rabbit stew. She was happy to say that Adam was awake and feeling much better. The news was the most delicious course on the menu. I was content to eat the remainder in solitude. It was going to be lonely, having to stay in the barn by myself for a while, but it was worth it to know that Adam might be on the mend.

The next morning Eve Anna brought a note of gratitude from Adam, along with breakfast. She left a pen so I could write on the back of the page. This is the contents of the letter I returned to him:

Dear Adam,

I had planned on sending you this note—that I have jotted down from memory—over ten years ago after our disagreement. Unfortunately, I never found the courage to mail it to you. Please accept this gift of love in the manner in which it was intended.

"Difficult Friendship"
It's hard for a man and a woman to be friends.
But if we were children again,
insulated from the harsh scrutiny of others,
our friendship could be unbridled.
The early years uncomplicated by sexual boundaries;
youthful innocence would protect us.
It would be just a boy and a girl,
embracing the shared treasure of kindred spirits.

Get well soon. All my love, your Rock Candy.

I went to bed that night with a deep sense of peace, knowing Adam had a good chance of survival. I slept soundly as if in a trance, until I was startled by someone slapping a large strip of duct tape across my mouth. The light from the full moon was streaming down from the loft window and outlining the menacing form of Captain Dick, who now had me pinned tightly inside my sleeping bag.

"Your precious Adam isn't going to come to your rescue this time, my little sweetheart."

I had to swallow my screams, that could not escape from my clogged mouth and wiggled helplessly inside my confining bed roll. The captain flipped me over like a hot dog in a bun, so that I was lying on my front and pinned me to the floor by sitting on my backside. He then unfastened my bag and grabbed hold of my flailing arms. I fought with all the strength I could manage, but my attacker was still able to tape my hands behind my back. Next, he unzipped my sleeping bag wide open and tossed me over onto my back, while ripping off my blouse in the same aggressive motion. I tried to dig my heels into the straw and squirm out from under him but his weight was just too much for me to bear.

"There's no sense fighting it, Honey. You're mine for the taking, so you might as well relax and go along for the ride."

For the first time in my life, I wanted to kill someone. There was that much hate and loathing in my soul. If there had been some way I could have stolen my gun from the captain, I would have shot him in the blink of an eye.

"Your nipples are so perky from the cold." He twisted at my breasts as if he was tuning a radio with his fingers. I tried to recoil from his touch, but there was nowhere to hide. Then he took his slobbery tongue and lapped at my chest. The moisture he left behind soon turned cold from the chill in the air, but my troubled mind would have preferred smouldering acid over his putrid spit. He mock drank of my bosom, like a thirsty lizard, for two eternities and then unfastened my pants.

"You won't be needing these." He raised himself to grab the cuffs of my jeans and then ripped them from my legs as if he was starting a lawnmower. I tried to sit up, but he forced me down with his foot. Then he held me down with one hand and removed my panties with the other. All the time I was trying to kick him in the head with no success. As a last resort I tried to soil myself in hopes of making my body offensive to him. Since I was either too cold or too frightened to perform that function, I tried sitting up again, but again the captain threw me to the floor.

"Lie still!" he shouted, slapping me across the face.

When I had recovered from the blow, he had his pants off. He was a large man. Every part of him was big. All I could think about was: "Oh my God, don't let him stick that thing in me!" Before I knew it, he was on top of me again trying to jam his leg between my knees; but I had them fused together with every ounce of strength I had remaining.

"Don't fight me or I'll cuff you again," the captain growled, his legs now between mine. He was ready to make his move.

But I was too frantic to heed his warnings. He boxed me senseless before I stopped resisting. Finally, there was no need to add more injury to my insult. My body went limp and I felt only numbness. The captain had triumphed over me again. My panic never stemmed from the fact that I was going to be raped; strangely, my greatest fear was losing my virginity. A little voice inside kept screaming for that part of me to be preserved until after the birth of my first child.

I stared blankly into my assailant's eyes, begging him with my tears to stop this atrocity. He only smiled sadistically and spit into his hand. He wiped his venom inside me and probed with his grimy fingers. A shiver of icy fear swept through my quivering body. I closed my eyes in dreaded anticipation as he fumbled to get inside me.

Suddenly, there was a loud, familiar metallic ring that brought me back from the edge. Then the captain collapsed in a lifeless heap on top of my quaking body. There were alarms going off in my mind everywhere. I did not understand what just happened, and I was smothering underneath the weight of his stinking body. Being suffocated by his blubber was only a slightly better fate than being raped by him. No matter how hard I tried, I could not get him off me. I was soon relieved to find someone else tugging at his arm to help roll his limp body from the top of mine.

As soon as I wiggled out from under his mammoth frame, I could make out Nicole standing in the moon light. She was wound up with his baseball bat poised to strike him again.

"Stand back," she advised. "I'm going to finish the bastard off."

I shook my head from side to side and screamed a muffled "No!" through my taped mouth. Since my request was beyond all comprehension, Nicole tore the duct tape from my mouth.

"As much as he deserves it, I wouldn't be able to live with myself." I said gasping for breath.

"Candy, your face is a mess. We can't just wait until he does this sort of thing again!" she insisted forcefully while removing the remainder of my duct tape bindings.

"There has to be another way."

"Let's tie him up then, until we think of something." Nicole set down her bat and helped me roll him on his back.

I found the captain's duct tape and then we proceeded to restrain him with multiple wrappings until we reached the end of the roll. Houdini himself could not have escaped from those bindings.

"Did he violate you?" Nicole asked.

"No, luckily he's just as bad an aim with his penis as he is with a gun." We both laughed in spite of the situation. "Speaking of my gun, where did he set it?"

We searched through the straw until we found my firearm. I cannot tell you how glad I was to finally get it away from the captain.

"Let's castrate the son of a bitch," Nicole said with excitement. "That's what they used to do with perverts like this."

"Go to the house and bring me a large flashlight, some disinfectant, dressings and some of those pre-packaged surgical instruments that I brought back from my trip." My immediate call to action proved to Nicole that I had approved of her idea. It would render him harmless without having to kill him. "I'll get dressed while you're gone."

While I was putting my clothes back on, I thought about my father. He never could have imagined, while he was teaching me to castrate calves back on the farm, that I would ever be able to put that knowledge to such good use. Because I had performed the operation hundreds of times on cattle, I was confident I could do a proficient job on the captain. My only uncertainty, however, was my trembling hands. I was still shaking violently from my ordeal.

Nicole had a huge grin on her face during the entire operation. She was happy to finally take her revenge. Separating the captain from his testicles gave me a certain measure of satisfaction as well. It was comforting to know that he would no longer be a threat to me. I had his gun and I had his balls; the man would be harmless without them.

"How did you know I was in trouble?"

"I heard the captain sneak out of the house. I'm sorry, but it took me a few minutes to realize what he was up to."

"I'm so glad you came when you did." I reached out and gave her a big hug of gratitude.

"What if he never wakes up?"

"Then we went to a lot of work for nothing," I stated, without sympathy, gathering up our things. "Unwrap all his upper body. Having to rip all that tape from his own hairy legs will be extra punishment for him."

Nicole gave me a high-five to let me know she appreciated my devious mind. She ripped the tape off of his upper half and then we left him to wake up in his own misery. We slept in the cab of the truck that night. Now there was a chance we were both infected.

Chapter Twenty-Four

SLEEP HAD A FIRM HOLD on me the following morning. My subconscious mind was protecting me from the inevitable pain that I was soon to experience from being awake. But eventually, I had to succumb to all the signals that were trying to roust me from my slumber. Eve Anna was hollering from the house and bouncing rocks off our truck.

"Hello, what's going on in there," her voice rang out in conjunction to the sound of a rock clanking against the truck's side panel. "Is something wrong?"

I opened my eyes slowly. I was now very aware of the pain from my injuries that I had received the night before. My eyelids were so badly puffed up, I only had slits to peek through. The morning light stung and made me cringe. I opened the driver's door and stumbled out to greet Eve Anna.

"My God, Candy. What happen to you?" Eve Anna was obviously shocked at my appearance and started running to my aid. I raised my hand, motioning her to keep her distance.

"Our Captain Dick was horny again last night."

"What happened?"

I told Eve Anna the whole story. When I got to the part about the operation, she was jumping up and down and clapping her hands.

"Bravo, Candy, bravo. That asshole finally got what he deserved."

"I suppose," I said with hesitation. I was feeling a little guilty for what I did in spite of all the horrible things he had done to me.

"Are you ready for breakfast?"

"I'm famished," Nicole replied from the open window of our pick-up truck.

"Bring us three servings please, Eve Anna," I requested.

She tilted her head and looked at me inquisitively before going back into the house. Her eyes told me, let the bastard starve.

She could not comprehend my show of generosity towards the captain. I knew what it was like to be rapt in an obsession. I have been to that dark place in a man's mind, that fuels volatile desires for a woman. I could understand why the weak might surrender to such a compulsion.

In a few minutes she was out with a tray. She had already prepared oatmeal and coffee. Nicole and I picked this up from the step and made our way to the barn. I tucked my 45 in my pocket, so that it would be in full view, and then took the captain his food. He was awake, dressed and completely free of duct tape.

"What did you do to me, bitch."

"I told you I would have your balls on a platter if you messed with me and my girls."

"You dumb cunt, you'll pay for this."

"Just be thankful you're still alive."

"You should have killed me when you had the chance!" he hissed.

"Do you want your breakfast, or not?" I set the platter down slowly; not taking my eyes off of him for a second. "If you would have kept your pecker in your pants, none of this would have happened."

"I'm glad I messed you up last night. Get out of my sight you stupid slut."

I backed away from him and hurried down the ladder. Nicole was standing guard with the rifle at the bottom. We had our oatmeal and coffee and then decided that we should move to another location for safety reasons. I backed the old truck up to the barn, so that we could load up some bales to take with us. By noon we had moved into the machine shop.

When Eve Anna brought us lunch, she told us that Adam was feeling much better and his leg was healing nicely. It was a huge load off my mind. Later that day I went to his bedroom window and tapped on the pane. I waved to him and smiled. It was a joy to see him sitting up with the appearance of well-being. His face brightened and he blew me a kiss. Then he called for Eve Anna to come open the window. I stepped back while she raised the sash. When she had moved to Adam's bedside, I returned to talk.

"Hi, Big Guy, how are you feeling?" I tried to give him a big grin even though it hurt to stretch those muscles on my face.

"I'm much better thanks. I owe you a large debt of gratitude. I'd be dead right now if it wasn't for you."

"That's what friends are for."

"But what about you?" His smile turned to a look of concern. "You and the captain really went to war last night."

"Yes," I admitted with a marked tone of regret. "It was a high stakes battle that I nearly lost, I'm afraid. But I'll heal, which is more than I can say for the captain."

"Old Double Dick got just what he deserved."

The rest of our conversation turned towards the extent of our aches and pains, because Adam must have sensed I was uncomfortable talking about my confrontation with the captain. All the time we talked, Eve Anna was playing the part of Adam's private nurse. She was checking his temperature, straightening the covers, fluffing pillows and offering him a sip of water. There was way too much physical contact for my liking. She was constantly patting him, stroking him and running her fingers through his hair. Neither of them noticed that I was irritated by her fondling. I took a civil leave of them and went to chop wood. It helped me take my mind off of my troubles and alleviate my frustration.

I continued to take meals to the captain, but I did not stop to chat. I had put up with enough of his abuse already. Six days after the operation, the captain snuck down from the loft and stole our pickup truck. I was upset with myself for being so negligent—leaving the keys in the ignition. Having wheels would only expedite his return and his subsequent revenge. I knew from experience that over twenty percent of the vehicles on the road had firearms in their trunks.

———•———

In the days that followed I came to Adam's window at least once a day and Nicole spent a lot of time talking to Randy at the opposite end of the house. They were missing each other terribly. It was a shame that I had to drag her into this quarantined situation, but the anticipation of finally being in a harmonious group when we returned made it all seem worthwhile. At least we thought that it would be free of hostility.

The day before the end of our self-administered exile, I went to Adam's window the same as usual; only this time the curtains had been closed. Naturally my curiosity got the best of me and I peeked in through a small opening left by the cloth not coming fully together. I was appalled to see Eve Anna up on the bed, naked from the waist down and straddling Adam. They were obviously having sexual intercourse. I cannot describe how seeing them engaged in the act of love made me feel. It definitely chilled me to the bone and made my stomach queasy. Even though I had given Eve Anna permission to be with Adam, I was ill prepared to witness the deed. My first reaction was that of anger, because I did not receive any advance notice. Then my anger was soon replaced by a complex, but passionate jealousy. I ran from the window troubled, hurt and confused. Was I upset because I was being protective of Adam or was I envious of him? I was not completely sure.

•———•

The next morning Nicole and I were able to join the others for breakfast. It was a bittersweet reunion on my part. Sweet because I was glad to be back in the group; bitter because there was a storm brewing within the unsettled social environment.

Since Adam was able to walk with assistance, he got out of bed and took his meal in the kitchen—against nurse's orders—so that we could all be together. He seemed very pleased to be in my company; he rarely let go of my hand throughout breakfast and was constantly rubbing my back and shoulders as well as fussing with my hair. He looked at me as if star struck, even though I must have been a sight; my face was beat up and I hadn't bathed or washed my hair in days. Eve Anna sat at the far end of the table, being quiet and sober.

I kept the tribe enthralled for several hours with stories of my adventures out in the world and with Nicole's and my battle with Captain Dick. Everyone gave their seal of approval for what we did to the captain and many of them expressed concern that I was not hard enough on him. By the time I had exhausted all my tall tales, Randy announced that the water he had put on the stove that morning was ready for Nicole's and my bath. It was only fair to let Nicole go first, because Randy had gone to all the work of heating the water. Adam joined me when it finally got to be my turn. I had at least an hour wait because they had been talking, splashing and giggling the whole time in the tub. After that, they headed directly to the downstairs bedroom.

I helped Adam sit on the floor beside the tub; then I undressed and lowered myself into the lukewarm water. It felt heavenly to wash the grime and any residue of Captain Dick from my body. Adam helped me wash my back, my hair and a couple of other strategic spots on my body. His eyes rarely left mine the whole time. After a thorough scrub, I reclined and we talked.

"Look, Adam, I'm getting a paunch," It struck me as funny, as I ran my hand over the slippery surface of my tummy.

"How's the pregnancy going, anyway?"

"Great, I rarely get sick in the mornings anymore and my energy level seems to be still good."

"I'm glad everything is going well after everything you've been through."

"It's been kind of wild since I saw you last, that's for sure."

"I can't tell you how glad I am to have you back and have the captain out of the picture."

"I wouldn't count the captain out just yet. He'll be back; I can assure you of that. He will want to get even for what I did to him."

"I guess we'll have to keep the door locked at night and have a gun close by at all times."

"Don't worry, I've already thought of that."

"I have a confession to make." His expression was apprehensive, like a dog caught chewing your favourite slippers. "Eve Anna and I have already started our little project."

"Without asking me first?" My voice sounded reproachful despite my intention.

"She told me you wanted us to start as soon as I was ready." He said in a sheepish defensive tone. "Besides you asked me…"

"It's okay, Adam." I interrupted. "I forgive you. I was upset for a while but I'm fine now."

"What do you mean, you were upset for a while?"

"The day you were doing it, I peeked in the window and saw you."

"Which day?"

"You mean you've done it more than once?"

"Now that she's tried it..."

"Stop! I've heard enough already. Let's change the subject, shall we?" I shivered, causing ripples to form in the suds; and it was not because of the temperature of the bath water.

"Lovely weather we are having," Adam joked.

I splashed him with a large handful of water and foam. Then I rose from the tub and kissed him on the forehead to show that I had forgiven him.

•———•

The next day was lovely indeed. It was unseasonably warm for the time of year. So warm in fact, Eve Anna and I were able to fetch eggs from the barn in our shirtsleeves. She seemed extra pretty this morning, but I was not in the mood to bask in her loveliness.

"Is something wrong?" she asked. "You look pissed about something."

"I'm mad about you and Adam." I did not look her in the eyes, but continued to gather eggs instead.

"You told me that he could be my first."

"I thought we had agreed that you should wait because of your miscarriage."

"I decided it would be less awkward if we started while you were gone."

"Are you sure you weren't just acting-out, because I left you behind."

"Come on, Candy. I'm not a frickin' three-year-old. Give me a break."

"I want you to stop trying to get pregnant with Adam." There was a mysterious, latent hostility stirring inside me.

"But you promised."

"That was before I had a chance to think this through. It would be best for everyone if you seek a relationship with Frankie." I was angry with Eve Anna now, because my unrequited feelings for her had caused me so much pain. And I detested the way my unconditional devotion to her made me vulnerable and weak. Her potent, seductive voodoo had roused dark and fierce emotions, that I had kept long hidden, deep inside me. The spell that she held over me acted like poison in my blood.

"But I'm not ready for that."

"I'll talk to Frankie about it tomorrow."

"Don't you dare!" Her hands moulded into a fist and she gave me a threatening glare.

"I think I know what's best for you." The explosive furore that was pent up inside me was clouding my mind and it felt like it was about to go critical.

"You're not the boss of me!" she shouted; pushing me backwards with both hands, crushing me against the partition between the stalls.

Letting my runaway emotions get the best of me, I slapped Eve Anna across the face in retaliation. She instinctively raised her hand to cover the red mark that my hand had left behind. She was visibly stunned by the ferocity of my reprisal and could only stare at me bitterly. Her glaring eyes pierced me like weapons. She stood motionless for a moment and then lunged forward. I did not offer any resistance as she came at me, but stood proud and defiant as she grabbed my blouse with both hands; I casually allowed her to rip it from my shoulders. Eve Anna stepped back and assumed a rebellious posture, daring me to even the score.

"I hate you!" she said, tears now starting to moisten her penetrating eyes.

"I hate you more," I said childishly, standing topless across the manger from her. I was enraged by the way my love for her debilitated me and empowered her, and I was filled with a misguided passion that wanted to hurt her in return. I stepped forward. Eve Anna raised her chin insolently and allowed me to disrobe her upper body in one swift and vicious motion. Then her eyes darted wildly and her teeth were bared. She seemed to be studying me intently, just as I was examining her. Her smooth breasts were larger now and her nipples stood out from the cold, like pink gumdrops nestled on new fallen snow.

"Bitch," she said with resentment, reaching out and viciously twisting my left nipple.

I cringed with pain, because my swollen breasts were tender. Not completely understanding my own actions, I grabbed Eve Anna around the shoulders and pulled her close to me. She resisted energetically, but I lunged forward and bit her on the earlobe. As she squirmed against me, her breasts felt cool and silky against mine, like I was brushing up against a flower.

"Snot-nosed brat!" I responded with hostility.

As I released her long enough to assess her expression, she growled, staring at me with starving eyes, and then kissed me with wild abandon. I was disarmed with a powerful rush of desire, just long enough to enable her to draw my lower lip into her mouth and sink her teeth into its sensitive tissue. I pulled away and screamed:

"Ow, that hurt, you little shit."

Eve Anna appeared to be momentarily shocked by what she had done to me. Her lips quivered as my blood dripped from the corner of her mouth. That picture of her: naked, untamed, seductive, bloodied, filled me with a potent, unfulfilled hunger that crumbled the foundation of my existence. I grabbed her by the neck and applied just enough pressure to make my actions symbolic. Then I licked my blood from her lips and kissed her as rowdily as she had kissed me; concluding with a nip to her upper lip that made her yelp in pain.

Eve Anna only ended our lip-lock long enough to exclaim, "Bad boy!"

Then she went after me again. Our aggressive fervour had now transformed into a frenzy of animalistic sexual desire. She probed my mouth with her warm tongue and we nipped at each other with forceful, sadistic pleasure. Eve Anna tugged at my breasts as she kissed and nibbled heartily. I was all too glad to reciprocate. Her young bosom was firm, like a ripe peach, and her skin felt like cream between my fingers.

"Oooo," I cooed with delight. "You little scamp, you."

Eve Anna then hooked her leg behind mine and toppled me. We fell as one into a soft mound of straw and tussled in an unyielding embrace. Her pelvis darted against my thigh as she pawed at me and mouthed my lips. We duelled with each other's tongues; parrying from one mouth to the other in a battle that neither of us cared who won or lost.

Eve Anna finally stopped the skirmish just long enough to say: "I love you, Sir."

Her voice was tender and heartfelt and now her kisses felt the same way. I delighted in her tears falling against my cheeks and her body quivering against mine. I kissed her softly in return and wiped her adoring tears from her eyes. Naturally, I was crying along with her, because she had now fulfilled my dreams.

"I love you too," I answered, hardly daring to leave her lips alone long enough to say the words. "I have loved you always."

We cried together and we kissed warmly for a long, long time. And we unendingly declared our love for each other. We made love as well as any two people could with their pants still on and I was not the least bit ashamed. Eve Anna's love had released a part of me, that I was afraid could never be unleashed. It felt good to have been set free.

Eve Anna started to laugh.

"Look at us," she said in hysterics. "That was quite a performance, wasn't it?"

"I'm sorry I hurt you," I said, touching her swollen lips with my trembling fingers.

"It was worth it, if it finally brought you to your senses." Eve Anna said with a smile.

"What would the P.T.A. think if they had seen our little exhibition?" Eve Anna and I laughed with delight.

"Now what?" Eve Anna asked looking at me queerly. "Do we tell the others?"

"Let's keep it secret for a while." I was too confused to make a decision. "At least until I have time to think this thing through."

"We had better get back to the house, before they suspect something," she said, rising from the straw pile and offering to help me up with her hand.

Our blouses were in tatters and most of the buttons were ripped free. We both looked a wreck compared to when we had left the house. We finished gathering the eggs and returned to our dwelling; self-consciously gathering the fabric of our shirts where our buttons had once been.

Lucky for us everyone was still in bed when we returned. We winked at each other and went to our respective bedrooms to find a new top.

"What the hell happened to you?" Adam asked when I entered the bedroom.

"It's a long story," I said latching the door behind me.

"I have nothing but time." He patted my empty half of the bed as he spoke, inviting me to sit and tell all.

"Eve Anna and I had a fight." I announced. "And something astounding became of it."

"What?"

"Eve Anna and I discovered that we are in love with each other." I dropped the bomb as gently as possible.

"Oh, is that all." He did not seem the least bit surprised.

"What do you mean, is that all?" I had expected it to be earth shaking news.

"Frankie and I have suspected it for some time."

"You're kidding me?"

"Frankie came to me some time ago and questioned me about you and Eve Anna. We could see it in your eyes and the way you acted when you were together. He assumed that you and she were lesbians, but I had to set him straight. I hope you don't mind that I let the cat out of the bag about you being transgender."

"No, I'm glad he knows the truth. It'll make things easier."

"So, what happened to your strong position against same-sex relationships?" he said with a smug, self-satisfied grin.

"It's amazing, isn't it? How quickly I abandoned my ideals in order to find love. My convictions seem so insignificant and petty now that I've been enticed with a chance to love and be loved."

"Where do we go from here?" Adam patted me on the back affectionately to show his approval.

"I'm going to call Eve Anna right away, if you don't mind."

I did not wait for Adam's permission, but got up right away and beckoned her to come into the bedroom. She entered the room tentatively; unsure of what was in store. I was surprised at how bruised and red she was around the mouth from me trying to devour her lips. It made me feel guilty for what I did to her, but then I realized I probably looked just as bad or maybe even worse. She was surprised to hear what Adam had to say about Frankie, but took the whole thing in stride.

"I guess I owe him an explanation," she said.

"Take your time. Wait until the time is right," Adam suggested.

"How do you feel about me being in love with your fiancée?" She lowered her eyes in a timid fashion as she asked.

"I knew that Rock and my relationship was going to be far from ordinary when I signed on," he admitted. Just because the 'he' in Rock is in love with you, that doesn't mean that she will love me any less."

"I'm sorry I have made things so complicated," I said.

"It's nothing that four rational individuals can't work out comfortably with a little understanding," Adam insisted.

"By the way, Eve Anna, you and Adam are welcome to continue with the project for as long as it takes you to get pregnant."

She kissed me very carefully, because we were both extremely tender in that area. Then she kissed Adam and left the bedroom in happy tears.

That morning at breakfast everyone could see a difference in Eve Anna and me. I explained that we had been in a fight, but had come to an understanding. Everyone seemed to be happy with that explanation for the time being.

Shortly after the dishes were done, Eve Anna asked Frankie if he would like to go for a walk. I guessed that it would be all out in the open soon. Oh, what a tangled web I had woven.

Chapter Twenty-Five

I HAD EVE ANNA TO thank for resolving all the sensitive issues concerning our love rectangle. Frankie apparently took the news well, because he was glad to hear that it was something other than a lack of physical attraction that was keeping them from becoming a couple. It was comforting to him to know that Eve Anna was sexually straight and was only attracted to the male in me, and that she found him to be a desirable young man. The fact that she was in love with me seemed insignificant to him as long as they could still be together one day. I think she did a good job of convincing him that there was still hope for the two of them. Now that her and my relationship was more stable, and because she was very taken with him, she could concentrate on learning to love him as well. And something she said to him while they were on their walk seemed to give Frankie all the confidence in the world.

"I can hardly wait to have your little brown babies," she evidently admitted.

We had now evolved into a very tight knit group and all of us seemed to get along wonderfully. Eve Anna was with child shortly after starting the project. I was a little worried about her becoming pregnant so soon after her miscarriage, but everything seemed to be coming along fine. Adam and Eve Anna's child was the first naturally conceived baby in this chapter of human history.

Helena, Nicole and I were also doing well with our pregnancies; other than the usual dry heaves in the morning and the odd drop kick to our bladders, everything seemed to be wonderful. The last few days, while I slept, Adam put his hand on my stomach and tried to feel the baby moving. Two nights in a row he woke me with his laughing—it all seemed so amazing to him. We are all due in the spring, just like most of God's creatures. I am looking forward to being a mother more than anything I have ever done in my life. Ain't that a kick in the teeth (if you can excuse my choice of words)?

Adam and I were married while I was approaching my thirtieth-fifth week of pregnancy. Frankie performed the ceremony and Eve Anna was my maid of honour. Adam danced with me afterwards, as I had prophesied. It was a very slow dance, but our hearts were in it and that was all that mattered. There was a strong outpouring of emotion at the party afterwards; everyone was very happy for us. Our union would help solidify the composition of the group.

That night the baby moved into the transverse position, surprising me with several kicks to the bellybutton. The next morning, however, the bladder shots were back in full force; he was in that position from then on. At night, I was beyond uncomfortable; I constantly tried to find the perfect sleeping position but tossed and turned because it was unattainable. Adam has been very patient with me. He is an excellent partner.

Three weeks before my due date, Blaine and Helena were wed. They both were adamant about having Helena's baby born into wedlock. I read from the Bible and helped them take their vows.

It was challenging, because I was having the first of my practice contractions throughout the day. By a lucky coincidence the girls and I had been in a nesting mood that week and had the house spotless and neat for the celebration.

Adam had allowed Eve Anna and me to sleep together on several occasions. We made beautiful love together, while adhering to strict guidelines that we had set for ourselves. It is a joy beyond all belief to be in love with such a beautiful and vibrant young woman. All my wishes have been fulfilled. The man in me is happier than I ever thought possible.

•———•

One night, several days after Blaine and Helena's wedding, I needed to go for a walk to work off some of the discomfort of my Braxton Hicks. Adam was happy to accompany me for the companionship and to strengthen his bad leg. There was a new moon that night, but there seemed to be a strange, heavenly glow lighting our way just the same. Adam looked up and discovered an extraordinary anomaly in the evening sky.

"Holy Shit!" he exclaimed with obvious excitement. "A star in Cassiopeia has gone supernova."

"That's unusual, isn't it?" I said, gazing skywards with fascination. The exploding star was the brightest object in the heavens; its luminosity surpassing that of Venus and the World Space Station. I was awe struck by its unusual—almost hypnotic—glow.

"I think the last one was way back in the early sixteen-hundreds and was recorded by Johannes Kepler. This is huge, Rock. It's too bad there are no astronomers here to observe it. Any cosmologist would give his left nut to see a celestial event of this proportion."

"I'm glad you're not an astronomer," I joked.

"I think it's a sign," he confided in a mysterious way. "I think something wonderful is about to happen."

"What do you mean?"

"I'm not sure. I just have this strange feeling of mysticism and gladness; like I am in the proximity of greatness."

"Wow, that's freaky, Adam." I was astounded by his take on the whole affair, but dismissed his star-struck outlook as nothing more than a misguided hunch; but Adam's theory was soon to gain credence, thanks to the strangest of allies.

That night I had an odd dream. Eve Anna was there helping me deliver my baby. The only strange part was, instead of a baby, I gave birth to a gleaming bundle of warm and mysterious light. I awoke with a start, overwhelmed with a feeling of euphoria. No, better than that—an orgasmic euphoria.

The next afternoon everyone went for a walk in the pasture with the exception of Nicole and me. We were having troubles with swollen feet and decided it would be best if we stayed home for the day. I was sitting on the toilet reading an old magazine and soaking my feet in the tub when I heard Nicole scream.

"Candy! Come here, quick."

I did not stop to dry my feet as I raced to her aid. She was standing beside the picture window holding my SKS rifle and my 45.

"Someone's coming up the driveway," she shouted with urgency, passing me my handgun. "I think it's Captain Dick."

I had to agree, because it was the same old pickup that he stole from me that was coming up the drive. I checked the guns to make sure they were in order and then we went outside to meet our adversary head-on.

"What a time for that son of a bitch to show up," I barked. Nicole and I could not have been in worse shape to contend with him—we were both barefoot and as pregnant as any two women could be.

The captain stopped the vehicle as soon as he saw his armed greeting party. He got out and crouched down behind his open door, sliding what looked like a rifle out with him.

"Don't shoot!" he pleaded.

"Get back in your truck; turn around and get the hell out of here as fast as you can, or you're a dead man," I shouted back.

"It's vital that I talk to you," he insisted as he slowly stepped away from the truck. He had a white flag tied to the end of his gun barrel and was waving it above his head.

"Let's shoot him now while he's in the open," Nicole insisted. "We might not get another chance."

"Let's hear what he has to say. Just don't take your sights off him for a second."

The captain started inching toward us, all the while waving his flag in his left hand and pleading for us to refrain with the outstretched gesture of his right. When he was about ten meters away, I raised my palm for him to halt.

"I bring great tidings from the Lord," he announced.

"It's a trick!" Nicole warned with good reason. "Shoot him! Shoot him now!"

I reached out and dropped the muzzle of her rifle with my hand. "Let him speak his piece."

"You're an unlikely messenger of God," I challenged.

"I admit that freely." His right hand shook at his side while he spoke. "Up until yesterday my mind was bent on evil."

"Why the change of heart?" I was satisfied to take part in his ridiculous game.

"I've seen angels."

"Shoot'im! It's a trick. I know it is." Nicole was getting frustrated with his outlandish story and my unwillingness to make my revenge complete.

I was suspicious of him myself, but for the life of me I could not see what he had to gain from his preposterous claims. I allowed him to continue.

"Have you seen the star?' he asked. "The star that heralds the coming of the next Messiah."

"We have seen a supernova, yes."

"The angels asked me to follow that star to you. For you will be the mother of God's child. You, Candy, have been the recipient of his immaculate conception."

Now I was ready to shoot him. His story was obviously part of an elaborate deception to catch me off guard. I raised my handgun and pointed it at his head.

"No! Please don't. As God is my witness, I speak the truth."

"I got pregnant from the semen sent to us in the Glenn, the same as everyone else. Don't try to feed me this Messiah bullshit."

"The semen capsule that you first inseminated yourself with was unlabeled. Is that correct?"

I tried to recall. Then it came to me: "Yes, I guess that's true."

"It was unlabeled, because it was put there by God."

Now I was confused. How could he have known about the mysterious vial? I was the only one in the clinic at the time. Maybe there were hidden surveillance cameras linked to the control room. I had suspected as much once before when he had guessed that I was a virgin. I had assumed he had overheard my conversation with Eve Anna.

Surely this was just more of his artful trickery. But the recollection of last night's dream hinted otherwise.

"Tell me more about the angels," I demanded.

"They came to me the same night the star appeared." He paused for a second to set his rifle on the ground. "I had acquired this gun and I was on my way back here to kill you."

His honesty was duly noted.

"The angels beckoned me to change my ways and accept God. They told me that I was to be the messenger to all that remained and announce the coming of His child. I was to bow down and worship you; for you are the bearer of the second coming." With this, the captain dropped to the ground and stumbled towards me on his knees.

Nicole followed him to my side with the muzzle of her assault rifle and we both watched in amazement as he clung to the fabric of my pant leg and begged for my forgiveness.

"I will do anything you want," he pleaded. "Just, please excuse me for what I've done. I was a monster to you and I hurt you in so many ways. I beg you to take pity on my soul and pardon me for my sins. I fear that I will never be invited to dwell in the house of the Lord, unless you can find it in your heart to forgive me."

Nicole and I looked at each other in total disbelief, for the captain now wept uncontrollably at my feet. In that instant the rest of the group, except for Adam who was lagging behind because of his wounded leg, came running around the corner of the house. They too were flabbergasted by what they saw. The captain was now lying flat on the cold ground, wailing pitifully and grovelling at the tattered cuff of my pant legs.

"What's going on?" Eve Anna asked with urgency. "We came as soon as we saw the vehicle."

I held up my hand and motioned to her for silence. I grabbed the collar of his shirt and pulled, saying: "Get up, Captain. I've heard enough for one day."

"Please, call me Richard. I don't deserve that title any longer." He raised himself to his feet and wiped away the tears that bathed his cheeks.

"You can take your meals with us and you can sleep in the barn. But if you try anything at all, you'll answer to me."

"That's very generous, thank you. But I don't want your pity; I only crave your forgiveness, because I won't be able to rest until I receive that precious gift from you."

"Go to the barn. I'll come and get you for supper."

"Yes, Mother. I am your humble servant." He hurried to the barn without looking back.

"What in the name of God has gotten into him?" Adam asked, now in the group.

"Adam, come with me." I took him by the arm and led him into one of the bedrooms and shut the door. Then I gave him a complete account of what had transpired while he was out for his walk.

"It sure makes you wonder, doesn't it?" he said after hearing my story.

"I'm completely baffled. You should have seen him, Adam. He's an opposite reflection of his former self. I'm convinced that he's not feigning this inexplicable transformation. I think his mind has snapped from being alone all this time, with nothing to keep him company but his guilty conscience."

"Or he could be telling the truth."

"Come on, Adam, give me a break. Why would God pick a transgender to have his child?"

"Where else would he find a beautiful virgin of your maturity?" he said laughing.

"I suppose you've got that right." I snickered along with him. "And the Big Guy does have a sense of humour, that's a given."

"From where I'm sitting, you're the perfect candidate. You're wise beyond your years, statuesque, spiritual, and you are the kindest, most giving and morally responsible individual I've ever met; not to mention the bravest. You've shown a lot of pluck to get us this far."

I was taken aback by his outpouring of flattery. "I love you for saying all those things, but I'm still not sure that I'm deserving."

"You shouldn't be afraid of being noble." He paused in contemplation then added: "Didn't Shakespeare say something in one of his plays..."

"Be not afraid of greatness: some are born great; some achieve greatness and some have greatness thrust upon them."

"Ya, that's the one... I never said anything before, but I had a strange dream last night."

"What kind of dream!" I was filled with an uneasy expectancy when I heard his admission.

"I dreamt that you were giving birth. But it wasn't a normal delivery. When Eve Anna pulled your child from the womb, there was a great feeling of elation and I was struck by a warm comforting light. It was emanating from the baby. Or the baby was engulfed in it, I'm not sure. Anyway, the baby seemed to be special; that much I remember for sure."

"Well, I'll be..." I could not continue because I had been overcome with tears. The whole concept was too much for me to handle. How could I cope with being the mother of a Godly child? I fell back onto the bed and curled up into a ball. I asked Adam to leave me alone while I grappled with the plausibility of such an occurrence. It was by far the most momentous development of my entire life.

I had to admit that a strange force had compelled me to choose the unlabeled vial that day on the Glenn. And I could not account for my determination to stay a virgin until the end of my pregnancy. What strange force had picked me to go on the mission in the first place? Clearly, the experiment that I submitted to NASA was poorly thought out. But perhaps the most convincing argument was the miraculous change in the captain; that could only have been achieved by divine intervention. The whole situation was too much of a coincidence for my liking. And of course, there was the appearance of the bright star in the heavens and the two separate, but realistic dreams that correlated with the captain's prophecy. Could this really be happening to me? Fortunately, I had conceived and carried the child quite unknowingly so far, but could I cope with the huge responsibility of bringing His child into the world? Would I—as strange a candidate as I could imagine—be a suitable mother to His second chosen son?

I lay in my bed and cried for an hour because there were too many difficult questions and not enough answers.

I was a little more composed by the time Adam called me for supper that night.

"I'll walk with you to fetch the captain," he said with reassurance, already in possession of my 45.

"You're not going to believe this," he said with reluctance, on the way to the barn. "But Eve Anna had the same dream as you and I had last night."

"No way!"

"It's true, I swear. Nicole said that Eve Anna almost peed her pants when she was told what the captain had to say. Her dream was exactly the same as ours, except she was the one delivering the baby."

"Wow... this whole situation is scaring the crap out of me."

"I don't know about you, but I'm starting to become a believer." Adam gestured with his hand to offer first entry into the barn.

I stepped in and shouted for the captain. He was down the stairs in an instant and very happy to see me.

"I'm glad to see that your face healed nicely. You are just as beautiful as you ever were."

I only offered a grunt of recognition.

"There were no complications from the surgery, by the way. I'm thankful for that, because I know there was nothing saying you had to be so meticulous. You could have just hacked them out with a dull spoon."

"I was definitely tempted."

"I know now that I deserved everything you did to me and more. I hope someday you'll find it in your heart to forgive me for the rotten things I've done."

I stopped. Adam and the captain took half a step more and then turned round to face me.

"If you've truly changed, Richard; and you are committed to spend the rest of your life for the good of the group, I'd say there's a chance for you."

"I have changed, Candy. Truly I have. Being in the presence of angels has altered my life forever. I've devoted the rest of my days to God and the little Jesus child you're carrying in your womb. If I can earn your trust, it would be a privilege to help you raise him."

"You're a believer now, are you?" I tossed out a sarcastic question.

"I was ever so wrong to think otherwise. You were right and I was wrong. There, see, I admit it. The old Captain Dick would never have admitted to making a mistake, ever. You know that."

"That's what makes this whole thing so scary," I said, just loud enough for Adam to hear, while I opened the front door to the house. "Enough talk, let's have supper."

"I haven't had a decent meal since I ran off," the captain said.

At the dinner table Richard gave a more detailed account of his meeting with the angels. His eyes were bright and excited as he spoke and his hands and arms wafted the air with wild exuberance. His enthusiasm was truly contagious and everyone was swept away by his interpretation of the scene. It was like looking at a totally different individual; and it was hard to dispel what he had foretold so convincingly. He also mentioned that the Divine voices stressed to him that God regards man and woman as being equal in value—I would learn differently later why this message was so important; but for now, I assumed it was directed toward Captain Dick, because he had been such a bastard toward women all his life—and that the reason society has unfairly demeaned and discounted females throughout history is only because of man's insecurities.

After supper Richard cleared the table and helped wash the dishes. Then he was content to sit in the corner chair and read the Bible until the generator was turned off. He knew now that he was wrong about the existence of God, but he was right about us needing to focus on building a utopia here on earth instead of pouring all our energies and resources into fighting over our differences. At bedtime he thanked us all for having him and returned to the loft. It was more like having a stranger in for a meal than the infamous Captain Dick. We locked the door behind him and I took my handgun to bed with me.

"What a day this has been," I said to Adam before we retired. He had to concur.

That night I had the same dream, only this time it was more real and more detailed than before. This time God spoke to me—or at least a voice spoke to me. He told me that He wanted me to have His baby and raise it with Christian family values, just as I had been raised. He said that the baby was a gift from Him to help with the development of our new civilization. I awoke with the same euphoric sensations as before.

"Adam." I elbowed him in the ribs a little too enthusiastically.

"Ow! What's the problem?"

"I'm going to have the child of God."

"What changed your mind?"

I explained the dream to him. And tried to explain the strong sense of purpose God instilled in me. But I did not try to describe the overwhelming connection that I made with Him.

Simple words would not be an acceptable medium for that type of communication.

A few days later, Nicole and I went out to the barn to gather eggs. I was having pains that morning, but I blamed the contractions as being false labour. While I was in the barn, my water broke. I laid down in the manger and asked her to run for Eve Anna and Captain Dick.

"Are you going to have your baby, right here in the manger?" she cried with excitement.

"Don't be silly, Nicole. That would be just too weird."

When Richard and Eve Anna returned, the captain picked me up and carried me to my bedroom. He is as gentle as a lamb now and treats everyone with kindness and respect. I have not told him yet, but I have forgiven him.

Naturally, I am committed to natural child birth. No fancy epidural or caesarean section for me, even if I wanted it. How the hell did I get myself into this predicament? I'm a small woman; will I even be able to have this baby?

This being my first child, I have already been in labour for eighteen hours. If I was a man, I would have gained a whole new respect for women. I have had lots of time for reflection while fighting to give birth. I am not afraid of having this baby anymore. In a way, this child is a huge comfort to me; because it is proof, beyond a shadow of doubt, that God loves me, in spite of my queer tendencies. I am now convinced that I can raise this child as well as anyone could. I shared my thoughts with Adam between contractions.

"There are so many things that I cannot wait to teach him, Adam. It will be exciting to see him walk for the first time and speak his first words. And he could not have better parents when it comes to his education."

"He couldn't have better parents, period." Adam insisted, kissing me on the forehead.

"Okay, Candy, I can see the head now," Eve Anna sounded excited. "Just one more big push."

I pushed until I felt the relief of the baby passing from my body. It cried as soon as it hit the harsh reality of the new world.

Then Eve Anna surprised us all.

"Congratulations, Candy. It's a girl!"

The beginning.

CPSIA information can be obtained
at www.ICGtesting.com
Printed in the USA
LVHW041934010623
748482LV00008B/96/J